SECRETS OF
EQUILIBRIUM

SECRETS OF EQUILIBRIUM

Jonathan E. Miller

THE CHOIR PRESS

First published in the United Kingdom in 2014 by
The Choir Press

ISBN 978-1-909300-26-2

www.jonathanemiller.com

To the memory of Suzanne Marchant (1967–1987).
With love and gratitude.

There exist two forces so fundamental in nature they shape the very universe around us. When chaos and order are balanced, harmony prevails. When not, unholy devastation.

William Cecil, Lord Burghley, Chief Adviser to Queen Elizabeth I on her Accession Day, 17th November 1558.

CHAPTER ONE

'How do you mean *weird*?' exclaimed Mr Hamilton in surprise, dodging out of the way of two elderly ladies jostling past them on the busy pavement.

Peering nervously through the window to check her boss inside couldn't see her, the trainee estate agent answered quickly: 'Look, all I know is when we went to the house, I waited in the car while Mr Ball went in to check it was all secure. About ten minutes later I watched him stagger out white as a sheet and throw up in the front garden. It wasn't nice, I can tell you.'

'What did Mr Ball say when he got into the car?' broke in Mrs Hamilton, glancing at her children, Hamish and Suzy, who were listening intently.

'Well, that's another weird thing,' continued the young trainee; 'he didn't want to talk about it. I asked him if he'd seen something, like, you know, a ghost or something, but he said he hadn't. He said he couldn't describe it, just that he was never going back in there again.'

'Have you been in the house, Karen?' asked Suzy, noting the name badge pinned to the lapel of her blue blazer.

'Well, given Slime won't go in . . .' She stopped abruptly, a look of horror crossing her face.

Hamish and Suzy smiled.

'Don't worry,' said Hamish sympathetically. 'We won't tell him.' Then chuckling quietly he added, 'It's a great nickname, though!'

Relieved, Karen reddened. 'Thank you,' she said, smiling. 'What I meant to say was because Mr Ball refuses to go in there, I'm the one who tends to show prospective buyers around. It's been ages since I was last in there, but I've never come across anything out of the ordinary. In fact, I like showing people around it. It's weird, but I think there's something comfortable about the old place.'

'Why hasn't Slime – I beg your pardon – Mr Ball told us about it?' asked Suzy, smiling conspiratorially.

1

'He hates the place,' she replied regretfully. 'He says it should've been demolished and redeveloped years ago, were it not for the old recluse who lives next door. And because it's been empty for about seventy years, it's—'

'*How* long?' spluttered Hamish.

'Yes, I know,' she replied, raising her eyebrows; 'it's amazing, isn't it?'

'That's the Second World War!' breathed Suzy distractedly, peering along the bustling high street.

Noting the homeless family's bemused expressions, Karen continued quickly. 'A few offers have been made on the place over the years,' she explained, 'but they all pulled out once the structural surveys were done. Nobody wanted to tackle the dry rot and subsidence. Personally I think it'd make a lovely home. But it does need a lot of work, which puts most people off. Mind you, it's been empty for so long that I reckon the seller might be prepared to accept a low offer for it.'

Mr Hamilton glanced at his wife apprehensively. 'What do you think?' he asked quietly.

Mrs Hamilton was silent for a long moment.

'Oh come on, Mum,' snapped Suzy impatiently, her words almost drowned out by the roar of a passing bus, 'what's there to think about? As Slime Ball so succinctly summed up our position just now, we've exhausted all our options. With our tiny budget it's not as though we're spoilt for choice. We've got nothing to lose by taking a look at it.'

'She's right,' added Hamish gloomily. 'Beggars can't be choosers. If you're serious about starting a new life down here in Cornwall then you're going to have to compromise about where we live.'

Stung by her children's criticism and undeniable logic, Mrs Hamilton looked at her husband and shrugged. 'They're right,' she replied guiltily. 'Our options are limited. We may as well look at all possibilities.'

Smiling sympathetically, Karen reached into her blazer pocket and withdrew a length of tattered grey string. Attached to it was a large brass key. 'I'm afraid my diary's packed today so I can't accompany you,' she said, handing it to Mr Hamilton, 'But please feel free to take a look around by yourselves. Drop the key off whenever you want. After all, it's not as if there's a queue of people waiting to see it.'

*

Steering the family's battered old blue Volvo into Porchester Road on the outskirts of the ancient market town of Warfield, Mr Hamilton pulled up in front of number 12b and laughed quietly. Peering up at the ruinous semi-detached flat-fronted Georgian town house, they all noted the decaying mildew-stained walls, boarded-up windows and a front garden so overgrown and strewn with litter it resembled municipal wasteland.

'No, I don't think so,' sniffed Mrs Hamilton dismissively. 'Drive on. There's no point even looking at it.'

'Hang on a minute,' Mr Hamilton said slowly, echoing Hamish and Suzy's sentiments. 'Okay, it's a bit run down, but—'

'Bit run down?' scoffed his wife in disgust. 'It's derelict. It looks like a forgotten tomb in an abandoned cemetery.'

'I grant you it's not going to win any prizes for first impressions,' said her husband patiently, 'but come on, we've got nothing to lose by having a look around. You said so yourself.'

Suddenly excited, Hamish and Suzy smiled at each other.

'I agree with Dad,' chirped Hamish, winding down his window to get a better look at the neglected edifice. 'It needs a lot of work, but there's a certain grandness to it.'

'Just imagine what it could look like,' Suzy exclaimed, leaning forward in her seat and pointing towards number 12a. 'Like next door!'

The contrast to the other half of the immense building couldn't have been greater. Where the mould-streaked walls of 12b were grey and crumbling, revealing patches of ochre brickwork, the pristine whitewashed walls of 12a gleamed in the glorious August sunshine. The front gardens too were polar opposites. Where 12a's was perfectly tended with a bowling-green lawn, 12b's was an uncultivated riot of brambles, nettles and weeds. Completing the chaos were old tyres, the rusting carcass of a long-defunct washing machine and a ripped mattress, its horsehair intestines exposed to the elements.

'It's no wonder the birds choose to perch next door,' chortled Suzy, climbing out of the car.

Mrs Hamilton surveyed the assault course of a barely visible path to steps leading up to the imposing but weathered front door. 'I'm not at all sure this is a good idea,' she muttered as her family set off excitedly. Peering up again at the great crumbling façade, she shivered involuntarily. 'Not good at all,' she sighed, watching her husband unlock the front door and lead their children inside.

Their footsteps echoing in the dank cavern of a hallway, Hamish and Suzy followed their father to a tall set of double doors. 'I wonder what's beyond here,' said Mr Hamilton, reaching for two grey porcelain knobs and pushing the doors open.

Gasping in unison, they gazed into a vast high-ceilinged room, its left wall dominated by a fireplace fringed by heavy grey marble surrounds, its right by two elegant floor-to-ceiling windows. Like stairways to heaven, diagonal rays of white sunlight penetrated the cracks between the wooden boards obscuring the view over the front garden, lending the immense grey shell an ethereal quality.

'It's like an aircraft hangar,' marvelled Hamish, stepping forward, his words echoing in the empty chamber.

'It's massive!' laughed Suzy, performing a full circle in the centre of the great room. The floorboards creaking underfoot, she turned to her father framed in the doorway. 'Where's Mum?' she asked, frowning.

Peering up at the high ceiling's ornate plasterwork, he was about to answer when they heard her shrill voice resonate from the hallway. 'That garden's an absolute disgrace,' she cried, her voice growing louder; 'do you know how much it will cost . . .' But her words petered out the moment she appeared in the doorway.

Amused by her astonished paralysis, Hamish and Suzy grinned at each other.

'Come on, sis, let's go and explore,' urged Hamish excitedly, hurrying towards the door.

Like archaeologists discovering a lost world, Suzy and Hamish toured the run-down house set over five floors with growing excitement. Tired and filthy from almost seventy years of neglect, its dated décor couldn't dampen their enthusiasm as they roamed up creaking stairs through large square rooms, progressively lower-ceilinged the higher they climbed. Despite its decrepit condition, the building retained many of its original features, from intricately decorated ceiling mouldings to elegant fireplaces in every room flanked by classical pillars. But decades of emptiness had taken their toll. From the dust and grime covering every surface to ancient cobwebs hanging from ceilings and doorways like gruesome tinsel, the entire place reeked musty and stale.

'There's no heating or electricity!' exclaimed Suzy in bemusement, wandering through another darkened room, scanning its peeling walls and flaking grey ceiling for signs of either. But there were none.

'Hey, sis, check this out!' came Hamish's startled cry from one of the rooms along the corridor.

Continuing to scan the walls for switches and radiators, she returned to the shadowy corridor. Then she heard it: the distinctive splashing of running water. Frowning, she rushed forward, her mind racing.

'Sis, come here!' called Hamish insistently. 'I'm in the bathroom.'

Reaching the open doorway, she stopped abruptly, unable to believe her eyes. Hamish was shrouded by a thick cloud of steam rising from an ancient bathtub in the centre of the bright room, its small frosted windowpane one of the few not boarded over.

'It's not possible!' she whispered, staring at the mist swirling up from the rusted tap's gushing spout.

'Be careful, it's very hot,' Hamish cautioned as she moved transfixed towards the curved high-sided Victorian bathtub set on four cast-iron claws.

He was right. The water was scalding. No sooner had she jabbed two fingertips into the steaming waterfall than she flinched, recoiling instantly. 'Have you tried the cold?' she asked through gritted teeth.

Shaking his head, he turned off the tap and reached for the cold. He tried turning it but it was rusty and stiff. Gripping the ancient handle tightly, he heaved with all his strength until it turned, slowly at first, then easier. Suddenly a deep rumble shook the floor and the spout coughed loudly. As if coming from the very bowels of the earth, constipated air locks hammered their way through the ancient piping. Hamish and Suzy grimaced at the sulphurous odours belching from the spout. But it wasn't long before the noxious gases gave way to sharp spurts of clear water. Suzy placed eager hands under the accelerating flow, but suddenly drew back, her freezing fingers icy and numb.

'Unbelievable!' she exclaimed, rubbing her hands together to restore circulation.

Frowning, Hamish turned off the tap. 'You're right, sis,' he muttered darkly. 'It's unbelievable. This house has been empty since the Second World War. The water supply would have been shut off decades ago.' Pausing, he looked at her with a mixture of concern and determination in his eyes. 'Look, sis,' he continued earnestly, 'I don't think we should tell Mum and Dad about this. It'd freak them out. We shouldn't say anything that might put them off this place.'

Suzy nodded. 'I agree,' she said, 'but it's unlikely we'll be able to afford it anyway. I don't know how much it's on the market for, but even in this ramshackle state I bet it's too expensive for us.'

'Sis, you might be right,' conceded Hamish, 'but I still think we shouldn't mention it.' Pausing, he smiled mischievously. 'Come on,' he urged, 'let's check out the top floor.'

They couldn't know it because they were upstairs when their parents walked into the airy bathroom, but their concerns were unnecessary. Amused by the old relics of porcelain furniture gracing the room, Mr Hamilton smiled at the ancient freestanding bathtub. Wandering around it, he casually turned on one of the taps.

'You don't seriously expect any water, do you?' scoffed Mrs Hamilton, crossing to the frosted windowpane and straining to peer out.

'Of course not,' he replied absentmindedly, studying the dry dusty surface of the enamelled bathtub. 'It's amazing to think that the last time this old thing saw water was seventy years ago.' He paused as a sudden thought occurred to him. 'Mind you,' he said, bending down to rub a finger through the dust, 'cleaned up, I bet it'd fetch a good price at auction. More than enough to replace it with a modern bath.'

*

Peering through a crack in the boarded-up attic window, Suzy looked across the tiled roofs shimmering in the heat to the spire of a church marking the centre of Warfield.

'I wonder who last lived here,' she said thoughtfully.

'It'd be interesting to find out,' acknowledged Hamish, crossing the attic to join her. 'It's weird to think that a house this amazing has been empty for so long. Even if it does have subsidence and dry rot, it's still a fantastic place.' Pausing for a long moment, he gazed out at the sun-kissed urban landscape. 'Sis, how do you feel?' he asked slowly.

Startled by the question, Suzy frowned. 'Now you mention it,' she said, 'I feel great!' She paused, deep in thought. Despite its run-down condition there was something about the house she found surprisingly comforting. Like a light mist leaving no corner untouched, there was a strange peacefulness about it she couldn't put her finger on. Then it dawned on her and she turned to Hamish, her voice a whisper. 'I feel like I belong here!'

Hamish smiled. 'Me too,' he murmured softly. 'It feels like we've come home, doesn't it?'

Suzy grinned. 'Come on,' she said excitedly, 'let's go and find out what Mum and Dad think.'

*

Reclining in his chair, Mr Ball had his back to them when the family entered the estate agency later that afternoon. Resting the heels of his polished brown brogues on the corner of his desk, he was speaking loudly into his telephone, unaware of the four clients waiting patiently behind him in the cheaply furnished office. With only three desks, two of them empty, it was clear that Ball & Co. was run as a tight ship and, judging from its owner's conversation, a highly lucrative one at that.

'Unless you add another fifty grand to your offer I'm not even picking up the phone to my client,' he boomed. 'It's a beachfront property, for God's sake. And remember, it's a seller's market so put up or shut up . . .'

Hamish and Suzy glanced at each other apprehensively and noted a similar look passing between their parents.

'. . . I don't think so,' countered the estate agent aggressively. 'I've got people lining up to buy that place, so another fifty grand's the minimum I'll accept.' He paused, listening impatiently to the person on the other end of the line. 'I know it's not *my* house,' he growled irritably, 'but I'm going to make sure my client gets the best price for it. After all, the higher the price the bigger my commission. So if you want it, you'd better come up with a better offer.'

Laughing callously, he slammed down the phone and turned to face his desk. His smile faded instantly. Sighing heavily, he raised his dark beady eyes to heaven. 'Twice in one day! To what do I owe this honour?' he asked sarcastically, feigning a yawn. 'I've already told you, we've got nothing on our books in your pitiful price range. So if you've grown tired of living in Mrs Miggins's grubby little boarding house then I suggest you go around to one of Warfield's finest supermarkets and invest in a couple of cardboard boxes.'

Appalled, Hamish and Suzy looked at their outraged parents struggling to maintain their composure.

Regarding the pinstripe-suited estate agent with loathing, Mr Hamilton took a deep breath. But when he spoke his tone was dignified. 'Mr Ball, you are without doubt the most odious little man I have ever had the misfortune to meet,' he said calmly, 'but I am grateful for one thing: that my daughter and son have witnessed the lowest form of pond life at an early age. You are the antithesis of all that is good in a role model, so I thank you for your tawdry little performance.'

Smirking at the estate agent's sudden fury, Hamish and Suzy observed his jowly face reddening and his left cheek beginning to twitch. His lips trembled and he ran an agitated hand through his thick, slicked-back blond hair. Opening his mouth, he was about to explode when suddenly the door opened and in walked the trainee estate agent. Sensing the tension, she closed the door slowly, staring warily at her boss. 'Is everything all right?' she asked hesitantly.

It was Mr Hamilton who found his voice first. 'Hello, Karen,' he said quietly. 'Mr Ball was just explaining to us the importance he places on maintaining good customer relationships.' Pausing, he withdrew the key from his jacket pocket and held it up by its frayed string. 'I was just about to explain to him that we'd like to make an offer to buy 12b Porchester Road.'

Mr Ball's puce complexion paled and he shot out of his chair. '12b Porchester Road!' he spluttered. 'How did you find out about that place?'

Smiling, Mr Hamilton glanced across at Karen and noted a look of horror passing across her face. Narrowing his eyes, he turned back to her boss. 'Were you trying to conceal it from us?' he asked suspiciously.

Shifting uneasily from one foot to another, the estate agent's arrogance deserted him. His darting eyes betrayed panic and when he spoke, his voice was a nervous stutter. 'No, no,' he protested, 'I didn't think you'd be interested.' He paused, scratching his bulbous nose. 'And anyway,' he continued sourly, 'I knew you'd never be able to afford it in spite of its terrible condition.'

'Is that so?' interjected Mrs Hamilton, a thin smile playing on her lips. 'And how much do you think the seller would be prepared to accept for it, Mr Ball?'

Momentarily lost for words, he stared at her blankly. 'I . . . I . . . can't remember,' he stammered in surprise. Sitting down heavily, he turned to his keyboard and punched in some details. Frowning at the computer screen, he glanced up and was about to speak when Karen crossed the room and handed him a plain manila folder.

'I think you're looking for this,' she said coolly. 'If you recall, you told me not to transfer the details of 12b Porchester Road onto the database.'

Mr Ball glared at her. 'I said no such thing,' he barked angrily, snatching the document from her outstretched grasp.

Smiling apologetically at the Hamiltons, she retreated to her desk.

'Let's have a look,' he muttered with a scowl, opening the brown folder marked *12b Porchester Road*. Inside was a single sheet of yellowed paper. Picking up the ageing translucent page, he scanned the tiny black print written on a post-war typewriter and smirked. 'Of course, I remember now,' he sneered, looking up at them. 'The seller wishes to remain anonymous. All dealings have to go through his representatives, an old firm of London solicitors, Peacock & Mayther.'

'So what's the price?' snapped Hamish impatiently, irritated by his pomposity.

'There isn't one,' he snarled, his eyes flashing anger. 'It's been so long since anyone enquired about the place, I'll need to consult the seller's representatives.'

'Then please do it,' Mrs Hamilton urged him softly, deflecting the agent's wrath away from her son.

Sighing heavily, he picked up the phone and dialled. Instantly impatient, he tapped his fingers on the desk, then absentmindedly picked up a yellowing card from the open folder. Holding the card up, he gave it a cursory glance, then threw it down as his call was answered and swivelled away from them to begin his solicitous exchange.

It was Suzy who recognised the old black and white photograph first. Frowning, she stepped forward and picked it up. 'That's strange,' she murmured hesitantly. Turning it over, she noticed the handwritten date: *12.12.1945.*

'What is it, sis?' asked Hamish, sensing her confusion.

'It must be a reverse image,' she muttered, passing it to him.

After studying the yellowing photograph for a long moment, Hamish exhaled noisily. 'That's no reverse image,' he exclaimed, holding it up for communal inspection; 'just look at the numbers on the front doors!'

'You're right!' declared Mrs Hamilton, reaching for the image of the flat-fronted building.

It was the condition of the two semi-detached homes that surprised them. As now, their appearances were exact opposites. But on the 12th December 1945, 12a Porchester Road wasn't the immaculate dwelling it was today. It was boarded up and run-down, a perfect replica of 12b today. In 1945, the house they were hoping to buy gleamed spotless.

'But the place is worth a fortune!' spluttered the estate agent incredulously, causing his startled clients to look up. Even with his back to them, they could detect his growing agitation from his twitching head movements.

'But for that price you may as well give it away,' he coughed disbelievingly, turning to face them. His eyes like saucers, his face suddenly paled and he spoke quickly, an expression of horror crossing his jowly features. 'No . . . no . . . that wasn't a recommendation, it was just a figure of speech,' he jabbered. Another pause. 'But . . . but what about my commission?' he asked plaintively, his shoulders sagging in resignation. 'Yes, I know it's remained unsold for almost seventy years but . . .' Flinching, he held the telephone receiver away from his ear. 'Yes, sir, 6 pm. I'll pass that on to them,' he said flatly. 'I understand, you represent the seller and I'm to execute your wishes as stated.' He replaced the receiver slowly, shaking his head in dismay. Pausing for a long moment, he studied the startled faces staring back at him.

When he finally spoke, all trace of animosity had disappeared from his voice, replaced instead by astonished resignation. 'I don't know what's going on,' he muttered, 'but it seems you've hit the jackpot. 12b Porchester Road is yours. And the price?' He paused, leaving the question hanging in the air as he looked at each of them in turn. 'The nominal sum of twelve thousand pounds,' he continued, shaking his head in disbelief.

Lost for words, Hamish and Suzy shot stunned glances at each other and turned to their gaping parents.

'I'm sorry, but I don't think I heard you correctly,' murmured Mr Hamilton, frowning.

Mr Ball shook his head, unable to believe what was happening. 'Regretfully, for reasons I cannot begin to understand, it appears you have a generous benefactor,' he intoned, rueing his lost commission. 'The owner, who wishes to remain anonymous, has instructed his representatives Peacock & Mayther to sell you the house for twelve thousand pounds on one condition: that first you meet the reclusive Mr McLeod next door. He's expecting you at six o'clock this evening.'

Hamish glanced at his watch. 'That's just over two hours from now,' he whispered uncomprehendingly.

'None of this is making any sense,' said Mrs Hamilton. 'Surely there's been some mistake.'

Sighing heavily, the flabbergasted estate agent ran the fingers of both hands through his hair. 'Look, lady,' he replied, raising his eyebrows, 'I wish it *was* a mistake. I'm losing money over this. It makes no sense at all. It's the first time I've ever come across a seller making an offer that the buyer can't refuse. Like I said, it appears you've got a generous benefactor who wants you living in that house.' Pausing, he frowned as a thought occurred to him. 'Perhaps you'll find out more when you meet the strange old buffer in number 12a,' he said. 'If so, let me know. I'd sure like to know what's going on.'

*

It was six o'clock precisely when Mr Hamilton pushed open the wrought iron gate to 12a's manicured front garden and led his family up the polished steps to the imposing front door. Admiring the burnished brass lion's head fitted to the centre of the glossy black door, he leaned forward, took hold of the fierce cat's hinged jaw and knocked twice. Immediately the heavy door swung open, revealing a cavernous hallway decorated entirely in brilliant white. As the late-afternoon sun projected their long shadows on to the sparkling white floor tiles, the four Hamiltons glanced at each other, surprised to find nobody there.

'Hello,' called Mrs Hamilton hesitantly.

Receiving no reply they entered cautiously, transfixed by the immense white space. Like a blank canvas awaiting an artist's paint, it was completely spartan, devoid of any fixtures or furniture. The only features breaking the white monotony of the high walls were five sets of double doors; two to the left, two to the right and one at the far end. All were resolutely white and all were closed. A bright light cast down from the ceiling reflected off the shimmering walls and floor tiles, accentuating further the scintillating white brilliance. But where the hall's appearance dazzled, its atmosphere positively startled. Warm and welcoming, it radiated contentment, optimism and peace.

'All it needs is a few fluffy white clouds and we could be in heaven,' murmured Hamish, summing up the sense of calm washing over them.

After what seemed like an eternity but was only a minute according to her watch, Suzy noticed a faint irregular ticking coming from behind the nearest set of double doors. Tentatively she reached for one of the white porcelain knobs and opened the door fractionally. Peering in, she was taken aback by a reception room so opulent it could have graced a stately home.

'Ah, my dear people, I'm so sorry to have kept you waiting,' came a jovial voice from behind, causing them to spin round. Startled, they observed an elderly gentleman emerging smiling from the doorway at the far end of the hall. 'I'm afraid I had some rather urgent business to attend to. The name's McLeod,' he announced, crossing the hall towards them and extending a wizened hand.

'It's a pleasure to meet you,' replied Suzy uncertainly, surprised at the strength of his handshake. Watching him greet her family, she had the strangest feeling she'd seen him before. But try as she might, she couldn't remember where.

'Welcome to my humble abode,' he chuckled, pushing open the door to the sumptuous stateroom and ushering them in.

Awe-struck by their lavish surroundings, they were momentarily lost for words.

Turning a full 360 degrees, they took in the roaring log fire framed by its giant marble surround, set under an equally large gilt-edged mirror that reflected an immense chandelier sparkling above them in the centre of the room. Oak-panelled walls gave way to ceiling-high bookcases containing hundreds of leather-bound volumes of various sizes and colours. Elegant and obviously valuable antique furniture abounded, including a grand piano in one corner and a large mahogany leather-inlay writing desk set between two tall sash windows fringed by gold silk drapes. Beyond, bathed in bright sunshine, lay the well-tended front garden.

'Please make yourselves at home,' chortled the elderly gentleman, enjoying the effect the room was having on them. Then gesturing towards a broad marble-topped table at the far end of the room, he continued warmly, 'And please do help yourself to refreshments. Then we can sit down and become acquainted.'

A considerable understatement, the so-called refreshments were exquisite. As befitting the majesty of their surroundings, a dozen platters of rare delicacies prepared by expert hands lay before them. After the family had helped themselves to cuisine fit for emperors, Mr McLeod waved them to one of two immense burgundy sofas facing each other in front of the roaring log fire. Settling himself opposite, Mr McLeod watched them eat, sipping tea from fine bone china.

Noting how the ocean liner of a sofa seemed to swamp its slightly built occupant, Hamish guessed him to be in his late sixties or early seventies. It wasn't until Mr McLeod looked directly at him that he noticed his startlingly blue cobalt eyes. Magnified by round wire-rimmed spectacles, his eyes resembled crystal clear sapphires that sparkled and penetrated with equal effect. His face – pale, thin and taut with an equine nose – would have appeared severe were it not for the neatly trimmed white beard softening his features. Flecks of golden light danced across his hairless head as the fire's licking flames reflected down from the chandelier's crystal drops.

Dressed in plain grey flannel trousers, a pale cream open-necked shirt and a threadbare brown tartan woollen blazer, Mr McLeod's sartorial appearance was no match for the elegant surroundings. Although he looked more like a kindly head gardener than an urbane lord of the manor, his dowdy image had one exception: his footwear – rich crimson velvet slippers with a sun-like monogram stitched in gold thread onto their soft uppers.

Smiling at their enthusiastic appreciation of his house-keeper's cooking, Mr McLeod sipped his tea. 'Thank you for coming,' he said softly. 'You probably think it's rather strange being required to meet me as a condition of your house purchase.'

'It had crossed our minds,' replied Mr Hamilton curiously, forking a succulent chunk of poached salmon into his mouth. 'We have no idea what's going on.'

Chuckling quietly, Mr McLeod went on, choosing his words carefully. 'Let's just say that the current owner and I go back a long way. A very long way. And he feels that I'm eminently qualified to determine whether you would be happy living in such ... such an exceptionally special house.'

'Exceptionally special?' repeated Mrs Hamilton, frowning.

Mr McLeod smiled. 'The house next door has remained unoccupied for almost seventy years,' he began softly. 'During that time, several families have tried to buy it. But unfortunately they weren't ... suitable. You see, the chemistry was wrong. And choosing a home is all about chemistry. It's possible to walk into a house and to know instantly whether you could live there or not. That certainty isn't due solely to rational likes or dislikes about a place – more often than not, those are just cosmetic issues, easily remedied. No, what governs the ultimate decision is the irrational. Does this place feel right? It's an intuitive thing. Instinctive. It's all about that sixth sense. The house has to *feel* right.'

Pausing, he took another sip of tea and looked at each of them in turn. 'And for a house to *feel* right,' he continued slowly, 'the *house* has to feel right.'

His guests stopped eating, silently replaying his cryptic words.

'Surely you're not implying the house next door is a living entity with feelings of its own,' ventured Mr Hamilton hesitantly.

'I'm implying nothing of the sort,' replied Mr McLeod, pausing. 'I'm stating it as fact.'

As one, they all stopped chewing and stared at him.

'But that's preposterous!' exploded Mrs Hamilton, her appetite deserting her.

Suddenly electric, the room's atmosphere crackled and Hamish felt the hairs standing on the back of his neck. Glancing at his shocked family beside him, he thought he saw the oak-panelled walls beyond turn a darker shade of brown. Hoping he'd imagined it, he attributed it to the fading light outside. But when he looked out, he could still see bright sunlight bathing the front of the house.

Watching Mrs Hamilton place her unfinished meal on a side table, Mr McLeod smiled at her sympathetically. 'But, my dear, tell me how you felt when you looked around the house,' he said softly.

Sensing his mother's difficulty gathering her thoughts,

Hamish glanced at Suzy and spoke quietly. 'I think the house is great,' he said. 'The weird thing is, I felt like I knew it already. It felt familiar and comfortable ... like we were coming home.'

Mr McLeod smiled and looked at Suzy. 'And how did *you* feel?' he asked, putting down his empty cup and saucer.

Frowning, she was silent for a long moment. Then, weighing up her words carefully, she spoke hesitantly, her tone puzzled. 'The house felt strangely tranquil,' she murmured. 'Like this house, it felt peaceful.' She paused, deep in thought. 'Now I think about it,' she whispered, 'I felt protected and safe there!'

Nodding slowly, Mr and Mrs Hamilton looked at each other. 'That's right,' they breathed incredulously.

Mr McLeod grinned broadly and clapped his hands. 'So you see, you're made for each other!' he declared. 'The chemistry's right! Now perhaps you'd be good enough to explain what plans you might have for it.'

Taken aback by his sudden change of direction, Mr Hamilton cleared his throat. 'I'd like to come back to the issue of chemistry in a moment,' he warned, 'but since you ask, there's obviously a lot of tidying up to be done. What's more, we understand there's some subsidence and dry rot, so we'll need to conduct a full structural survey to establish the extent of the problems.'

'Oh, I don't think you need to concern yourself with such matters,' said Mr McLeod, waving a hand. 'I can assure you that any survey will conclude that the house is structurally sound and fit for habitation on an immediate basis.'

'But previous surveys scared people off,' protested Mrs Hamilton.

'That's correct,' chuckled Mr McLeod knowingly; 'it's quite extraordinary what a survey can reveal, particularly when a house doesn't like the people trying to buy it.'

Shocked, Mr and Mrs Hamilton glanced at each other apprehensively, a mixture of disbelief and suspicion in their eyes.

'Well, if that's the case,' conceded Mr Hamilton uncertainly after a long moment, 'then we don't intend to make any structural changes. We like the layout of the house as it is. But it does require modernising. We're going to have to install central heating and electricity. And after we've replaced the floorboards and re-plastered the walls, we'll have to redecorate it entirely inside and out.'

'And the gardens are a disaster area,' added Mrs Hamilton quietly. 'They need a great deal of work if we're going to restore them to their former glory.'

'I see.' Mr McLeod paused, a troubled look clouding his gaunt features. 'I grant you the house needs a good lick of paint and there's no doubt the gardens require a lot of work. But I'd advise you to spend some time living in it before taking a hammer to it in any way. As I mentioned earlier, it's an exceptionally special house and you'll need to take time getting to know it, just as it will need time getting to know you.'

Mrs Hamilton shivered involuntarily.

'Don't be afraid,' Mr McLeod urged her, sensing her disquiet, 'As you've already experienced, the house is your refuge, a safe haven where you'll be protected for as long as you live there. Remember, it's no coincidence that after seventy years you're moving in. Just as you have chosen the house, so too it has chosen you.'

Intrigued and suddenly excited, Hamish smiled at his mother. 'Come on, Mum,' he said. 'Trust your instincts. It's a fantastic house. We'll all be safe and happy there.'

With all eyes on Mrs Hamilton, nobody noticed the troubled look momentarily passing across Mr McLeod's face as he reflected on the boy's confident words of encouragement. Sighing heavily, he forced himself to smile. 'Now, I'm sure you've got some questions for me,' he said, 'but before we start I must warn you, please don't feel frustrated if my answers fail to provide you with immediate clarity. I promise that in time, you will come to understand.'

Surprised by his cryptic disclaimer, Suzy went first. 'How long have you lived here?' she asked.

Mr McLeod smiled thinly. 'Time is a complicated business, my dear Suzy. Let's just say for longer than I care to remember.'

'Who last lived next door?' countered Hamish, surprised by his ambiguity.

'A young family not unlike yours,' he replied gravely.

Irritated, Hamish pressed on. 'What happened to them? Where are they now?' he asked impatiently.

'They moved on,' replied Mr McLeod vaguely. Then, sensing his answer wouldn't satisfy his persistent inquisitor, he continued softly. 'My dear boy, let me assure you, the family who last lived next door did so happily until they decided to move overseas. I'm not entirely sure where they all are now – no doubt the mother and father are long dead – but I do know that the boy continues to live locally.'

Detecting a momentary sadness to his voice, Mrs Hamilton noted his posture sagging as if deflated by some past memory. 'Mr McLeod, you say the house next door is a living entity. How's that possible?' she asked apprehensively.

'I'm afraid there are some things in life you just have to accept,' he replied quietly, leaning back in the sofa, 'and that's one of them.'

'But there must be a reason,' she pressed.

Hesitating, he looked at her thoughtfully. 'Do you believe in God?' he asked after a long moment.

'Well, yes, I do,' she replied, frowning.

'And what evidence do you base that belief on?' he asked.

Momentarily lost for words, she stared at him blankly, a flicker of understanding beginning to dawn on her.

'Just because you can't see the other side of the mountain doesn't mean it doesn't exist,' he explained. 'Sometimes, you just have to accept it's there.'

Suzy frowned. 'Why did the house choose us after so many years?' she asked.

Leaning forward on the oversized sofa, Mr McLeod rested his chin on clasped hands. 'Harmony!' he stated simply. Then noting their blank expressions, he laughed softly. 'Allow me the indulgence,' he continued, amused. 'Six weeks ago, after a prolonged battle with the local council, you lost your home – a smallholding in rural Northumberland. The modest swathe of rough land you've farmed tirelessly for many years is set to become a new housing estate. After years of hardship striving to harness the unpredictable nature of land and climate, your efforts were dashed by greedy property developers and duplicitous officialdom. With the meagre proceeds of your forced sale, you fled here to Cornwall in search of a warmer climate and a more balanced life.'

Astonished, they all stared at him in disbelief.

'But how could you possibly know that?' spluttered Mrs Hamilton incredulously.

Ignoring her question, Mr McLeod smiled knowingly and continued. 'The same balance you seek in life also exists within your family. Mr and Mrs Hamilton, you are perfect complements to one another. Mr Hamilton, you thrive on risk and uncertainty while your wife craves stability. She enjoys the familiarity and certainty of the known, of planning and working within clearly defined processes. That's why she's applying for jobs in local government.

'But you, Mr Hamilton, you detest bureaucracy and rigid structures. You're far more comfortable working in an ever-changing environment. Overcoming new challenges appeals to your natural spirit of adventure. You can build or fix almost anything you set your mind to, which is why you were such a good farmer. It also explains why you're talking to the banks about setting up your own landscape gardening business.'

Then turning his attention to Suzy and Hamish listening spellbound, he smiled mischievously and went on. 'Complex and evolving balances also exist in your children. Even judging by their appearances, it's clear that Suzy is modest, practical and highly artistic. And Hamish, he's an extrovert, impulsive with a healthy disregard for rules. Always keen to explore the unknown and push the boundaries, he's often grateful for his older sister's steadying influence.'

Taken aback by the unerringly accurate descriptions, Suzy and Hamish turned to each other, their questioning eyes seeking out the same answer: *how does this stranger know so much about us?*

Watching them in amusement, Mr McLeod noted their silent exchange.

Taller than most fourteen-year-olds, Suzy wore loose-fitting clothes in a self-conscious attempt to camouflage her height. She was currently dressed in one of her father's old navy blue V-necked sweaters over a white T-shirt and a long flowing navy skirt, her flat-heeled ballet pumps chosen specifically to minimise the height differential with her peers. With long straight brown hair, large hazel eyes, high cheekbones and luminous olive skin, her striking looks belied a keen intelligence. But where her school grades impressed, it was her precocious talent as an artist that set her apart. As she searched her brother's blue eyes for answers, the only outward sign of her prodigious artistic gift hung in the form of her brightly coloured earrings: homemade rainbow titanium shells.

Separated from her by just eleven months, Hamish contrasted sharply with his neat, colour co-ordinated sister. He sported faded denim jeans holed at the knees, a once white but now grey T-shirt and grass-stained trainers, his unkempt shock of blond curls crowning his effortless dishevelment. But despite their differing appearances, Mr McLeod could tell their bond was strong. Gazing at each other at a loss, they shook their heads in silent defeat.

'What I've been describing to you is balance,' continued Mr McLeod. 'Or harmony. That's why the house has chosen you. And why you have chosen the house.'

Her mind racing, Suzy stared at him, unable to work out how he knew so much about them. Then it dawned on her. Most of it was public knowledge. The local newspapers had chronicled their campaign against the property developers. And her countless awards for painting had generated widespread media coverage in the north of England. But why would a complete stranger living in Cornwall be interested in them? Unless, she reflected darkly, he was part of some conspiracy. Suddenly unsettled, she took a deep breath, about to interrogate him, when Hamish spoke.

'But balance between *what* exactly?' he asked, intrigued.

Regarding them solemnly, Mr McLeod was silent for a long moment. When he replied his tone was grave. 'Within the universe there exist two competing forces, so fundamental in nature that most people overlook them,' he intoned.

'You mean good and evil?' interjected Hamish.

Mr McLeod shook his head. 'Those are merely human conditions,' he said dismissively. 'No, the universal struggle revolves around two forces far more powerful than those. What I'm talking about are *chaos* and *order*. When they're balanced, harmony prevails. That's what you can feel in this building. It's also what the building senses in your family.'

Forgetting her conspiracy theory momentarily, Suzy frowned. 'So what happens when chaos and order fall out of balance?' she asked guardedly.

Looking suddenly tired, Mr McLeod sighed. 'I'm afraid the answer to that question is rather complicated,' he began, his words measured and precise. Pausing to gather his thoughts, he was about to continue when there was a knock at the door.

Startled, his expectant audience looked up to see a small silver-haired woman appear in the doorway. Wearing a white apron over a black dress, she coughed politely. 'I'm sorry to interrupt you, Mr McLeod,' she said timidly, focusing on the back of her employer's hairless head, 'but I'm afraid you have another visitor.'

'Ah, Mrs Gibbs, come in,' responded Mr McLeod without turning. Then addressing his guests opposite, he continued light-heartedly. 'Allow me to introduce my housekeeper. Not only is Mrs Gibbs an exceptional cook but she's the very soul of discretion.'

Wiping her floury hands on her apron, Mrs Gibbs smiled at them fleetingly. 'I'm pleased to meet you,' she announced. Then turning her attention back to Mr McLeod, she continued cautiously, a troubled look clouding her lined features. 'Mr McLeod, he insists on seeing you immediately. He says it's urgent, that it can't wait.'

'I'll be with you in a moment,' replied Mr McLeod, smiling apologetically at his guests sitting opposite.

'He says it's a matter of life and death …' she protested uneasily.

Mr McLeod was silent for a long moment. 'Very well,' he sighed reluctantly. Then levering himself out of his seat, he gestured to the far end of the room. 'I'm sorry for this unwelcome interruption,' he said solemnly, 'but please do help yourselves to some more of Mrs Gibbs's fine cooking. I'll be back again shortly.'

Wordlessly, they watched him depart. His anxious-looking housekeeper closed the door behind them.

'That sounded ominous,' muttered Hamish, getting to his feet and wandering over to a tall bookcase. Tilting his head to one side, he scanned the titles embossed into the leather spines.

'Anything interesting?' asked Suzy, crossing the room to join him. Stopping in front of the nearest window, she marvelled again at the impeccably manicured front garden bathed in the early evening sunlight.

'It's a historian's paradise,' he said, studying the chronologically ordered tomes. He guessed many of them were first editions, judging from their ancient leather bindings. Suddenly a thought occurred to him and he turned around, scanning the room's furniture. Like the books, everything was antique. It was then he noticed the giant globe dominating the far corner and wandered over to it. Set in a heavy oak cradle, the brown leather sphere, worn and scuffed from centuries of use, outlined the earth's borders and boundaries in intricate shiny gold leaf. He pushed it gently, examining its surface, and frowned. 'Hey, sis, check this out!' he hissed, glancing across at their parents in animated conversation in front of the fire.

'What is it?' she asked curiously.

'It's a globe!' he teased her, smiling.

'Very funny,' she replied, nudging him in the arm. 'I can see it's a globe, but what's so special about it?'

'Take a look for yourself,' he urged her, stepping aside.

Intrigued, Suzy leaned forward. Rotating the globe slowly, she noted the exquisite gold calligraphy labelling its geography and frowned. 'But how can that be?' she whispered uncomprehendingly.

Hamish shook his head. 'Don't ask me,' he muttered. 'That thing must be hundreds of years old. But it shows what the world looks like today!' He glanced across at their parents, still engrossed in conversation, before turning back to his sister, a curious mixture of excitement and disquiet flashing in his eyes. 'Do you know what I think, sis?' he asked. 'I think what we've heard today is just the tip of the iceberg. I can't help feeling there's a lot more to this place that Mr McLeod isn't telling us.'

Suzy nodded. 'I think you're right,' she agreed. 'Did you notice his reaction when I asked him about chaos and order falling out of balance?'

'I sure did,' he replied, frowning, distracted by a tall grandfather clock that stood sentry-like, guarding the door. 'Look at *that*,' he urged her with a barely-perceptible nod of his head.

Perplexed, Suzy followed his gaze and spotted the oddity immediately. As they moved across to the towering mahogany timepiece, it became clear that it was like nothing they had ever seen before. Instead of having one face like normal grandfather clocks, this clock had three: one on each of the three sides facing into the room. And within each copper face sat a smaller dial, making a total of six clocks in all. But what surprised them was that each clock told a different time.

'Listen!' whispered Suzy, studying the clock's inner workings through its glass door.

Irregular in both pattern and volume, its deranged ticking emanated from six long pendulums swinging erratically, one behind the other.

Just then Mr McLeod returned, a troubled look etched into his drawn features. Closing the door quickly, he noted their interest in the multi-faceted sentry. 'She's a beauty, isn't she?' he murmured surreptitiously, glancing across their parents. Standing in front of the fire, they had stopped talking and were watching him expectantly. 'I'm sorry, but I'm afraid we're going to have to cut short our meeting,' he announced solemnly. 'Something's come up that requires my immediate attention.'

'I hope it's nothing too serious?' asked Mrs Hamilton, crossing the room towards him.

Mr McLeod smiled at her reassuringly. 'It's nothing that can't be resolved,' he replied. Then reaching into his woollen blazer, he withdrew a brown leather wallet. 'Before you go there's something I must give you,' he said, slipping out a small white card and handing it to Mrs Hamilton. 'This business card will save you a lot of time and frustration.'

Frowning, Mrs Hamilton read out the inscription quizzically. '*Chimes & Sons, Discreet Removals?*'

Mr McLeod nodded. 'They're the only removal firm permitted to deal with this property,' he explained. 'I can vouch for them personally. Rest assured, their rates are competitive and their service is second to none.' Then looking up at the imposing clock, he opened the door and continued quickly. 'My dear people, it's been a pleasure meeting you. I'm so sorry to cut short our meeting, but I really must be getting on.'

Peering into the hallway, they gasped in astonishment. Nothing could have prepared them for the sight that greeted them. No longer bathed in brilliant white, it now glowed fiery red. Like a spectacular sunset, its immense surfaces blushed crimson.

'It's like a furnace without flames,' whispered Hamish, detecting a change in the building's atmosphere. Like Suzy, he sensed tension. The peaceful calm that had accompanied their arrival had gone, replaced instead by something different; something unsettling, something dangerous.

Observing their reactions, Mr McLeod nodded imperceptibly and stepped forward, motioning for them to follow. 'Remember we share an exceptionally special building,' he advised them solemnly, escorting them through the radiant but disconcerting glow towards the front door. 'You'll soon accept the ways of the house as completely normal. As I said earlier, please take time getting to know it.' Then bidding farewell to each of them in turn, he opened the front door.

Outside, the day's shadows were at their longest when the Hamiltons stepped into the porch. Squinting west, they hesitated at the top step. Despite the clear dusk sky, the air was still, the atmosphere hot and oppressive. Suddenly they felt a warm wind blow up from nowhere, whipping at their hair and clothes, increasing rapidly in strength.

'Look at the horizon!' gasped Suzy, pointing.

'Dear God,' murmured Hamish, transfixed by a roiling wall of darkness reaching high into the heavens, racing towards them.

An apocalyptic sight of epic grandeur, the seething bank of black clouds rolling rapidly east was turning dusk to premature darkness. Eerie rumbles of distant thunder grew steadily louder as lightning flashes illuminated the raging mass converging over Warfield. Stifling humidity enveloped them and heavy drops of cool rain began peppering the ground. Watching the advancing storm in fearful wonder, they knew its savage ferocity would be like nothing they had ever experienced before.

'Come on, let's get into the car before it strikes,' yelled Mr Hamilton above the buffeting gale howling like a chorus of demons.

They were about to make a run for it when they suddenly heard Mr McLeod's voice behind them.

'The tempest begins,' he bellowed, causing them to spin round, startled by his words.

Silhouetted in the blood-red doorway, his dark spectral form appeared sinister.

'Hurry!' he shouted. 'Get under cover as soon as you can.' Then without warning the door slammed, leaving four bewildered faces staring at the polished head of a fierce lion.

CHAPTER TWO

'They're here!' cried Hamish, careering into the hall and almost colliding with his sister.

'All right, calm down,' muttered Suzy, watching him throw open the front door.

'Calm down?' he replied, sounding hurt. 'Come on, sis, where's your sense of anticipation? We've been looking forward to this moment for months, ever since we left the farm. Our days of living out of a suitcase are finally over. Today we're going to be surrounded with our own things.'

Standing in the doorway, they both watched the blue and white removal truck cough to a halt.

'That's unusual,' muttered Suzy, noting the distinctive signage emblazoned across the lorry's high side: *Chimes & Sons, Discreet Removals, Established XXXX.*

The cabin doors sprang open and four men in matching blue and white overalls climbed down. Shielding their eyes against the dazzling early morning sun, they stood on the pavement, peering up at the building.

'What's taking them so long?' asked Hamish.

'They're probably wondering who in their right minds would want to live in such a dump,' replied Suzy humourlessly.

Moments later the silver-haired man waved to them. 'Good morning!' he called jovially, leading his team through the front gate. 'I never thought I'd see *this* day.'

Hamish and Suzy frowned.

'What do you mean?' called Hamish, aware of his parents joining them in the doorway.

The senior man laughed. 'Because of the weather, of course,' he chuckled, climbing the steps. 'Torrential rain one minute followed by clear skies the next. And flurries of snow after that. Surely you've read the newspapers. The past week's been the hottest and coldest in living memory. The weather's been so extreme it'll keep the weathermen scratching their heads for years trying to figure out what caused it.' Reaching the top step, he paused to catch his breath. 'It's always the same with this place; it takes years for a job to come along, and when it does the weather holds us up.' Smiling warmly, he extended a giant ham of a hand to Mr Hamilton. 'The name's Chimes,' he announced. 'Bob Chimes. And these three likely lads are my boys Amos, Roger and Bert.'

The 'boys' nodded curtly as their names were called. It was obvious where they'd inherited their powerful barrel-like physiques. Younger replicas of their father without the lacquered silver hair and craggy wrinkled features, they resembled bulldogs, reflected Suzy. 'Aren't you a bit old to be shifting heavy furniture?' she asked, wincing at the strength of the older man's handshake.

'Suzy!' exclaimed Mrs Hamilton, shocked. 'What sort of a question is that? You apologise right now.'

Sighing loudly, Suzy rolled her eyes. 'What's wrong with that?' she grumbled. 'It's a fair question. He's an old man.'

Taken aback, Hamish looked at her. Ever since they'd arrived that morning she'd been acting strangely.

'Don't worry, Mrs H,' laughed Chimes. 'Suzy's right. My lifting and carrying days are long gone. I'm just here to make sure these toe-rags do a good job. I'd never unleash knuckle, knuckle and knuckle here on such a prestigious job without supervising it myself.'

'Prestigious job?' repeated Mrs Hamilton in surprise.

'That's right,' said Chimes, nodding. 'Our family has carried out the removals for this building for as long as anyone can remember. Number 12 Porchester Road's been part of our family tradition for generations. Yeah, this old building's been good to us.'

Hamish couldn't contain his curiosity any longer. 'What does the XXXX stand for?' he asked, pointing at the lorry.

'Wouldn't *we* like to know?' replied Chimes, raising his eyebrows. 'It's a bit of a family debate, that one. Nobody really knows how long we've been in the removals business. We've done the family tree an' all that, but the trail goes cold at around 1760. Don't ask me why, but I reckon we've been in discreet removals for longer than that. We don't even know where the *discreet* bit comes from, just that it's been handed down over the years.' Pausing, he looked up at the building and smiled. 'The old girl's looking a bit tired on your side,' he continued. 'You've got your work cut out there, all right. Mind you, Mr McLeod's half looks the very picture of health. I don't suppose you'd mind us taking a look around before we start unloading? It's been years since I was last inside and I know the boys are keen to have a look around.'

'Of course, be our guests,' said Mrs Hamilton, stepping aside. 'I would offer you a cup of tea, but I'm afraid the kettle and mugs are in the back of your lorry.'

'You couldn't anyway,' mumbled Suzy. 'There's no electricity, remember?'

Mrs Hamilton glared at her. 'What's got into you?' she hissed angrily.

'Don't worry,' soothed Chimes. 'We've got a couple of thermos flasks in the cab. I think we could all do with a good cuppa before we start work for the day.' Then turning to his sons, he issued his instructions and watched them descend the steps. 'Right then,' he barked, clapping his hands. 'Let's have a look inside. I'm intrigued to see what the old place looks like after all these years.'

Brushing past the Hamiltons, he headed straight for the cavernous living room. Surveying its peeling walls, he crossed over to the nearest window and peered out. Below, lying haphazardly in the overgrown garden, were the filthy wooden boards ripped down from the windows earlier that morning to let daylight flood in for the first time in seventy years. 'She feels just the same as she did all those years ago,' he sighed. 'It's priceless.'

Standing by the grand fireplace opposite, Suzy looked from Chimes to her brother apprehensively. 'I wouldn't call it priceless,' she muttered. 'Something's changed. I don't know what. But something's wrong.'

'Sis, lighten up!' Hamish urged her quietly. 'You've been like a bear with a sore head ever since we arrived here this morning.'

'I know,' she grumbled. 'The moment I walked in, I felt tense and uneasy.' Pausing, she looked at him expectantly. 'Don't *you* feel it?' she asked.

Frowning, Hamish shook his head slowly.

'I was with my Gramps when I last stood here,' Chimes continued wistfully, surveying the view outside. 'It was just before the end of the war. I was sixteen. Every house in the street had been bombed, all except this one. Why the Germans ever targeted this part of Cornwall I'll never know. I mean, what strategic purpose could an ancient market town like Warfield have had? Anyway, I remember looking out of this window at the ruins around us. And despite the devastation and constant fear we all lived under at the time, I felt as I do right now: protected and safe. Yep, it's a priceless feeling all right.'

'Why were you here in the Second World War?' asked Hamish, intrigued.

Turning away from the window, Chimes smiled at him. 'We had the job of relocating a young family who'd been living here,' he explained. 'I remember it took us about three days. We didn't see anyone. According to Gramps they'd already moved on.'

Suzy frowned. 'So where did you take their belongings?' she asked.

Hesitating momentarily, Chimes noted their expectant faces. 'To Southampton docks,' he replied guardedly. 'Beyond that, I can't say anything. Remember, *Discreet Removals* is our family motto.'

Frustrated, Mrs Hamilton sighed. 'Mr Chimes, I'm sorry if we appear overly inquisitive but we're new to the area,' she explained. 'We don't know much about this house or its history and we'd like to learn more. So if you don't mind my asking, how do you know Mr McLeod?'

Chimes smiled. 'Mr McLeod and I go back a long way,' he said, with a laugh. 'He's a true gentleman. But you'd know that, having met him yourselves. The very fact that we're standing here having this conversation means we've got two things in common: Mr McLeod and this old building. And if it wasn't for Mr McLeod, this place wouldn't be here now.' Suddenly his face darkened. 'And God help anyone who tries to damage it,' he added menacingly.

'What do you mean?' asked Mr Hamilton, startled.

Smiling humourlessly, Chimes explained: 'Five years ago, the local council decided to redevelop this property. They deemed it out of character with the rest of the street. They wanted to demolish it and replace it with a block of flats. Can you imagine that? After surviving the war, it came under attack from property developers and the local council. As you can imagine, Mr McLeod wasn't happy about it all.'

'We know how he felt,' murmured Mrs Hamilton, glancing at her husband.

Chimes continued gravely. 'He fought them using every legal means possible but still the bureaucrats won. They slapped a compulsory purchase order on the place. Then late one evening, Mr McLeod called me. He asked me to collect four council officials the following morning and bring them here for a meeting.' He paused, laughing softly. 'The following day, the four officials were waiting for me outside the council offices. I could tell they were nervous. Nobody spoke for the entire journey. I waited in the van as they all went in. Then about half an hour later, the front door burst open and they all came piling out. They couldn't get out of there fast enough. I'll tell you this: I've never seen such fear in a man's eyes as I did when they clambered back into the van. As I drove them home, three of them kept mumbling incoherently about a hellish pit and fiery conflagration while the fourth one just sat silently rocking backwards and forwards.' Savouring the memory, Chimes chuckled. 'The compulsory purchase order was revoked the very next day. And during the course of the next two years, each one of those four council officials committed suicide without ever revealing what they'd seen.'

Horrified silence greeted the end of his story.

'Do you have any idea what they saw?' ventured Hamish after a long moment.

'Nope, and it's none of my business,' replied Chimes. 'All I know is this is an exceptionally special house, but why I couldn't tell you. The point is, none of us would be here if we weren't meant to be.' Then noting Mr and Mrs Hamilton's harrowed expressions, he smiled at them sympathetically. 'Mark my words, you'll be happy here,' he reassured them. 'But a word of advice: *always* place your full trust in Mr McLeod.'

Startled, Hamish and Suzy glanced at each other anxiously. Each knew what the other was thinking: just who was their new neighbour, and what could he possibly have done to drive four people to take their own lives?

Swallowing hard, Suzy was about to speak when the dull thud of heavy footsteps interrupted her thoughts.

'Right then, time for a cuppa,' announced Chimes as his three sons entered the room. Sensing the heavy atmosphere, they placed their boxes down wordlessly and began serving the refreshments. 'When we've finished,' continued Chimes, rubbing his hands together enthusiastically, 'I suggest we unload everything into this room. It'll make a good temporary base while you clean up and redecorate the rest of the house.' Pausing, he looked across at Mr and Mrs Hamilton, still staring at each other. 'If that's all right with you, of course?' he added.

But Mr and Mrs Hamilton didn't respond.

Watching them lost in thought, Hamish could tell they were having doubts. 'Mum, Dad, we're going to be fine...' he began. But before he could continue, a terrible dread stirred deep within him. Feeling suddenly sick, he grabbed Suzy's arm. 'Something's wrong!' he hissed in alarm. 'I can feel it too!'

*

It was lunchtime when Mrs Hamilton discovered the brown box marked *kitchen utensils* in the partially-constructed cardboard wall at the far end of the room. Lifting it down, she ripped off the packing tape and began rummaging inside. 'Where's that cutlery?' she muttered to herself, pulling out a white plastic kettle.

Watching amused from the other side of the room, Chimes posted another chip into his mouth and licked his greasy fingers. Smiling, he glanced across at Hamish and Suzy sitting on the floor opposite, eating their fish and chips out of newspaper. He noted their glum expressions and winked at them mischievously. 'Put the kettle on, Mrs H,' he called across. 'I could murder a brew.'

'Very funny, Mr Chimes,' replied Mrs Hamilton, handing a knife and fork to her husband as he unwrapped his meal, 'and how exactly do you suggest I do that?'

Laughing quietly, Chimes climbed to his feet and walked over to the box. 'Well now, I never thought I'd need to teach someone how to use one of these,' he chortled, picking up the kettle and heading for the door. Returning a minute later, he placed the now-full kettle in the centre of the floor. 'Gather round, it's time for an important demonstration,' he announced playfully, positioning the electric cord and plug in a straight line behind the kettle.

Intrigued, everyone got up and formed a circle around him.

'Ladies and gentlemen, allow me to introduce you to this kettle of water,' he continued theatrically. Then pausing, he smiled at Suzy. 'I'd like you to be my attractive assistant and kindly press that button for me,' he said, pointing at the switch on the kettle's handle.

Irritated, Suzy raised her eyes to heaven. 'Duh, it's not plugged in,' she said testily.

Chimes's smile faded. 'Just indulge me,' he said, a hint of impatience entering his voice.

Suzy sighed loudly. Reluctantly, she reached down and pressed the button.

'Impossible!' exploded Mrs Hamilton as the orange light came on. But the crackle of convection proved it was working.

Observing their disbelief, Chimes smiled, recalling his own astonishment in 1945 when his grandfather had switched on an unplugged lamp. It had been the first of several revelations he'd experienced that day. And now almost seventy years later, he mused, he was revealing the same secrets to others. 'You'll find that all of your electrical appliances work,' he said with a laugh. 'You may as well cut off all the cords and plugs for what use they'll be. What's more,' he added, grinning at their bemused expressions, 'despite the absence of central heating or air conditioning in this house, the temperature always stays the same. It doesn't matter whether it's summer or winter, the temperature remains a comfortable 24 degrees Celsius all year round.'

'But how's this all possible?' whispered Mr Hamilton in dismay.

Chimes shrugged his shoulders. 'It beats me,' he replied. Suddenly, his face darkened and he fixed his sons with hard eyes.

'And I don't need to remind you that whatever happens in this house stays in this house,' he growled menacingly. 'Remember, Discreet Removals is our code, never to be broken.'

Watching each brother nod slowly, Hamish shuddered to think what fate might befall them should they ever break their blood code. But chillingly, he suspected it might be fatal.

'There's something else you should see,' announced Chimes, brushing past them and heading towards the door.

Following him into the hall, they watched him close the front door. Then, turning to face them, he gestured to four open doorways leading off the hallway into bright sunlit rooms. 'Hamish, I'd like you to close all the doors,' he instructed softly.

Hamish frowned. Then, compliantly, he crossed to the nearest door. Unsure whether the throbbing in his ears was the sound of his footsteps or his racing pulse, he circled the hall, gradually extinguishing the daylight. Reaching the final doorway, he hesitated and peered back at the puzzled group of on-lookers standing in the gloom. Each face wore the same quizzical frown. Then, taking a deep breath, he closed the door and darkness enveloped them.

'Mr Chimes, is this really necessary?' came Mrs Hamilton's indignant voice from the blackness. But before she could continue, the hallway gradually illuminated, bathing them in brilliant white light. Astonished, everybody peered up at the ceiling.

'What the ...' exclaimed Mr Hamilton, desperately trying to rationalise the anomaly in physics he was witnessing. For the light was radiating from each of the hall's expansive surfaces.

Amused, Chimes laughed softly. 'Let there be light!' he declared.

Mrs Hamilton looked at him. 'I don't suppose there's any point asking you how all this is possible?' she asked.

Chimes shook his head. 'I'm afraid not,' he replied. 'Your guess is as good as mine. As you can see, the house possesses fantastical energy, but where it comes from I have no idea. I think the only person who knows the truth about this place lives next door.'

Hamish and Suzy glanced at each other. *Mr McLeod*, they mouthed silently.

*

The late afternoon sky was paling when the last box was set into the brown cardboard wall dominating the far end of the now-overcrowded room. Wiping their brows, Hamish and Suzy wearily surveyed the temporary family encampment.

'It looks like a second-hand furniture warehouse,' observed Suzy, yawning loudly.

At one end a double bed had been set against the boxes, while two single beds occupied the far corners nearest the door. A jumble of furniture filled the space in between. Tables, chairs, wardrobes and sofas were stacked alongside desks, chests of drawers, shelving units, pictures and rolled-up carpets, filling the room with the entirety of the family's worldly belongings. Narrow aisles criss-crossed the cluttered emporium, providing access to the beds, windows and door.

'It's not going to win any prizes for interior design,' conceded Chimes, chuckling at the live-in storeroom. 'But at least it's a start. The way your parents are slaving downstairs in the kitchen, you'll be moving into the rest of the house in no time at all.' He paused, studying their pale, drawn faces. 'You both look cream-crackered,' he said, smiling. 'I think you've done enough for one day. But before you finish up there's something I'd like you to do for me.' He reached into the chest pocket of his blue overalls and withdrew a white envelope. 'I'd like you to deliver this next door,' he said, handing it to Suzy.

Frowning, she read out the handwritten name quizzically. 'Mr McLeod?'

'That's my invoice for today's work,' explained Chimes. 'Mr McLeod always insists on paying it himself. I was going to drop it off later, but the boys and I need to help your parents downstairs, so I'd like you to deliver it for me.'

Hamish and Suzy glanced at each other apprehensively.

'Don't worry,' Chimes said, sensing their disquiet, 'you'll be fine. Just be sure to trust what he has to say.'

*

Pushing open the front gate to 12a Porchester Road, Suzy

noticed that the bowling-green lawn had sprung an unwelcome guest. Standing defiantly in the centre, a bright yellow dandelion was basking in the fading sunlight. Inspecting the surrounding flowerbeds, she could see the green flecks of infant weeds beginning to push their way up through the loamy soil.

'Mr McLeod's obviously got more important things on his mind than gardening,' she observed.

But Hamish didn't hear her. Fixated by the lion's head, he'd gone ahead and was already climbing the polished steps towards the glossy black door.

Suzy rushed after him. 'Do you think he's in?' she whispered as they came to a halt.

'There's only one way to find out,' he said, reaching up and flipping the big cat's hinged jaw.

Immediately, the door swung open and standing before them was Mr McLeod.

'Come in, I've been expecting you,' he said, smiling weakly. Then, after gesturing for them to enter, he led them slowly through the crimson hallway and into the familiar stateroom.

Hamish and Suzy stopped abruptly, surveying the opulent room through disbelieving eyes.

'What's happened?' exclaimed Hamish, shocked.

Like a vibrantly coloured oil painting dulled by age and grime, the room's once-dazzling appearance had faded. Everything about it, from its previously rich and lustrous panelled walls to its gleaming furniture, looked tired and dull. Even the burgundy sofas in front of the smouldering fire appeared worn and threadbare. But it wasn't just the room's appearance that had deteriorated; its atmosphere had changed too. No longer warm and welcoming, it felt oppressive and claustrophobic.

'It looks the same but everything's changed,' murmured Suzy, looking up at the chandelier's lifeless crystal drops.

'What's happened?' repeated Hamish, glancing at Mr McLeod. It was then he noticed that their elderly host appeared different too. Gaunt and frail, he looked exhausted. But more than that, he looked considerably older.

'I'm afraid it's a rather long story,' he replied wearily. 'But before I explain, I'd like you to tell me how you're both feeling.'

Hamish hesitated. 'I feel tense, ill at ease,' he said, frowning, 'like I'm going to be told off for something I've done wrong.'

'Me too,' sighed Suzy. 'I've been feeling on edge all day.'

Mr McLeod smiled thinly. 'My dears, what you're experiencing is *anxiety*. It's permeating every fibre of this building.'

'*Anxiety?*' repeated Hamish, confused. 'But how? Why?'

With a heavy sigh, Mr McLeod ushered them over to the giant globe in the corner of the room. Pushing the ancient sphere gently, he gazed at its brown leather surface. 'You'll both recall what I said about chaos and order during our last meeting,' he said quietly. 'When they are balanced, harmony prevails. But Suzy, you asked me what would happen if order and chaos ever fell out of balance. Well, I'm afraid the answer to that question can be found right here.' He tapped the globe as he spoke.

Hamish and Suzy noticed a red blush on its worn surface.

'The Middle East?' whispered Suzy uncertainly.

Mr McLeod nodded. 'Yes,' he replied solemnly. 'Note how the borders of that region have become blurred. What you can see there is a manifestation of order and chaos falling out of balance. Unless current differences can be resolved, conflict will soon engulf the region. And the outcome of that conflict will shape how the world looks in the future. It's regrettable, of course, but I'm afraid that's the way life is.'

'I don't understand,' said Hamish, confused. 'But why would conflict in the Middle East lead to ...' He paused, searching for the right words, then gestured to the room. '... lead to this ... to anxiety here?'

'It wouldn't,' replied Mr McLeod, tapping the globe again. 'Take another look. Do you notice anything different?'

Hamish and Suzy examined the sphere again.

After a long moment, Hamish exhaled noisily. 'It's fading!' he gasped, pointing at the intricate gold markings. 'The borders and boundaries of the whole thing are disappearing ...'

Suzy wasn't convinced. 'Surely it's just the light in here ...' she countered.

But Mr McLeod shook his head. 'No, I'm afraid Hamish is right,' he said sadly. 'The globe's markings are disappearing. The world as we know it is coming to an end.'

Suddenly afraid, they stared at him wide-eyed.

'The end of the world?' whispered Suzy, aghast.

Gesturing for them to follow, Mr McLeod led them across to the large writing desk set between the two tall sash windows. Opening the top drawer, he withdrew six clear golden cubes. 'Amber,' he announced, holding one up, 'a yellow translucent fossil resin derived from extinct coniferous trees. Each one of these six cubes contains a trapped insect.'

Confused, they watched him stack one cube on top of the other to build a golden column on the green leather inlaid surface.

'Imagine that this cube represents our three-dimensional world as it exists today,' he said, pointing to the top cube. 'In the present, the powerful forces of chaos and order are constantly opposing each other, shaping how the world will look in the future. That's what the globe is showing us in the Middle East. The future, which doesn't exist, is being modelled in the present.'

Then pointing to the five cubes below, he went on. 'But the universe is far more complicated than mankind currently understands. There are other dimensions in time and space. These five cubes represent dimensions in history. They form the foundations on which our world has been built. The problem is that chaos and order are just as active here as they are in the present. But if chaos and order fall out of balance in the past, then...' He withdrew the bottom cube.

Horrified, Hamish and Suzy watched the tower collapse.

'So what the globe's showing us,' said Hamish after a long moment, 'is that somewhere in history, chaos or order is about to prevail over the other in a way that means the world as we know it will be destroyed forever.'

Mr McLeod nodded slowly. 'Precisely, young man,' he sighed wearily. 'The consequences are unimaginable.'

Suddenly aware of the irregular ticking in the background, Suzy gestured towards the imposing sentry guarding the door. 'That grandfather clock,' she said, 'that's got something to do with all this, hasn't it?'

Mr McLeod smiled at her perceptiveness. 'Yes,' he said,

crossing over to it. 'The universe consists of an infinite number of dimensions. But chaos and order possess only enough energy to compete in six dimensions at any one time if they stand any chance of prevailing over the other.' He patted the mahogany long case gently and continued. 'This ancient timepiece is tuned automatically to whichever six dimensions have chaos and order in conflict.'

Suzy peered up at the multiple clock faces and frowned. 'So which five historical dimensions are they competing in?' she asked.

'Shifting sands, my dear,' replied Mr McLeod, opening the grandfather clock's glass door. 'They're constantly changing, but they always target shallow pools in time.'

'Shallow pools?' she repeated quizzically, watching him adjust the swing width of one of the pendulums.

'The clues can be found in our history,' he said, inserting a key into a clock face and cranking it up. 'Chaos and order always compete on the historical sites of previous conflicts where one either triumphed over the other or came close to prevailing. They compete in precarious moments of history where the prospects of victory are greatest. Historical weak points. Shallow pools in time.'

'1940,' murmured Hamish, reading a four-digit combination dial set into the larger of the two faces on the side of the clock.

Mr McLeod sighed heavily. 'The Second World War,' he said. 'I'm sure that period will be a permanent site of conflict. The chaos and anarchy of pre-war Germany paving the way for a new order intent on ruling the world. Such devastation.'

Hamish checked his wristwatch. 'Mr McLeod, why's the clock tuned to the present showing the wrong time?' he asked, frowning.

Momentarily unsure how to provide a simple answer to such a complex question, Mr McLeod hesitated. 'Cutting a very long and complicated story short, my dear boy,' he said, 'time is the most relentless force in the universe – impossible to stop or move forward. But this clock stands over a universal point that enables me to manipulate time by slowing it down to suit to the requirements of harmony in each one of those six dimensions . . .'

Continuing to study the strange clock, Suzy noted six dates

spanning centuries and the reality of what they were hearing began to dawn on her. It was like a bad dream, she thought. Only this wasn't a dream at all. It was real. The world was coming to an end. And somehow she and Hamish were part of it. Her mind raced. Dread and fear congealed into panic and she felt sick. She willed her anxieties to subside but still Mr McLeod's gentle voice continued tormenting her. Bowing her head, she forced herself to breathe deeply. Suddenly she heard a stifled sob and realised it was the sound of her own voice. 'Stop it. Stop it!' she cried. 'I don't want to hear any more. This is madness. It's all madness. Why are you doing this? Why are you telling us? I want to go home. I want to get out ...'

Alarmed, Hamish grabbed her by the shoulders. 'Sis, calm down,' he urged her, shaking her gently.

'Calm down?' she cried. 'Calm down? What's there to be calm about? We only came here to deliver this invoice and before we know it, we discover the world's coming to an end—'

'You're right,' interjected Mr McLeod, placing a hand on her shoulder, 'the enormity of what you've learned is difficult to comprehend. You should go home now and rest. It's been an exhausting day for you both.'

Hamish looked at him angrily. 'Now hang on a minute, you can't stop there,' he protested. 'You've got to explain how all this is possible. And Suzy's right. Why are you telling *us*?'

Mr McLeod looked at Suzy for a long moment, then shook his head. 'No,' he said, 'the answers to your questions will become clear soon enough. Now is the time for rest.'

Frustrated, Hamish sighed, about to protest further, but Mr McLeod raised his hand.

'You've heard enough for one day,' he said firmly. 'It's time for you to go home and rest. But before you go, you must promise me one thing. Never reveal any of this to your parents. For to do so would put their lives in great danger. You must trust me on this. Never tell your parents.'

Hamish and Suzy stared at him blankly.

Mr McLeod smiled. 'Good,' he said. 'Now come, I'll show you out.'

*

'I must be coming down with flu or something,' groaned Mr Hamilton, crawling into bed. 'My limbs ache and I've got a pounding headache.'

'Me too,' sighed Mrs Hamilton, climbing in beside him. 'I've felt worse as the day's worn on.'

'We're all exhausted,' said Mr Hamilton, yawning loudly. 'It's very late. We just need a good night's sleep.'

Listening from their beds at the far end of the giant storeroom, Hamish and Suzy peered at each other through the fading gloom. Each knew what the other was thinking: they were all suffering from the same symptoms of anxiety overload.

Falling back into his pillow, Hamish yawned and stretched, luxuriating in the comfort of his warm bed. Peering up at the ceiling, he noted how the pale light radiating from its immense surface was fading rapidly. He turned on to his side, pushing all thoughts from his tired mind. It was time to switch off, he told himself. Mr McLeod was right. Now was the time for rest.

Within moments, the room's faint light gave way to darkness and the soft breathing of deep sleep filled the air.

At first Suzy thought she was dreaming. But as she climbed towards consciousness, she heard it again: the sonorous clunks of ancient plumbing. Refusing to open her eyes, she turned over, willing sleep to embrace her again. But the metallic clunks were becoming more persistent. Sighing heavily, she turned over again, cursing the disturbance, when she heard Hamish's voice above her.

'Sis, wake up!' he hissed.

'I'm awake,' she groaned. Reluctantly, she opened her eyes and saw his silhouetted face inches from hers. A pale golden halo shone above him.

'That sound,' he whispered. 'It woke us both up, didn't it?'

'So?' she replied irritably.

'Well, it hasn't bothered Mum and Dad,' he whispered, peering into the blackness beyond. 'So there must be a reason. Come on, let's find out where it's coming from.'

'You *are* joking, aren't you?' she asked. 'If you think I'm going to go chasing around this house in the middle of the night, you can think again.'

Suddenly, a loud metallic bang made them both jump and Hamish spun round.

'What was that?' whispered Suzy nervously.

Hamish shook his head, contemplating the door. 'Come on, let's find out,' he murmured slowly.

Suzy looked at him in alarm. 'No way,' she hissed, 'I'm staying here.'

'All right, I'll go by myself and leave you alone,' he said.

'Alone?' she replied uncertainly. 'But Mum and Dad are here . . .'

Hamish smiled. 'That's true, but they're asleep and you're not,' he said, 'so you'll just have to lie there listening to the strange noises all by yourself.'

Suzy narrowed her eyes. 'Sometimes, Hamish, you can be a real pig!' she spat.

Hamish grinned and picked up her blue dressing gown. 'I know,' he said, passing it to her. 'Come on, let's go.'

With a resigned sigh, Suzy pulled on her gown and together they crept over to the door, their narrow path illuminated by a tunnel of golden light. Slipping silently into the blackness of the hallway, they closed the door quickly and stood motionless, waiting for a sound to guide them. Unease swelled in the pit of Suzy's stomach and she reached out for Hamish's arm. Agonising seconds ticked by like minutes. Then slowly, like a fiery red sunrise, crimson light flooded the space around them, transforming the hallway into a giant furnace.

'It looks like next door,' whispered Suzy, tugging her brother's arm. Robed in the black and white stripes of his beloved Newcastle United, he stood immobile, like a monochrome statue, his senses on full alert. 'Maybe the noises have stopped,' she added hopefully.

'Maybe,' murmured Hamish distractedly, scanning their fiery surroundings.

Suzy glanced at him nervously. She could tell he was coiled, ready to spring at the slightest cue. 'Hamish, I want to go back to bed,' she whispered.

Just then another metallic bang made them both jump and Hamish wrenched his arm from her grasp. 'Come on!' he cried, bolting for the stairway opposite.

Suzy's heart sank. 'Hamish, no!' she pleaded, but it was too late. He'd already reached the stairs and was thundering down to the basement. With an anguished moan, she lurched after him. But when she reached the stairs, he'd gone.

'Hamish, where are you?' she called, peering down into the darkness. But he didn't answer. Tentatively, she began climbing down, her unease congealing into fear. Swallowing hard, she struggled to keep her voice steady. 'Hamish, where are you?' she repeated, breaking into a cold sweat. But still there was no response. Another bang jarred her nerves and she stopped abruptly. Peering back up the stairs, she contemplated retreat, but one look at the sinister red hallway persuaded her to carry on. Taking slow deep breaths to quell her rising panic, she stepped down unsteadily, using the walls for support. Light-headed and faint, she cursed him silently. 'Hamish, answer me!' she implored. Then, out of the darkness, she heard his voice and her relief was immediate.

'Sis, I'm in the long room,' he called. 'Come quickly.'

Her legs like jelly, she stumbled down the remaining steps and turned left into a room running along the front of the house, its peeling walls stained by damp and mould. It was then she saw him, standing in the centre, bathed in the white light of a full moon streaming in through two squat windows. Distracted by the stale brown carpet, he was probing its threadbare surface with his slippered feet.

'What are you doing?' she asked quietly, her pulse still racing.

But Hamish didn't respond.

Watching him lost in thought, Suzy's fear and relief exploded into rage. Summoning up every ounce of strength she could muster, she marched over to him and punched him in the chest with both fists.

Caught by surprise, Hamish exhaled loudly and sprawled backwards, his arms wheeling like demented windmills. With a groan, he crashed into the wall, lost his footing and collapsed to the floor heavily. Wincing in pain, he stared up at her through disbelieving eyes.

'Don't you ever do that to me again!' she shouted. 'Don't you ever leave me alone like that again!'

Sitting himself upright against the wall, Hamish grimaced. He'd never seen her so angry before, and it took him several moments to gather his thoughts. Then, slowly, realisation began to dawn on him. 'Sis, I'm sorry,' he said, holding his shoulder. 'I'm sorry. I should have thought . . . I should have realised . . .'

'Yes, you should,' she snapped. 'Don't you ever leave me alone like that again! Do you hear me?'

Hamish looked up at her and nodded weakly. 'I promise,' he said.

She saw the remorse in his eyes and her anger dissipated as quickly as it had flared. 'Thank you,' she said, bending forward and offering him her hand.

Accepting it gratefully, Hamish hauled himself back to his feet and leant against the wall, rubbing his chest. 'That was some punch,' he said, smiling through the pain. 'Remind me never to pick a fight with you again.'

Suzy laughed softly. 'Let that be a lesson to you,' she said. 'Now tell me what's so interesting about the carpet.'

Hamish led her to the centre of the room. 'Here,' he said, pressing the floor with his foot. 'Do you feel anything strange?'

Frowning, Suzy pressed the carpet with her sheepskin slippers. Immediately, she felt it yield, a slight depression in its worn surface. 'What is it?' she asked slowly.

Hamish shook his head. 'I don't know,' he said, 'but if you trace it with your feet, it makes a square . . .'

'A *square*?' she repeated in surprise.

Hamish nodded. 'The last bang we heard came from directly below here,' he said.

'Are you sure?' she asked doubtfully.

'Sis, I'm certain of it,' he said. 'The moment I walked over this spot, I nearly jumped out of my skin.'

Suzy frowned. 'But we're in the basement,' she said. 'There shouldn't be anything below here but foundations.'

'Precisely,' he replied.

Suzy shivered involuntarily. 'What do you think it is?' she asked uneasily.

'That's just what I was trying to figure out when you bowled me over,' he replied. Then moving across to the wall, he bent down and slipped his fingers under the edge of the carpet. 'There's only one way to find out, though,' he said, taking a deep breath and pulling with all his might.

A loud staccato crack filled the air as the ancient carpet relinquished its fixing tacks. Hamish staggered backwards, hauling it away from the wall. When he was sure he'd cleared the target area, he stepped on to the carpet's fold to prevent it from rolling back, then retraced his steps. Intrigued, Suzy went to help him and together they folded back the green felt underlay.

Nothing could have prepared them for what they found. For set into the grey concrete floor was a trapdoor, a frayed rope-handle protruding from one side.

Hamish whistled softly. Crouching down, he swept a hand across the rough wooden surface and tapped it with his knuckle. 'I wonder where it leads?' he murmured, taking hold of the rope with both hands and glancing up at Suzy.

Instantly, she saw the gleam of excitement in his eyes and her blood ran cold. 'Don't even think about it!' she hissed in alarm.

But it was too late. He was already heaving at the frayed handle. With every sinew, he tugged at the door as if his life depended on it. Ignoring Suzy's increasingly frantic pleas, he knew it wouldn't be long before she found the courage to intervene.

Suddenly, a sharp hiss filled the air and the trapdoor moved, slowly at first, then easier, as if a sealed vacuum had been broken. His veins popping, he staggered backwards, raising the door to its full height. Then moving forward, he caught hold of it and lowered it gently to the floor. Sweat glistened on his forehead and he straightened up, staring in disbelief at a stone spiral staircase.

'If you think I'm going any further, you can think again,' muttered Suzy grimly.

Ignoring her, Hamish knelt down. 'I wonder where it leads?' he murmured, noting how the dark granite steps looked polished and worn from centuries of use.

'I don't know and I don't care,' replied Suzy flatly.

Hamish looked up at her, puzzled. 'Aren't you just a little bit intrigued?' he asked. 'Don't you think we've come too far to turn back now?'

Suzy glared at him. 'Stop it!' she hissed. 'Just stop it! I've had enough of all this. I'm not going any further.'

'You haven't got a choice,' he replied matter-of-factly.

'What do you mean?' she asked, nonplussed.

Hamish stood up. 'Neither of us has a choice,' he said. 'Whether we like it or not, we're here for a reason, just as Mr McLeod and Chimes have explained. Look, sis, we've been woken up by strange noises on our first night here and they've led us to this place. There's no way it can be a coincidence. Something's going on that involves the two of us. That's why Mum and Dad are asleep upstairs now and why Mr McLeod told us we couldn't say anything to them.' Pausing, he pointed to the steps. 'I think we'll find some answers down there,' he went on, 'and the way I see it, you've got three choices. You can either go back to bed, wait here, or you can come with me.'

Taken aback, Suzy stared at him for a long moment. Despite her anxieties, she knew he was right. No matter how much she wished for this nightmare to end, she realised the time had come for her to face up to whatever it was they were involved in. 'All right,' she sighed, 'I'll come. But on one condition: promise me you'll never leave me alone.'

Hamish smiled at her warmly. 'Sis, I swear it,' he said sincerely. 'I swear it. Now come on, let's go.'

Pressing the cold walls with the palms of their hands, they braced themselves in the corkscrew stairwell, fearful of losing their footing on the steep polished steps. Within moments, the last glimmer of moonlight disappeared and dense blackness swallowed them.

'Sis, are you all right?' asked Hamish, stepping down blindly. He could hear her short laboured breathing above him and knew she was struggling.

'Yes, but I can't see a thing,' she replied hesitantly, the tremor in her voice betraying her fear.

Peering down at where his feet should be, he was about to agree when suddenly he noticed a faint golden glow on the circular wall below him. At first he thought his eyes were playing tricks on him but as he continued down, the light grew steadily brighter. 'Sis, there's light down here!' he hissed. 'I can see light!'

Suzy's stomach curled into a knot. Although she was desperate to escape their dark confinement, she knew that light meant they were probably nearing their destination. And that made her shudder. 'Hamish, slow down,' she whispered urgently.

Sensing her panic, Hamish stopped and looked back. 'Don't worry, I'm not going to leave you,' he said soothingly. 'Put your hand on my shoulder and I'll guide you down the rest of the way.'

Reaching out, she found him in the darkness and Hamish realised she was trembling.

'Sis, listen to me,' he whispered, placing his hand on hers, 'there's nothing to be frightened of. Trust me. We're going to be fine. There's nothing to be afraid of. Do you hear me?'

Comforted by his touch and the strength of his conviction, she began to relax.

'Do you hear me?' he repeated insistently.

'Yes,' she replied, continuing to draw solace from him. 'You'd better lead on.'

'Good, now keep hold of my shoulder,' he said, stepping down. 'Look, the light's getting brighter.'

Sure enough, Suzy saw his silhouette appear against the wall and she breathed a sigh of relief. Silently, they continued their descent, grateful for the golden light guiding their way, until suddenly, without warning, they emerged through an arch and stopped dead in their tracks.

Lost for words, they stared in disbelief, mesmerised by the spectacle before them.

'Dear God,' murmured Hamish, struggling to take in the enormity of what they were witnessing.

Bewildered, Suzy released her brother's shoulder and stepped forward. 'What the ...' she began to say, but her words petered out as she stared up at a concrete ceiling some hundred and twenty feet above them. Surveying a vast rectangular cave, she guessed it covered the combined surface area of numbers 12a and 12b Porchester Road above them. But while the scale of the subterranean cathedral was breathtaking, what it housed was truly astonishing.

Together they stepped forward, marvelling at what appeared

to be an ancient stone circle rising titan-like from the earthen centre of the cave, comprising twelve gigantic blocks each measuring sixty feet in height and twelve feet thick. It was clear from their weathered surfaces that each irregular stump had been fashioned over centuries of climatic extremes. Approaching in stunned awe, they noted six terraced steps contained within the stones, leading down to a circular pit.

'It looks like a miniature Roman amphitheatre,' breathed Suzy, peering down into the golden arena.

Touching the nearest stone, Hamish noted how the golden light radiating from each of the cave's surfaces seemed to soften the grey hue of the colossal granite block.

'Beautiful, isn't it?' came a voice from behind, causing them to spin round.

Startled, they saw Mr McLeod appear smiling from another arch at the far end of the cave.

'What you're looking at is the answer to all of your questions,' he called, crossing the uneven ground towards them. 'My dear people, allow me to introduce you to Equilibrium, the only point in the entire universe where chaos and order are always balanced and where harmony prevails.'

His mind swirling with questions, Hamish didn't know where to begin. 'How old is it?' he asked quickly.

Chuckling at the boy's ability to ask such simple, yet complex questions, Mr McLeod replied, 'It's as old as mankind but as young as the universe.'

Infuriated by his cryptic response, silently blaming him for the emotional rollercoaster she'd just endured, Suzy glared at him. Her patience finally snapped. 'Mr McLeod, we want answers, not riddles,' she growled. 'Now please tell us what this is all about.'

Mr McLeod nodded, a grave expression settling across his face. But inwardly, he was delighted. Suzy's outburst helped to confirm why she'd been chosen. Intellectual obfuscation infuriated her. What she thrived on was straightforward facts. Her ability to assess situations clearly and come up with the appropriate course of action was one of her great strengths. In short, she possessed an abundance of common sense, if not always the confidence to act as her instincts dictated.

'The henge before you consists of twelve obelisks,' he explained, 'and it marks the site of Equilibrium, the only stable point in the universe where the forces chaos and order cancel each other out to create perpetual harmony. Six of these stones represent order and six represent chaos. You'll recall that chaos and order compete in six dimensions: five historical dimensions and the present. Since—'

Like a bombshell, a thought struck Hamish and he interrupted. 'Did you just say six of order, six of chaos in six dimensions? But 666 is the sign of the devil!'

Mr McLeod smiled knowingly. 'Don't dwell on religious imagery, young man,' he said. 'Instead, consider the two extreme outcomes of that three-digit equation. If chaos or order were to prevail in all six dimensions then, I grant you, the outcome would indeed be hellish. But if harmony prevailed in each then the result would be far more heavenly, wouldn't you agree?'

Taken aback, Hamish and Suzy looked at each other in amazement.

Mr McLeod continued. 'Equilibrium's mystical properties and supreme power have made it a source of conflict since time immemorial. Indeed, the very name of this town attests to its history. The armies of chaos and order have fought over Warfield for centuries, knowing that to control it would result in victory for all eternity.'

'But why build a house over it?' asked Suzy, frowning.

'To protect it,' he replied. 'To try and hide it from those who would misuse it. After centuries of war and suffering, a remarkable man emerged from those dark ages to restore peace. To do so, he built over this site and formed a circle of government charged with maintaining harmony. The castle he built was called Camelot and his government comprised twelve Knights of the Round Table.'

Stunned, Hamish and Suzy gazed spellbound at the ancient stone circle. 'King Arthur,' whispered Suzy incredulously. 'This is his Round Table ...'

Mr McLeod smiled. 'Indeed it is,' he said. 'But of course King Arthur and Camelot disappeared in time. And ever since then, this site has been hidden by a series of buildings, each of them unassuming yet strong enough to disguise the immense energy emitted by Equilibrium.' Pausing, he looked at the stone circle thoughtfully and continued. 'Sadly, though, I'm afraid nothing can disguise Equilibrium's peak surges.'

'Peak surges?' repeated Hamish quizzically.

'Do you recall last week's tempest?' asked Mr McLeod by way of explanation. 'That was caused by your arrival here.'

Bemused, Suzy had a sudden thought. 'King Arthur couldn't have been an agent of chaos or order,' she said, 'otherwise he'd have abused his position and misused Equilibrium. And you, you're protecting all of this as well . . .'

'And don't forget you and Hamish,' interrupted Mr McLeod. 'We all share a very rare trait. Inner balance. My dear Suzy, the reason why you and your brother were brought here is that individually your personalities and beliefs are perfectly balanced. And as a pair, you complement each other beautifully, futher enhancing that balance. Your youth is an advantage. You're still open-minded, exploring your formative years, questioning and challenging the world around you. Because you're still developing rationally, emotionally and spiritually, you're perfectly qualified to navigate the fine tightrope between chaos and order. Apart from a very few exceptions, older generations don't have this ability because they've become too set in their ways. Their personalities and beliefs have become too closely aligned with either chaos or order. Only those who have inner harmony may enter Equilibrium.'

'*Enter* Equilibrium?' they chorused uncomprehendingly.

'Look into Equilibrium and tell me what you see,' Mr McLeod said softly.

Hamish frowned. 'It looks like rock or concrete,' he said.

'Look closer,' advised Mr McLeod, watching them closely.

Hesitantly, they climbed down to the bottom step and leaned out. With a sharp intake of breath, they saw their own reflections.

'Now touch it,' instructed Mr McLeod quietly.

Cautiously, they knelt down and touched the surface with the tips of their fingers, causing ripples to appear.

'It's a liquid mirror!' exclaimed Suzy, submerging her hand in the tepid pool. A moment later, she withdrew it and realised her hand was dry. Her blood ran cold and she cried out, 'Mercury!'

'Don't worry, it's not mercury,' Mr McLeod assured her quickly. 'It's similar, but it's not toxic or poisonous. In fact, it's quite harmless.' Then, sensing her relief, he explained. 'Like mercury, it's a heavy silvery metal that's liquid at or near room temperature. But this form of quicksilver is unique to this very spot. It's the most perfect doorway in the universe, acting as a hermetic seal to prevent the time or space of any one dimension seeping into another.'

'So this is the entrance to history!' whispered Hamish, surveying the pool.

'Yes,' replied Mr McLeod, 'but only for those qualified to pass through it.'

'What would happen if someone unqualified like, say, Mum or Dad tried to pass through it?' Hamish asked.

Mr McLeod looked at them for a long moment, then shook his head. 'That would be impossible,' he said gravely. 'If anyone without inner balance even looked at Equilibrium, they wouldn't see the serene liquid mirror we do. Instead they would experience the nightmare of their opposite force in appalling clarity. Quite simply, they'd be exposed to their own personal hell.'

Shivering involuntarily, Hamish and Suzy recalled the fate of the four council officials. And each knew then that their parents must never discover the secret hidden beneath them.

CHAPTER THREE

'1597!' exclaimed Hamish in astonishment.

Mr McLeod nodded. 'The reign of Queen Elizabeth I,' he replied gravely. 'The tipping point is close at hand. Events are unfolding in that dimension that, if left unchecked, will result in either chaos or order ascending over the other such that the world as we know it will come to an end.'

'But I don't understand, why would the Elizabethan era be a shallow pool?' asked Suzy, confused. 'Wasn't it supposed to be a Golden Age?'

'It was crucial to the development of the modern world,' conceded Mr McLeod. 'When Bess ascended the throne, England was a poor and minor power on the edge of a Europe torn by religious and political strife. By finding a middle way between the ideas of Catholics and Protestants, she united her people under a single Anglican Church and brought peace and stability to her kingdom.

'And you're right, Suzy. Her reign did indeed charter a Golden Age. England became a successful and wealthy trading nation. Arts, culture and learning flourished. Shakespeare was in his prime. Sir Walter Raleigh founded Virginia in North America in the Queen's name. Sir Francis Drake circumnavigated the world for the first time. Queen Elizabeth's contribution to the world as we know it cannot be overstated.' He paused, noting their expectant expressions, then continued. 'But her forty-five-year reign was also beset with conflict, plots and rebellion. For most people it was a terrible time to live. Plague and starvation wreaked havoc, while the constant threat of invasion by Spain created fear throughout her kingdom. It was a very uncertain period when the precarious harmony she managed to achieve could so easily have been destroyed by a great number of social, political and religious crises.' Hesitating, he looked at each of them in turn. 'I'm afraid that once again, chaos and order have converged on this period and are waging a war that will have catastrophic consequences unless you can restore harmony there.'

Hamish and Suzy stared at him in disbelief.

'*Us?*' spluttered Hamish.

'It's why you were brought here,' he replied. 'Time's running out. You're the only people who can save the world as we know it.'

Suzy swallowed hard, the familiar tide of panic once again threatening to engulf her. 'I can't,' she whispered, reaching for Hamish's arm. 'This can't be happening.'

'My dear Suzy, you have no choice,' said Mr McLeod firmly. Then he gestured to Equilibrium and held out his hands to them. 'It's time for you to accompany me into Equilibrium. I can assure you, you'll be perfectly safe. Just close your eyes and hold your breath before you go under.'

His pulse racing, Hamish looked at Suzy and saw the terror in her eyes. Quickly, he took hold of her hands. 'Sis, listen to me,' he implored urgently. 'Remember what Chimes said. Always place your full trust in Mr McLeod. We're going to be all right. I know the unknown's frightening but you're not going to be alone. I'll be with you. And Mr McLeod will be with us too. What we've learnt is too important to back away from now. Mr McLeod's right. We have no choice. We must go. But I swear to you, I'll never leave you alone.'

For several moments, they remained locked in silent communion. Then, as one, they turned to face him.

'We're ready,' announced Hamish quietly, leading Suzy to the top step.

Mr McLeod smiled at them gratefully. 'Thank you,' he said, stepping down.

Following him down to the silver pool, they stopped at the bottom step, staring into Equilibrium.

Mr McLeod looked at them, standing hand in hand, and noted the tension in their faces. 'Ready?' he asked gently.

Suzy looked at him and he saw doubt and trepidation in her hazel eyes.

But what *she* saw startled her. For peering into his azure eyes, she was struck by their tenderness, consoling and reassuring in equal measure. And when he spoke, his tone had an ethereal quality to it. 'Fear not,' he said soothingly. 'I remember only too well my emotions when I first entered Equilibrium. Like you, I was uncertain and afraid. But as my guide said to me, now I say to you – be not afraid, for this is your destiny.'

From nowhere, a gossamer calm descended on her and she stared at him in astonishment.

Mr McLeod smiled knowingly. 'Good,' he said, and together the three of them stepped down, their feet disappearing into the tepid pool. As they descended terraced steps beneath the surface, the silver liquid rose up, gradually submerging their waists and then their chests. Hesitating momentarily to take a deep breath, they each closed their eyes and slipped below the surface into Equilibrium.

Despite closed eyes, Hamish and Suzy marvelled at an irresistible white light at the end of a long tunnel, drawing them effortlessly towards it. The steps they descended seemed to float beneath them as they drifted weightlessly towards the celestial brilliance. Experiencing joy and contentment beyond their wildest dreams, peace and harmony suffused their very souls. Aware of each other's presence, they felt such euphoria that their spirits seemed to soar as if at one with the universe. They approached the wondrous light and their serenity intensified. Then they arrived. Climbing the submerged steps, they broke the surface and, opening their eyes, they gasped at the spectacle towering over them. Like an immovable guard of honour, twelve giant blocks surrounded the pool from which they were emerging dry.

'It can't be, we're back where we began!' exclaimed Hamish, confused.

'We are and we aren't,' chuckled Mr McLeod. 'Take a closer look around you.'

Climbing the terraced steps, Hamish and Suzy performed a full circle, taking in the familiar ancient stones. It was then they realised the walls and ceiling of the vast space looked different. No longer made of concrete, they were constructed from crumbling red bricks separated by the greyish hue of ancient mortar. And on either side wall, where once had been entrances to spiral staircases, wooden stairs led to two doorways some sixty feet above them.

A wave of recognition broke over him and Hamish laughed. '1597,' he called. 'Equilibrium begins and ends in the same place. The only changing variable is time.'

'Well done!' Mr McLeod congratulated him, smiling. Then turning to Suzy, he said, 'Now, that wasn't so bad, was it? Most people have to wait a lifetime to experience something like that.'

Silently chastising herself for her earlier fear, Suzy smiled sheepishly. 'It was beautiful,' she admitted. 'Out of this world.'

Leading them up a rickety wooden staircase to the door on his side of the house, Mr McLeod turned an ancient iron handle and pushed on it hard. The heavy door creaked loudly and Hamish and Suzy gasped. For what they saw wasn't the basement room of a Georgian townhouse. It was a long gloomy corridor. Faint yellow light from wall-mounted candles danced and flickered at regular intervals, casting bright spots on the low, whitewashed ceiling. Stepping forward onto grimy flagstones, Mr McLeod noticed their bemused expressions.

'Prepare yourselves for the unfamiliar,' he said, his words echoing in the long chamber. 'The familiar no longer exists. The only constant is Equilibrium. All else is changed.'

Just then a loud metallic clunk startled them and the end of the corridor illuminated as a heavy door groaned open. Holding their breath, Hamish and Suzy watched the silhouette of a bent figure appear, tapping a wooden cane on the stone floor. 'Is that you, McLeod?' the elderly gentleman called out, shuffling forward.

'My dear Genin, it's so good to see you again!' called Mr McLeod, laughing softly.

Hamish and Suzy watched the two men greet each other like long-lost friends. It was clear from their awkward embrace and patted solicitations that they shared a close bond. Although they both possessed grey beards and hairless heads, any resemblance ended there. Judging from his severe stoop and walking stick, Genin was clearly the more senior. But what struck them most were his clothes.

'I'd like to introduce you to some friends of mine,' said Mr McLeod, gesturing to Hamish and Suzy.

Genin smiled at them, revealing a mouth full of blackened teeth. 'So these are the young people you've told me so much about,' he said, shuffling forward and extending a wizened hand. Introducing himself, he looked Hamish up and down. 'Interesting stripes, young man. I'm delighted that the fashions of the future remain exactly where they are. We're going to have to dress you properly if you're going to blend in here.'

Hamish looked at Genin's baggy white shirt with its frilled neck, knee-length brown breeches over pale stockings, and he groaned inwardly.

'You must be hungry after your long journey,' Genin continued, ushering them into the dimly-lit room from which he'd just emerged.

Coughing as they entered, Hamish and Suzy noted a smouldering log fire billowing acrid smoke into the long narrow room. Two squat mullion windows with small diamond-shaped leaded panes provided the main source of light, while four wooden chairs positioned around the fireplace indicated that the sparsely furnished room was the principal living area.

Inviting his guests to make themselves comfortable, Genin shuffled off in search of refreshments.

'Mr McLeod, how do you know Mr Genin?' asked Suzy the moment the door had closed.

'Genin and I go back a long way,' he replied. 'Just as I am the custodian of Equilibrium in the present, he's its guardian in this dimension.'

With one ear on the conversation, Hamish wandered over to the nearest window. Peering through the uneven glass, he stared in astonishment at the early morning view outside the front of the house. Below him was a dirt yard sloping down to three dilapidated, thatched barns. Inside one, he could see a primitive plough and two yokes for the oxen that hauled it. A dozen or so hens roamed about, pecking at the stony ground. Opposite was a sturdy wooden gate, beyond which ran a narrow rutted track fringed by tall hedgerows. On either side, a patchwork of small green fields separated by dry-stone walls stretched for as far as the eye could see. And it suddenly dawned on him that in the sixteenth century, Equilibrium was disguised as a remote farmhouse.

Behind him, Suzy was about to continue her questioning when the tapping of wood on stone signalled Genin's return. Following him in was a large, rotund matron carrying a tray.

'Allow me to introduce you to Mrs Potts, my housekeeper,' he said, directing her to the table at the end of the room. 'I don't know what I'd do without her. She's a loyal servant and the very soul of discretion.'

Wearing a plain brown, loose-fitting floor-length dress and a white linen headscarf, the ruddy-cheeked servant placed the tray down obediently. Then, nodding once respectfully, she left the room without saying a word.

'Now, my friends, please help yourselves to breakfast,' Genin urged them enthusiastically.

Feeling surprisingly hungry, Hamish and Suzy sat down and helped themselves to large chunks of dark bread, creamy yellow butter, golden honey and boiled eggs. Beginning to eat, they were instantly struck by the delicious flavours of the plain fare.

'We have much to discuss before you depart today,' said Genin as he and Mr McLeod sat down opposite. 'You've both got a long journey ahead of you.'

Hamish and Suzy stopped eating and looked at him warily.

'Depart?' repeated Suzy. 'Just the two of us? What about Mr McLeod?'

Looking pained, Mr McLeod shook his head. 'I'm sorry, but I can't leave this site,' he said. 'To do so would leave Equilibrium exposed, without one of its custodians. And that, my friends, would contravene one of the most fundamental laws of harmony.'

Observing their concern, Genin chuckled quietly. 'You won't be going alone,' he said. 'I've seen to that.' Then picking up a pewter jug, he filled four earthenware cups and handed them out. Smiling, he raised his cup to Hamish and Suzy. 'Here's a toast to a successful quest,' he proposed.

'I'll drink to that,' acknowledged Mr McLeod solemnly.

Feeling uneasy, Hamish and Suzy drank. But the moment they tasted the liquid, they recoiled, their faces twisting in disgust. Resisting the urge to spit it out, they swallowed, wincing as the bitter drink slipped down.

'What's that?' spluttered Hamish, grimacing into his cup.

'Why, it's ale, of course,' replied Genin, nonplussed.

'Beer for breakfast!' exclaimed Suzy.

Mr McLeod laughed softly. 'I should have warned you,' he said. 'Most people drink ale in the sixteenth century because the water isn't clean.'

'What's it made of?' asked Hamish, examining the cloudy contents of his cup.

'Malt, water and aromatic herbs,' replied Genin proudly. 'I make it myself. And you'd better get used to it because we drink about a gallon of it every day.'

'*How* much?' exclaimed Suzy.

'About four and a half litres,' explained Mr McLeod, smiling. 'But it's so weak in alcohol that it doesn't generally impair people's ability to function normally.'

Hamish tasted it again and pulled a face. 'It's going to take a lot of getting used to,' he muttered grimly.

'It's an acquired taste, my friend,' replied Genin, wiping his mouth with his sleeve. 'I'd wager that by the time you go home, you'll both have developed a taste for it.'

Unconvinced, Hamish and Suzy bit into some honeyed bread to get rid of the sour aftertaste.

As he watched them from across the table, Mr McLeod's smile faded. And when he spoke, his tone was deadly serious. 'Before we prepare you for your journey, there are some things you must understand,' he said. 'Your task here is to restore the harmony between chaos and order. To do so, it's vital that you disregard any concepts of good and evil or right and wrong. You're not here to act as your conscience dictates. Imbalance is the only enemy. And it's quite possible that what you consider to be right or good is actually contributing to the current imbalance. If restoring balance means having to align yourselves with what you think is wrong or evil, then I'm afraid that's exactly what you must do. It's imperative that you always remain ruthlessly impartial.'

'But how will we recognise the imbalance?' asked Hamish uncertainly.

'Chaos and order in their extreme manifestations share a

common outcome,' he explained: 'pain and suffering. Whether it's the chaos of rampant anarchy or the order of totalitarianism, the outcome is always the same. The symptoms are readily identifiable. Your challenge is to identify the cause and neutralise it.'

'Where will we find this imbalance?' asked Suzy, frowning.

Smiling at her incisiveness, Genin replied. 'The symptoms can be found throughout the land, but the epicentre of imbalance appears to be London.'

'Then that's where we must go,' she said, causing Hamish to look at her in surprise.

Mr McLeod grinned and nodded at Genin, who reached into the pocket of his breeches and withdrew a small black satin pouch. Placing it on the table, he loosened the drawstring and removed a circular gold object attached to a long chain. Holding it up to Hamish and Suzy, he pressed a clasp at the side of the shiny device and a circular lid sprang open. Behind it was the strangest pocket watch they'd ever seen.

'This is the only timepiece of its kind in the entire universe,' Genin explained.

Spellbound, Hamish and Suzy counted three dials. Four arms rotated around a central fulcrum, three of them black and one red.

'It looks complicated,' continued Genin, noting their perplexed expressions, 'but if you look at it closely, it's actually rather simple to read. As you can see, there are three fixed bezels or dials running around the edge of the timepiece. The outer bezel features the traditional markings of a compass with one arm trained to the earth's magnetic north. The second dial shows a standard clock with two hands. And the third bezel makes it unique; this one is a barometer that gauges imbalance and harmony.' He paused, allowing them time to study it. 'Whenever the red arm points to the equivalent of 12 o'clock or "H", as marked here,' he explained, pointing, 'harmony prevails. But if it points to the left of 12 o'clock then imbalance exists, with chaos the prevailing force. As you can see now, it's pointing to the right of twelve, which means order's responsible for the imbalance.' Suddenly his face darkened. 'Whatever happens, you must never allow this arm to reach its extremes,' he warned gravely. 'For if it ever reaches the equivalent of a *quarter to* or a *quarter past* the hour, shown here by the markings "C" and "O", then chaos or order will have triumphed and the world you've come from will be destroyed forever.'

Shivering involuntarily, Suzy reached out and took the precious timepiece from Genin's grasp. Examining it, she closed the sprung lid and turned it over in her hand. It was then she noticed a familiar symbol engraved into its polished outer casing; it was like a full sun with twelve straight geometric rays.

'What's this symbol?' she asked, recalling the same symbol stitched into Mr McLeod's crimson velvet slippers.

'That's the Sign of Equilibrium,' replied Mr McLeod softly.

'Of course!' whispered Hamish. 'The round pool surrounded by twelve stones.'

'Ah, the mystical properties of the number twelve,' mused Genin distractedly. Then, noting the quizzical frowns opposite, he explained. 'It's no coincidence that the number twelve is so symbolic in religion and time. Think about it. In the Old Testament, Jacob had twelve sons, who were the progenitors of the Twelve Tribes of Israel. Jesus had twelve apostles. There are twelve months in a year. The Western Zodiac has twelve signs, as does the Chinese Zodiac. A new day begins at the stroke of twelve midnight, with the sun highest in the sky at twelve noon. The minute hand of a clock turns twelve times as fast as the hour hand. The basic units of time can all perfectly divide by twelve. It's all because the universe and the number twelve are perfectly aligned.'

His lecture over, he leaned forward and fixed them with hard eyes. 'Look after that timepiece well,' he warned. 'Under no circumstances allow it to fall into other hands. If at any stage you think it's going to be taken from you, destroy it. For if it falls into enemy hands, our cause is as good as lost.'

Hamish and Suzy looked at each other, the same question running through their minds.

Suzy answered first. 'I'd prefer you to look after it,' she said, handing it to him.

Weighing it in his hand, Hamish was struck by how light it was when he saw a momentary look of concern cross Mr

McLeod's face. 'There's something you're not telling us,' he said quietly.

Mr McLeod sighed heavily. 'My friends, it would be remiss of me to send you on this quest without spelling out the danger you face,' he said. 'You're about to become embroiled in the most dangerous conflict in history, a conflict in which neither chaos nor order desires harmony. You'll have help, of course, we've seen to that, but ultimately your success or failure will depend on you. I have complete faith in you; you wouldn't be here if you weren't up to the task in hand. But you must trust your instincts and believe in yourselves. You must believe that anything is possible. And, very importantly, you must never give up. For situations only become lost when those involved lose their belief.'

Reflecting on his advice, Hamish was about to ask a question when there was a gentle knock at the door. Looking up, he and Suzy saw Mrs Potts appear in the doorway.

'Master, the clothes are ready,' she announced quietly, addressing the back of his hairless head.

Genin smiled at them, revealing his rotten teeth. 'It's time to get you dressed,' he said. Then, without turning, he issued his instructions. 'Mrs Potts, take Suzy upstairs and help her dress. And make sure that Master Hamish's clothes are laid out for him in the principal bedroom.'

Smiling at them warmly, the housekeeper acknowledged their presence for the first time and gestured for them to follow.

*

'It's very itchy,' complained Suzy, trying to keep her balance on the three-legged stool. 'And the colour's rather drab. Can't I wear something brighter and more comfortable?'

'No, no, remember the sumptuary laws,' muttered Mrs Potts, slipping another pin into the waist of the floor-length pale blue dress.

'The *what?*' asked Suzy in surprise.

Mrs Potts stopped working and looked up at her. 'Don't tell me you've never heard of the sumptuary laws!' she exclaimed.

Suzy looked at her blankly.

'Well I never!' she said, resuming her needlework. 'The

sumptuary laws control what people can spend their money on. Queen Elizabeth introduced them to restrict the colour, style and materials of the clothes people are allowed to wear.' Tilting her head to one side, she stepped back to review her handiwork, a frown creasing her fleshy forehead. Adjusting another pin, she smiled with satisfaction and continued. 'You see, clothes are an easy way of identifying rank and privilege. We lower classes can only wear clothes made from wool, linen or sheepskin in certain colours such as pale blue.'

'You're joking!' laughed Suzy disparagingly.

'And why would I joke about something so serious?' snapped the housekeeper.

'Serious?' repeated Suzy uncertainly.

'Of course!' she replied in consternation. 'The punishments for flouting the sumptuary laws range from fines to execution. It doesn't matter if you can afford the finest clothes in the world; if your status in society doesn't permit it then you're not allowed to buy or wear them.'

'But that's preposterous!' exclaimed Suzy.

'I grant you it must be frustrating not being able to buy something you can afford,' replied Mrs Potts. 'But it'd be wrong if every woman went around looking like the Queen, wouldn't it? I think it's only right that royalty wears ermine while lesser nobles have to make do with fox and otter. After all, the status of royalty must be preserved.'

'But surely it would be better if society was classless,' Suzy said thoughtfully.

Mrs Potts froze. 'That's treasonous talk!' she hissed. Then, wagging a finger at Suzy, she continued sternly. 'Mind what you go around saying,' she warned. 'That type of free talk will get you strapped into the ducking stool. The punishments for loose-tongued women are severe. A word of advice: never forget your lower class status or your place as a woman.'

Taken aback, Suzy stared at her. 'My place as a woman?' she repeated uneasily.

'Dear Lord,' sighed Mrs Potts in exasperation. 'Woman in her greatest perfection is to serve and obey man. You must learn to keep your own counsel, be loyal, dutiful and supportive.'

Suzy's heart sank.

Sensing her disquiet, Mrs Potts took hold of her hand and patted it gently. 'My dear, I don't know where you've come from and I don't want to know,' she said, smiling. 'But you're clearly unfamiliar with the modern rules of English life. You've got a lot to learn. But I can tell you have a kind heart and a good head. So whatever it is you're here to do, just remember to think twice before you speak or act.'

Dispirited, Suzy nodded weakly.

'Good,' replied Mrs Potts matter-of-factly. 'Now take off that dress and I'll go and adjust it.'

Changing back into her blue towelling robe, Suzy handed the dress to her and watched her bustle out.

Alone in the small whitewashed room with its single bed and solitary chair, Suzy crossed over to the window and gazed out. In the distance, beyond the patchwork of fields and grazing sheep, she could see the spire of a church surrounded by the thatched roofs of half-timbered houses that made up Warfield in the sixteenth century. As feathery smoke plumes drifted up from the chimneys, she marvelled at the sunny rural idyll.

'So near yet so far,' she murmured, considering how close she was to home, yet separated by over four hundred years. Suddenly an overwhelming sense of isolation gripped her and she pressed her forehead against the cool glass, breathing deeply, resolving not to succumb to panic.

'Are you all right?' came a worried voice from behind her. Startled, she spun round and saw Hamish standing in the doorway. No longer wearing his black and white stripes, he looked like an actor from Shakespeare's Globe Theatre. Grinning at her surprise, he turned in a circle. 'What do you think?' he asked, laughing.

Resplendent in a brown leather jerkin over a loose-fitting white linen shirt, he was wearing knee-length brown woollen breeches, cream stockings and leather boots laced up to his calves. A russet woollen flat cap completed his lower-class look.

'It's all too clean, of course,' chortled Mr McLeod, standing behind him, 'but a few days on the road will see to that.'

Laughing, Suzy embraced Hamish warmly.

Watching from the hallway, Mr McLeod and Genin glanced at each other apprehensively. Each knew what the other was thinking. It was more than possible that the bond between brother and sister would be tested to breaking point, if not destroyed irrevocably. But it was a risk they had to take. Restoration of harmony was their only priority. And if that meant sacrifices had to be made, then so be it.

Bustling up the stairs, Mrs Potts brushed past them in the cramped hallway and laid the coarse woollen dress on the bed. 'We'll be down in ten minutes,' she said brusquely, shooing Hamish out of the room and closing the door.

'What's up with her?' asked Hamish, peeved.

Genin laughed softly. 'It's called Mother Hen syndrome, dear boy,' he said. Then, with a pointed look at Mr McLeod, he added, 'And Mother Hen's fearful for one of her chicks.'

*

They were in the smoky living room when Mrs Potts ushered in the pretty peasant girl. Blushing at the approving stares, Suzy accepted Genin's hand and sat down in front of the smouldering fire, smoothing the white linen apron tied around her waist.

'Sis, you look amazing!' exclaimed Hamish. He noted how her hair had been scraped back from her forehead and tied in a plait under a white linen headscarf, accentuating her high cheekbones and luminous olive skin.

'I told you pale blue would suit her,' said Mrs Potts, admonishing Genin playfully. She nudged Suzy in the shoulder. 'He'd have had you wearing yellow if it had been up to him.'

'Thank *you*!' replied Suzy, feigning horror, but she was genuinely relieved by the housekeeper's intervention. The thought of undertaking their mission dressed like a banana was too awful even to contemplate.

Mrs Potts touched her arm lightly. 'And remember what I told you, my girl,' she cautioned. 'Think!'

Suzy nodded. 'Thank you,' she whispered. 'Thank you.'

Excusing herself, Mrs Potts left the room. Genin waited until the door had closed before he got up and shuffled across to open a wooden cupboard in the corner, from which he withdrew two small cloth bundles. Returning to the fireplace, he handed them to Mr McLeod and sat down.

Noting the grave demeanours of the men, Hamish and Suzy watched them expectantly.

Clearing his throat, Genin began. 'When you arrive at your destination, a small village north of London, you'll be taken to a house where you will be safe. The head of the household and the gentleman who will help you goes by the name of Jeremiah Graves.' Pausing, he reached into his doublet and withdrew a small scroll. 'When you meet him, give him this letter,' he said, handing it to Suzy. 'It's proof of who you are and the nature of your business. Make sure you look after it well, for without it, your quest will be over before it's even begun.'

Examining the plain scroll, Suzy noticed that it had been sealed with red wax. And pressed into it was the Sign of Equilibrium.

Mr McLeod coughed, a troubled expression lining his tired grey features. 'My dear people, I sincerely hope you never have to use these,' he said, handing a small bundle of cloth to each of them.

Cautiously, they unwrapped the brown linen parcels. Inside each, they discovered an ivory-handled dagger in a plain leather scabbard. Whistling softly, Hamish studied the intricately carved ivory and recognised the roaring lion immediately. It was identical to the one protecting Mr McLeod's front door. Simultaneously, they pulled the weapons from their scabbards and were struck by the Sign of Equilibrium engraved into both sides of the glinting steel blades.

'I know the thought of having to use them will seem barbaric and abhorrent to you both now,' continued Mr McLeod gravely. 'But you must keep them with you at all times and use them if necessary. They are unique and will protect you when you need them most.'

Shuddering at the prospect, Suzy glanced at Hamish tucking his weapon inside his jerkin. 'Do I have to take it?' she asked tremulously.

Mr McLeod nodded and, reluctantly, she tucked it into the pocket of her apron, along with the scroll.

'What's that noise?' asked Hamish. A distant rumble like rolling thunder was growing steadily louder.

Genin smiled. 'See for yourself,' he said, gesturing towards the window.

They both got up and crossed the room quickly. Peering out, they saw Mrs Potts across the yard, opening the gate. She was waving to someone down the track. Then slowly an ox came into view, ponderously towing a high-sided wooden cart, its four hefty wheels crunching and cracking their way across the uneven stony surface.

Hamish laughed softly. 'It looks like our taxi's arrived.'

Perturbed, Suzy turned to the two men sitting by the fire. 'How far is it to London?' she asked apprehensively.

'About five or six days,' replied Mr McLeod, chuckling, 'or more depending on the weather and road conditions, of course.'

CHAPTER FOUR

'Are we nearly there?' called Hamish wearily, leaning forward on the unforgiving bench. Grimacing, he stretched his aching spine.

'Not far to go now,' cried their portly, long-bearded driver, smacking the ox on its huge hind. A low chuckle came from under his wide floppy-brimmed hat. 'We're making record time,' he announced. 'I've done this journey more times than I care to remember and four days will be the quickest yet!'

'Oh boy,' muttered Suzy grimly, sandwiched between her brother and the driver. 'I shudder to think what a slow journey would be like.'

Like her brother, Suzy ached all over. Lacking any suspension, the cart transmitted every rut and pothole directly into their bodies. And because the ramshackle roads they travelled were nothing more than unkempt dirt tracks, the painful shockwaves were frequent.

'At least it's not raining,' said Hamish, trying to lighten her mood.

But any mention of the weather was a mistake because it was one of the main causes of Suzy's gloom. The unremitting heat and humidity of the mid-summer days had been intolerable at times, never more so than when they'd crossed the vast expanses of open moors. Even their normally stoical driver had grumbled about the unseasonally high temperatures, but the combination of pain, heat, dust, sweat and merciless flies had reduced Suzy to scowling paralysis.

Hamish knew there was nothing he could say or do to alleviate her suffering, so he decided to ignore her. Peering up the track ahead, he compared it with the wide, open roads of the twenty-first century and was grateful for the arching tree canopy overhead, shielding them from the sun's glare. A riot of tall foliage grew on either side of the high banks, accentuating the lane's narrowness and creating a verdant tunnel for mile after mile.

Trundling past a group of weary peasants walking in the same direction, Hamish was struck by the warmth of their greeting towards their driver. It was clear from their good-natured banter and bawdy wisecracks that he was a familiar and much-liked traveller. At first, Hamish and Suzy had been surprised by his lack of provisions, but as their journey progressed, it became apparent that everything he needed was available en route in return for a small quantity of the wool they carried.

A daily pattern quickly emerged. As dusk approached, they would pull up outside a cottage where their driver would engage the man of the house in friendly barter. Once a deal had been struck, Hamish and Suzy would help tend to the ox before joining their hosts in their smoky hovel for a meagre ration of stew and bread, washed down with as little ale as their thirsts could tolerate. After supper, Hamish and Suzy would retire hungry to straw beds in the barn while their driver continued drinking with the man of the house over a game of cards. Under coarse woollen blankets, sleep came surprisingly easily after a long day's arduous travel. Then at dawn they'd be woken up by the shrill scream of a cockerel and, after a quick breakfast of bread and ale, they would be back on the road.

Living rough had taken its toll on their new clothes and Suzy resented her bedraggled state. But what distressed her the most was the lack of any hygiene. Sixteenth-century England stank. Sanitation was non-existent and the first towns and villages they'd passed through had shocked them to their core. The narrow streets were open sewers and the stench was gut-wrenching. A vile sludge of human excrement, decomposing animals and all manner of stinking waste lined their route. Compounded by the heat, the pungent reek had made them both retch, adding to the filth below.

Disconcertingly, their driver appeared immune to it, but they soon discovered why. He had problems of his own. They wondered if he'd ever washed in his life. And being squashed next to him, an experience much like that of being squashed next to an exceptionally large foul-smelling cheese, only exacerbated Suzy's discomfort.

Relieved that their journey was nearing its end, Hamish

reflected that if there was one positive from the last four days, it was that their sixteenth-century makeovers were now complete. Filthy and dishevelled, they were indistinguishable from everyone they saw along the way.

'I can't take much more of this,' muttered Suzy darkly as another merciless pothole jarred them.

Ignoring her, Hamish leaned forward in his seat. 'Is Westy your real name?' he called across.

'No, of course not,' replied the driver, laughing. 'Mind you, it's been so long since anyone's called me Thomas Stubbes, it might as well be. I'm called Westy because I hail from Land's End in the west country.' Leaning forward, he squinted at Hamish and went on, a hint of curiosity in his voice. 'And judging by that accent of yours, you're not from around these parts either.'

Opening his mouth, Hamish was about to reply when the driver cut him off. 'I don't want to know!' he snapped. 'If there's one thing I've learnt in this life, it's what you don't know can't harm you. These are uncertain times so the less I know about you, the better. Don't get me wrong, you both seem like nice people, but I'm only taking you north of London as a favour to Mr Genin. You're his business, not mine.' Then, leaning back in his seat, he began whistling tunelessly.

Taken aback, Hamish and Suzy shot surprised glances at each other.

'What do you mean, uncertain times?' called Hamish.

Westy stopped whistling and eyed him suspiciously from under his brim. 'You really aren't from around here, are you?' he said, more of a statement than a question. Then, stroking his thick, matted beard, he studied their blank faces thoughtfully and decided to explain. 'Well, for starters, there's the nobility and merchants growing richer while us ordinary folk struggle to survive. Death's hand is on the shoulder of most people in this land. The failed harvests of the past five years have done it for many. Unable to afford the higher prices, they starve. And if that doesn't kill them then the plague does. So it's no surprise violence and lawlessness grips the land. God help anyone who's foolish enough to travel at night. You see, most folk are so desperate they've got nothing to lose by thieving. And if they're caught, the hangman's noose gives them a swift way out.' He paused, a troubled expression clouding his features. 'Then there's the landlords throwing people off their land to make way for sheep. Families who've worked the land for generations forced from their homes with nothing and nowhere to go. And they can't go to the monasteries for help any more because Henry VIII destroyed them when he abolished the Catholic Church. Queen Elizabeth's religious settlement might have satisfied some folk, but there are many who'd like a return to Catholicism. That's why Her Majesty fears an invasion from Spain. And if that wasn't enough, there's the Puritans. Those Protestant fanatics don't think her religious settlement's gone far enough. If it was up to them, they'd ban every pleasure in God's name. Not that most folk have any pleasure ...'

'But it's not all bad,' broke in Hamish, recalling Mr McLeod's lecture. 'England's trade with the rest of the world is booming. The country's becoming more powerful and things like the arts are flourishing.'

Westy regarded him warily. 'So there *are* some things you know,' he said after a long moment. 'You're right. The rich are getting richer, but most folk are starving and dying.' He paused, a look of derision passing across his face. 'And as for the arts, don't make me laugh,' he spat. 'There are only two reasons why the nobles fund the theatre: to ingratiate themselves with the Queen and to divert the people's attention away from the misery of their everyday lives. You mark my words, Her Majesty's court is nothing more than a greedy bunch of corrupt scavengers. Wealth, land and power's all they care about. They care nothing for the people.'

'But you, you're making a good living, aren't you?' ventured Suzy hesitantly, avoiding his breath.

'I wouldn't say good,' he replied gruffly. 'I make ends meet, if that's what you mean. But that's largely thanks to Mr Genin. If it weren't for his generosity, most of Warfield would be destitute.'

Suddenly a stiff breeze blew up from nowhere, whipping up clouds of dust, forcing Hamish and Suzy to cover their faces.

'Looks like a storm's brewing,' called Westy, peering up at a gunmetal-grey cloudbank rolling ominously towards them.

'Typical, isn't it; we've been praying for rain for months and now that the harvests have failed, we're in for a deluge. Mind you, at least we should make cover before it breaks. There's Islington ahead.'

Squinting into the distance, Hamish and Suzy saw a group of houses huddled around a church, indistinguishable from the many towns they'd passed along their way.

'That's Islington?' spluttered Suzy in surprise.

Westy nodded. 'Aye,' he replied gravely. 'And the way that sky's looking, we can't get there soon enough.'

Bemused, Hamish and Suzy marvelled at their destination surrounded by rolling countryside, comparing it to the sprawling concrete metropolis of their cousins' central London home.

'Westy, what's the population of London?' called Suzy, leaning into the buffeting wind.

'I'm not rightly sure,' he cried, smacking the ox and urging it on. 'The plague's reducing the numbers all the time, but it's a lot. I'd wager it'll be about two hundred thousand.'

Hamish and Suzy looked at each other, the same thought running through their minds: *substantially fewer than the eight million living there now*.

They rumbled over a wooden bridge crossing a fast-running brook and turned left into a cramped high street flanked by narrow timber-framed houses. With overhanging upper floors, the two-storey black and white buildings with tiny windows and steeply pitched roofs were interspersed by occasional alleyways.

Shielding their noses from the stench, Hamish and Suzy watched the hustle and bustle of sixteenth-century street life with undiminished fascination. The din of hooves and coach wheels on the cobbles, the yells of traders, brawling drunkards and jostling pedestrians hugging the walls to avoid the open sewer all combined to create a wall of sound in which people shouted to be heard. Rumbles of distant thunder grew steadily louder and people became frantic as they rushed to complete their business before the impending downpour.

'You two wait here,' called Westy, pulling up outside a tavern. 'I won't be long.'

'That's out of order,' grumbled Hamish, watching him

clamber down and disappear into the King's Head. 'I know we've been on the road for four days, but at least he could drop us off before going to the pub.'

From their raised seat, they watched a drunkard reel out of the tavern and collide with a passer-by who was seeking the sanctuary of the covered pavement. Stumbling off balance, the drunkard reached out instinctively and grabbed the startled pedestrian by the arm. Like dancers in a macabre waltz, they twisted and turned, trying desperately to regain their balance. But the drunkard slipped and, arms flailing, they both pitched backwards into the open sewer. Grimacing, Hamish and Suzy watched them trying to get up on the slippery cobbles. But no sooner had one of them found their feet than the other dragged him back into the slick. Roaring obscenities, the outraged pedestrian finally clambered to his feet and lashed out, landing a heavy boot into the drunkard's throat. With a sickening crunch, his head snapped forward and he collapsed back motionless.

Horrified, Suzy sprang to her feet. 'Somebody call the police!' she screamed, pointing at the soiled pedestrian stumbling away without a backward glance.

People stopped what they were doing and looked at her, surprise and confusion in their eyes.

'Sit down!' snapped Hamish angrily, grabbing her sleeve. 'There aren't any police! Or telephones for that matter!'

The blood drained from her face and Suzy sat down heavily. 'Oh my God, I didn't think!' she whispered, panic-stricken. She could see people talking among themselves, still staring in a way that made her very uncomfortable. 'I didn't think!' she repeated angrily, berating herself.

Suddenly a woman's unintelligible cry rang out as an upstairs window flew open. Looking up, they realised it was a warning because no sooner had she called out than the sloppy brown contents of a chamber pot rained down, landing on the retreating pedestrian, plastering his head and shoulders.

Just then a clap of thunder exploded overhead and heavy raindrops began falling, sending everybody scurrying for cover.

'You two, come here!' came a sharp voice from behind, causing them to spin round.

It was Westy. Standing in the tavern's doorway, he was trembling with rage.

Hurrying down, they approached him nervously.

'Westy's witch!' he yelled at Suzy. 'That's what they're calling you! That mumbo jumbo you just screamed and this storm's got people talking.' He fixed Hamish with hard eyes. 'You'd better control that wench if she's going to survive. I want nothing more to do with you. I've fulfilled my promise to Mr Genin and brought you this far. You're on your own from now on.'

Shocked, they watched him climb up onto his cart.

'But you've got to take us to Jeremiah Graves,' implored Suzy, grabbing his boot.

Looking down at her, Westy saw the fear in her eyes and his anger subsided. 'These are uncertain times,' he said, scowling. 'People are afraid and superstitious. Across the land, loose-tongued women like you are being executed for witchcraft. You've got to understand. If you don't keep your counsel, you'll be burned at the stake.'

Oblivious to the cool rain falling on her face, Suzy nodded weakly. 'Jeremiah Graves,' she pleaded, looking up at him. 'Please . . .'

'He's in there,' replied Westy gruffly, gesturing towards the tavern. 'Sitting at the back, by himself.'

'Thank you,' she whispered, releasing her grip. 'Thank you.'

Smiling thinly, Westy smacked the ox. 'Good luck,' he called, pulling away. 'And remember, you heard nothing from me.'

Watching him disappear down the street, Hamish reached for Suzy's hand. 'Come on, let's get out of this rain,' he said, turning towards the tavern.

Apprehensively, they entered the busy hostelry and stopped abruptly. The noisy room fell silent as everyone turned to look at them, mistrust and animosity etched into their grimy faces. Unnerved, Hamish and Suzy surveyed the gloom. An open fire coughed acrid wood smoke into the low-ceilinged tavern, stinging their eyes and throats. Peering beyond the groups of drinkers huddled around small tables to the long narrow bar, they noticed that even the buxom barmaid had stopped serving and was eying them suspiciously.

'This ain't no place for Westy's witch!' came a gruff voice from the shadows, causing Suzy to shudder. More than anything else she wanted to flee. But she knew they had no choice. Her legs like jelly, she stepped forward onto the wooden floorboards strewn with rushes. Straining to see into the furthest shadows, she was about to call Graves's name when she spotted a lone figure sitting hunched over a table, his back against the far wall. Glancing at Hamish, she gestured for him to follow and together they approached the figure cautiously. He was obscured by a hooded black cloak – the only features visible to them were his two pale hands clutching a leather tankard – but they could see he was powerfully built.

Her mouth dry, Suzy swallowed hard, trying to keep her voice steady. 'Are you Jeremiah Graves?' she croaked.

Time seemed to slow as they waited for a response. Then after what felt like an eternity, the brooding figure emitted a low menacing growl. 'Who's asking?'

Aware of the eavesdroppers around them, Suzy reached into the pocket of her filthy apron and withdrew the scroll. 'We were told to bring you this,' she said quietly, placing it on the table.

'No!' hissed Hamish in alarm, lunging for the document.

But it was too late. With lightning reflexes, the hunched figure reached out and grabbed it.

Horrified, Hamish and Suzy held their breaths, watching him break the seal of Equilibrium. Agonising seconds ticked by as he unfurled and read it. Then rolling it up, he pushed it back across the table.

'You are Jeremiah Graves, aren't you?' implored Suzy, castigating herself for another potentially catastrophic mistake.

Slowly, the hunched figure moved back in his seat and pulled back his hood.

Looking down at him, Hamish and Suzy met his malign gaze and shivered involuntarily. Black and cold, his eyes transmitted anger and loathing in equal measure. Like an alabaster death mask, the pale skin of his thin, gaunt face was stretched taut over sharp features. With long black hair scraped back into a ponytail, he exuded menace from every pore. Staring at him through wide fearful eyes, Suzy noted how the only colour in his severe white face came from the red patches of broken capillaries on each sunken cheek. Taking a deep breath to steady her nerves, she was about to repeat her question when, without warning, he stood up, pushing the table out of his way and sending the tankard and scroll flying. Terrified, Hamish and Suzy leapt backwards.

'Follow me!' he growled under his breath, pulling up his hood and brushing past them aggressively, heading for the door.

His heart racing, Hamish detected an uneasy restlessness in the tavern. It was then he realised that nobody was looking at him any more. Or Suzy. Instead, all eyes were locked on to the departing figure in the full-length cloak.

With trembling hands, Suzy quickly retrieved the scroll and went after Hamish, noticing too how people were cowering away from the terrifying stranger marching past.

Outside, day had turned to premature dusk. Torrential rain was bouncing off the cobbles as they pursued the stranger down the deserted street. Half-running to keep up, they sought the dry sanctuary of the covered walkway, noting how the open sewer was swelling rapidly. Suddenly, the stranger turned right into a dark, narrow alleyway. And then he was gone. Camouflaged by his cloak, he'd melted into the blackness. Rivulets of water cascaded down from the roofs and it was only the squelch of his boots on the sodden ground that gave his position away.

'I can't see a thing,' complained Hamish, entering the muddy alley. Grimacing at the stench, he pulled up his collar against the rain, trying not to imagine what he was stepping in.

Behind him, Suzy was having similar thoughts. Hitching up her skirt above her ankles, she was on tiptoes, hoping the foul sludge wouldn't breach the top of her shoes.

Out of the darkness, they suddenly heard rapid banging followed by the clunk of a metal bolt. A heavy door groaned open, casting a shaft of yellow light into the dark alley. And silhouetted ahead of them was the cloaked stranger, impatiently signalling for them to enter.

Stepping on to scattered rushes, Hamish and Suzy entered a small, dimly-lit room. Opposite them, a fire crackled under a blackened pot, bathing the cramped living quarters in a warm orange glow and filling it with the delicious aroma of cooking. Their empty stomachs grumbling, they surveyed their simple surroundings, noticing a wooden table laid for two people. In its centre stood a tall candle, its flickering flame supplementing the firelight. Their hearts racing, they turned to the cloaked stranger behind them and gasped. For what they saw wasn't a malevolent death mask. Instead they were staring at a smiling face, full of warmth. His black eyes twinkled with amusement as he watched their amazement at his transformation. Then shuffling out from behind him, having closed the door, a frail white-haired woman appeared, clutching a wooden ladle. Wearing a filthy apron over a russet woollen dress rolled up at the sleeves, she crossed to the fireplace and began stirring the pot.

'Jeremiah Graves ...' whispered Suzy after a long moment, watching him remove his wet cloak and throw it over the back of a chair.

'Welcome to my humble abode,' he replied, his deep voice as warm as his smile. 'I've been looking forward to meeting you.'

Suzy's relief was overwhelming. 'Thank God,' she murmured.

Hamish frowned. 'But why were you so angry with us?' he asked, oblivious to the steam rising from his wet clothes.

Their host laughed softly. 'It's an act,' he explained. 'These are dangerous times. I can't trust anybody. So when I'm in public I keep everyone at arm's length by behaving with extreme hostility. That way, I can go about my business unhindered, choosing only to deal with those who might be able to help me.' Pausing, he noticed them studying his clothes. From his linen shirt under an open doublet to his breeches, stockings and boots, he was dressed entirely in black. 'And my clothes add to the effect,' he said with a laugh. 'Graves by name, grim by nature. It's no surprise that people call me the Reaper.'

Behind them, the housekeeper stopped stirring and glanced up at him nervously.

Jeremiah met her gaze and continued quickly. 'Now please have a seat,' he said, ushering them to the table. 'You must be hungry after your journey. We've prepared a special rabbit stew to celebrate your arrival.'

Gratefully, Hamish and Suzy sat down on wooden stools,

watching the unnamed cook ladle thick broth into two wooden bowls and deliver them to the table. Immediately, they picked up their spoons and began eating ravenously.

Watching them, the old woman smiled sympathetically. 'I'll fetch you some bread,' she said, heading for the only other door in the room.

Watching her disappear into what looked like a pantry, Hamish and Suzy wolfed down the stew, unable to recall eating anything so exquisite in their lives. By the time she returned, they'd emptied their bowls. Placing a loaf on the table, she cut thick slices and watched them help themselves. Then without asking, she collected their bowls and re-filled them.

Sitting in front of the fire, Jeremiah watched them thoughtfully. 'That was some entrance you made back there,' he said. 'Suzy, your driver was so frightened by your performance he couldn't get out of the inn fast enough. And the locals, they were afraid too.'

Suzy stopped eating and felt her cheeks flush. 'I'm sorry, it won't happen again,' she said, recalling Mrs Potts's advice.

'Don't worry, your secret's safe with me,' he said. 'But you've both got to be careful about what you say in future. By drawing attention to yourselves, you could jeopardise your mission.'

Just then a thought struck Hamish and he groaned inwardly, annoyed at their carelessness. At no point had they verified the identity of the man professing to be Jeremiah Graves. For all they knew, the man sitting opposite them could be an impostor, an agent of chaos or order lulling them into a false sense of security. 'How do you know Mr Genin?' he asked suspiciously.

Suzy glanced at him and knew instantly what he was thinking.

Startled, their host was silent for a long moment. Then, smiling knowingly, he stood up, removed his doublet and walked over to the table. Sitting down, he placed his left arm on the table and untied the frilled cuff of his linen shirt. Slowly, he rolled back the loose-fitting sleeve to reveal his sinewy forearm. And then they saw it, a black sun-like symbol tattooed into his pale skin. 'Need I say more?' he murmured, observing their relief.

'Mr Graves, what's causing the imbalance between chaos and order?' asked Suzy, getting straight to business.

Clearing the table, the housekeeper froze and looked at him fearfully.

Jeremiah's face darkened. 'Leave us alone,' he growled, infuriated by her reaction.

Disconcerted, Hamish and Suzy watched her quickly gather up the empty bowls and retreat to the pantry.

Jeremiah waited for the door to close before he continued. 'There's an ill wind blowing through England,' he said grimly. 'I'll tell you all about it tomorrow. But first you must rest.'

'Why can't you tell us now?' asked Hamish.

Jeremiah shook his head. 'I'll tell you tomorrow,' he repeated firmly, leaving no room for discussion.

No sooner had he spoken than an anguished moan came from behind the door. Jeremiah's eyes flashed anger. 'Wait here,' he growled, getting up and disappearing into the pantry.

Taken aback, Hamish and Suzy heard the low murmur of heated conversation and looked at each other uneasily.

'What's going on?' whispered Suzy. But before Hamish could reply there was a loud crash, like crockery shattering. Suddenly, the pantry door flew open and Jeremiah stormed out, his face like thunder. Ignoring them both, he grabbed his doublet and cloak, threw open the front door and marched out into the night.

The elderly housekeeper came bustling out of the pantry. 'I'm sorry you had to witness that,' she said, crossing the room and closing the front door quickly.

When she turned around, Suzy could tell she was on the verge of tears. 'I'm sorry, but we haven't been properly introduced,' she offered gently. 'My name's Suzy and this is my brother Hamish.'

Taking a deep breath, the housekeeper smiled at them. 'I'm Mary, Jeremiah's mother,' she replied, her voice strained. 'As you can tell, things are rather difficult at the moment.'

Hamish frowned. 'Why were you arguing?' he asked innocently. Then, horrified, he watched as the woman began to cry, her tiny shoulders rising and falling with each racking sob.

Suzy glared at him. 'Well done!' she snapped sarcastically.

Then getting up, she rounded the table quickly and placed an arm around Mary's shoulders. Carefully, she led her to a stool and urged her to sit.

Dabbing her tears with her apron, Mary sat down gratefully. Looking up, she saw Suzy's questioning eyes and she sighed. 'My dear, Jeremiah's under terrible pressure,' she explained apologetically. 'It's a long story, but rebellion is in the air. Like he said, he'll tell you all about it tomorrow.'

'But isn't there anything *you* can tell us now?' pressed Suzy gently.

Mary looked down at her hands and shook her head slowly. 'No,' she whispered sadly. Then, climbing to her feet, she motioned for them to follow. 'I'll show you to your beds now.'

Following her into the pantry, Hamish and Suzy surveyed the cramped room, its whitewashed walls lined with rough shelves supporting a variety of earthenware storage pots, wooden boxes and bulging sacks. Illuminated by several candles, they noted irregular joints of dried meat hanging from iron hooks fixed into the low beams supporting the floor above them.

'Where's Jeremiah gone?' asked Hamish warily, stepping across broken pottery.

'Back to the King's Head,' replied Mary, stopping at a narrow staircase in the corner. 'As you may have heard, I didn't want him to go.' She waved for them to go up ahead of her.

Intrigued, Hamish and Suzy climbed the steep stairs and emerged in a spartan room occupying the entire first floor. Bathed in moonlight, it contained just one item of furniture: an ornate four-poster double bed. Her spirits soaring at the prospect of a good night's sleep in a proper bed, Suzy went over and sat down, testing the lumpy mattress. Hamish crossed over to the small window.

'I'm afraid that's Jeremiah's bed,' explained Mary, carrying a candle. 'I've made up two beds for you over there by the wall.'

Disappointed, Suzy went over to inspect the makeshift bedding arranged on the bare floorboards. Kneeling down, she pressed one of the two thin beds placed along the wall and her heart sank. 'Straw,' she muttered grimly.

'Hey, sis, come and have a look at this,' hissed Hamish excitedly, looking up at the night sky.

Suzy went over to join him. 'Wow,' she breathed reverentially, taken aback by the glittering spectacle on show. The storm clouds had dispersed leaving a clear night sky, the brilliance and depth of which they'd never seen before. Like millions of diamonds sparkling in an infinite black backcloth, the starry universe shone majestically.

'No light pollution,' murmured Hamish as they watched a meteor shower strafe the sky.

Behind them, Mary coughed politely and they turned around. Her face was bathed in the yellow glow of the candle she was holding and she looked troubled. 'Please, make yourselves comfortable,' she said mechanically, gesturing to their beds. 'If you need anything during the night, you'll find me downstairs.' Then without another word, she turned and left.

Hamish and Suzy looked at each other. 'Something's wrong,' whispered Suzy uneasily. 'I don't know what's going on, but something's definitely wrong.'

Hamish nodded slowly. 'That's why we're here,' he said, looking sombre. 'As Jeremiah said, he'll explain everything tomorrow.' Pausing, he saw fear in Suzy's eyes. 'Come on, let's get some sleep. I'm sure things won't seem so gloomy in the morning.'

Unconvinced, Suzy smiled thinly. 'I'm sure you're right,' she conceded, accompanying him over to their beds.

'Look, why don't you take the bed in the corner?' suggested Hamish. 'That way, if Jeremiah comes back drunk, he's more likely to stumble on me rather than you.'

Grateful for his kindness, Suzy lay down and pulled the coarse blanket up to her chin. Staring up at the ceiling, it wasn't long before she heard his gentle snores and she wished that sleep would embrace her too. But her mind was racing. Her sixth sense screamed danger and no matter how hard she tried, she couldn't shake off her sense of foreboding. Finally, fatigue overwhelmed her and she drifted off into fitful slumber.

*

In his dreams, Hamish smiled reassuringly. He needed to calm his sister, who was calling his name. She sounded frightened, panicked even. He smiled at her again, about to offer some soothing words when he felt her touch, patting his cheek urgently. It was then he realised it wasn't a dream. It was real. And Suzy was terrified.

'Wake up, Hamish, wake up,' she hissed, her throat constricted by fear.

Hamish sat bolt upright. 'What is it?' he asked, his pulse racing.

'Listen!' she gasped, holding on to his arm.

Then he heard them: the aggressive bellows of angry men. 'Where are they?' boomed one. 'Tell us now!' howled another.

They heard Mary's voice, pleading and pitiful. 'Leave them alone!' she cried. 'They're only children. Leave them alo—' Suddenly there was a crash and her voice fell silent.

Instinctively, Hamish and Suzy stood up as one. Holding each other tightly, they retreated into the corner of the room, terrified by the din of smashing furniture. Then they heard words that made their blood run cold. 'Up here, up here,' came a guttural bellow. 'We've got them cornered. They're all ours now.'

Quaking, Suzy gripped her brother, causing him to wince. 'This can't be happening,' she whimpered. 'This can't be happening . . .'

Embracing her protectively, Hamish placed himself between her and the intruders climbing the stairs, the heavy thud of their boots causing the floorboards to shake. Suddenly a short heavy-set figure appeared from the stairwell, followed by a taller one. Unable to make out their features in the darkness, Hamish and Suzy could sense their hostility from across the room.

'The boy will come with us,' snarled the squat barrel-shaped figure, taking a step forward. 'But the witch stays here.'

'No,' cried Suzy instinctively, holding on to her brother tightly. 'You can't, you can't . . .'

When the intruder spoke again, his voice was deathly cold. 'I said . . . the boy will come with us . . . now!'

His muscles coiled, Hamish tried to loosen Suzy's grip on him. 'Sis, let go,' he whispered. 'For both our sakes, let go.' His mouth was dry and his words almost stuck in his throat. Adrenaline coursed his veins and he knew that flight was out of the question. Their only option now was to fight. But to do so, he needed to be free.

'No,' whimpered Suzy, holding on to him, 'I'm not letting you leave me.' Stifling a sob, she buried her face in his shoulder.

Impatient, the powerfully-built figure marched over to them.

Watching him in the moonlight, Hamish saw that he was dressed in black and his lower face was obscured by a black scarf. But what struck him most were the eyes. Black and cold, they flashed evil and menace in equal measure.

'Let go of the witch,' the man growled. 'I won't ask you again.'

Frustrated, Hamish shook his sister. 'Sis, let go,' he hissed through gritted teeth. But she refused.

Then without warning, powerful hands grabbed them roughly by their upper arms and began prising them apart. Suzy yelped with pain but still she held on. Like a limpet, she clung to her brother as if her life depended on it. A cruel chuckle filled the air and suddenly their arms were free. Then, with a sickening thwack, a giant fist slammed into the side of Suzy's face. Like a rag doll, her body went limp and she collapsed to the floor, slipping through her horrified brother's arms.

Cowering over his stricken sister, Hamish peered up, tears of outraged fury clouding his vision.

'Get up and leave the witch alone,' snarled the thug, laughing callously. 'She deserves to be burnt at the stake.'

White-hot rage consumed him and for the first time in his life, Hamish wanted only one thing: to kill. Howling like a wounded beast, he sprang at the savage, clawing at his face, seeking out the soft tissue of those sadistic eyes. Caught by surprise, the attacker recoiled, screaming as claw-like fingers penetrated the socket of his left eye. Reaching behind him with his free hand, Hamish sought to liberate the lethal blade tucked into his breeches. Desperately he groped for it, but it wasn't there. Then with awful realisation, he remembered he'd tucked it under his mattress before going to sleep. Summoning up all his strength, he clenched his fist and aimed a blow at the howling brute's thrashing head. But just as he was about to unleash the hammer, his arm became snared. Clinging to the face of one attacker and trying to liberate his arm from the other, Hamish exhaled loudly as something heavy crashed over his head and he too slumped to the floor unconscious.

CHAPTER FIVE

Suzy groaned and opened her eyes, blinking rapidly in the darkness. Disorientated, it took her a moment to remember where she was. Then it hit her like a sledgehammer and she gasped. 'Hamish,' she whispered, raising her head off the floorboards, scanning the blackness. But in her heart, she knew he was gone.

Her head throbbed and she tasted blood. Tentatively, she touched her cheek and flinched. Suddenly a wave of nausea washed over her and she hauled herself up on to her hands and knees. Retching violently, convulsions racked her stomach and throat. Oblivious to everything but her own despair, she began to sob.

Finally, she clambered to her feet. Patting the bed and walls with her outstretched palms, she edged her way unsteadily across to the stairs, pausing at the top step to gather herself. Below she could hear shuffling and looked down to see the faint glow of a candle. Forcing herself to breathe deeply, she descended slowly, anxious not to lose her footing. But the moment the pantry came into view, she stopped abruptly, taken aback by the destruction.

Without exception, everything had been smashed; shelves torn from the walls, storage pots shattered, sacks ripped and their grain spilled among the rushes. Even the joints of dried meat that had hung from the ceiling had been hacked into pieces and lay among the debris. And standing in the middle of it all, broom in hand, was Mary. Dazed, with a trickle of blood running from a cut above her left eye, she was attempting to sweep the floor.

'Are you all right?' asked Suzy quietly.

But the elderly housekeeper didn't respond. As if in a trance, she continued jabbing aimlessly at the mess.

'Are you all right?' she repeated, crossing over and touching her arm.

Like a startled rabbit, Mary jumped and spun round, a mixture of shock and fear in her wide eyes.

'What is it?' asked Suzy quickly.

Mary's shoulders sagged. Tears welled up in her eyes and she looked at her despairingly.

Suzy frowned. 'What is it?' she repeated, a hint of impatience entering her voice.

Mary glanced away nervously and resumed her sweeping.

Slowly, a seed of horrified realisation germinated in Suzy's mind. As she recalled Mary's argument with Jeremiah and their determined refusal to explain what was going on, a deep anger stirred within her. Her instinct had been right. Something had been wrong, very wrong. The pieces of the puzzle were falling into place and as the grotesque picture they formed became clearer, Suzy's outrage exploded. 'You knew!' she spat, grabbing Mary by the shoulders and shaking her violently. 'You knew! You knew and you let it happen!'

'No. No!' cried Mary sobbing. 'You don't understand ...'

'Release her!' came a sharp voice from behind, causing Suzy to wheel around.

Framed in the doorway, Jeremiah pulled back his hood and Suzy saw his pained expression.

'It was my fault,' he admitted quickly, noting her badly swollen cheek. 'The reason why you heard us arguing last night was because Mary was against it. But I had no choice ...'

'No choice?' snapped Suzy, her voice quivering with fury. 'You welcomed us into your home, a place where we were supposed to be safe, and you allowed us to be brutalised and my brother taken ... and you've got the nerve to say you had no choice ...' She paused, breathing heavily. Then without warning she lunged at him, pounding his chest with iron fists. 'I hate you! I hate you!' she screamed.

Making no attempt to stop her, Jeremiah stood motionless, his teeth clenched, absorbing the blows. He knew it was mild punishment for an act of betrayal so monstrous it was unlikely that his own mother would ever forgive him.

Eventually the fire of her wrath ebbed and the blows softened, then ceased. Exhausted, she stood before him, her head bowed, sobbing pitifully.

'It's time for some explanations,' he murmured, embracing

her gently and stroking her hair. Then ushering her into the living room, he gathered an upturned stool and sat her in front of the smouldering fire. Kneeling down, he set about rekindling the glowing embers.

'Why?' she whispered, surveying the ransacked room. 'Why?'

Jeremiah got up and removed his cloak. 'No words can adequately convey the shame I feel tonight,' he said, draping it over the upended table. 'It was a desperate act of last resort. And for that I am truly sorry.' He paused as Mary came in and sat down. Then he took a deep breath and continued, his voice a soft murmur. 'Suzy, life in England is terrible for most people. The failed harvests of recent years and higher food prices mean that ordinary people are starving. Higher rents have swelled the number of vagabonds living rough in towns and cities across the land, and the plague is adding to their misery. People are talking openly of rebellion. But to make matters worse, there's something else fuelling their discontentment; something else so sinister it's pushing them to the very brink of revolution.'

'What?' whispered Suzy, frowning.

'Abductions,' broke in Mary, glaring angrily at her son.

Suzy looked at her blankly.

'Oh, we don't know who's responsible for them,' she said bitterly. 'The main targets seem to be young men – mostly vagabonds and boys living in households perilously close to destitution. The upper classes are turning a blind eye to them. As far as they're concerned, the removal of such scum from society is a good thing. You see, they blame them for the lawlessness and violence gripping the land. And it's this lack of sympathy and willingness to help that's adding to people's resentment.'

'You used us,' said Suzy flatly.

Jeremiah sighed. 'I had to get someone on the inside whom I could trust,' he said. 'I spread the word that my orphaned niece and nephew were coming to live with me, an expense and responsibility I could ill afford.'

'You mean we could both have been taken tonight!' exclaimed Suzy, more of a statement than a question.

'It was possible,' conceded Jeremiah. 'A few girls have been taken, but the majority have been boys.'

The ghastly nightmare was becoming clearer to her. 'So the reason you went back to the King's Head after storming out of here was to show everyone that the coast was clear,' she deduced.

Jeremiah glanced at Mary, who had begun crying softly. 'Yes,' he said.

Bewildered, Suzy shook her head. 'So what do we do now?' she asked.

'We put you to work,' he replied matter-of-factly.

'*Work?*' she exclaimed.

Jeremiah nodded. 'I understand you're a talented artist. Painters are in great demand right now. The nobles and upper classes are commissioning more portraits of themselves and their families than ever before—'

'But how's that going to help?' she snapped, interrupting him.

Jeremiah fixed her with hard uncompromising eyes and when he spoke there was a hint of menace in his voice. 'My sources tell me there's a studio in London producing a suspiciously large number of portraits of just one person. You're going to find out who it is.'

*

It was the sickly stench of decomposing flesh that assaulted Hamish as he climbed towards consciousness. As if slapped in the face, he snapped awake, recoiling at the all-enveloping fug. Stifling a powerful urge to retch, he tried to reach for his face but his hands were tied behind his back. Frantically, he writhed in the darkness, twisting his wrists when something hard crashed into his stomach, driving the wind from him.

'Keep still!' came a muffled voice beside him. 'There's no room to move!'

Hamish coughed and the rancid smell raced up his nose, striking him at the back of his throat. Willing the pain and nausea to subside, he lay motionless, concentrating on breathing only through his mouth. Gradually, his torment eased and he became aware of the noises around him. Judging by the groans, it was clear that there were others suffering too. Then he heard the familiar rumble of wooden wheels on uneven stony ground and an unsettling thought occurred to him. Was this cart transporting the dead as well as the living? It would certainly explain the smell, he thought miserably.

As he lifted his head to peer into the blackness, taking care not to move his limbs, his cheek brushed against coarse fabric and he realised why he couldn't see. His head was encased in a sack. But surely, he reasoned, the rough cloth should be filtering out some of the smell. Unless, of course, it was the source. Cautiously, he tilted his head, trying to get his nose closer to it, and baulked. The smell of death was unmistakeable. Grimacing, he shuddered to think what dried fluids were causing its stiffness.

After what felt like an eternity, officious shouts from outside signalled their journey's end. The heavy wheels ground to a halt and he felt movement around him. He could tell from the anguished cries that disembarkation had begun when powerful hands grabbed his ankles and heaved him out, dumping him to the ground painfully.

'Get up!' came a menacing growl above him.

His pulse racing, he got to his knees and climbed unsteadily to his feet. Specks of daylight penetrated the fabric and he sensed his captor moving closer. Then, without warning, rough fingers encircled his throat and he cried out. Helpless to defend himself, he tried retreating but the vice-like grip dragged him back viciously. 'Come here; I'm not going to kill you yet, boy,' snarled his attacker, tugging at the cord securing his hood and ripping it off.

'You ...' wheezed Hamish, blinking rapidly. He was staring into the glowering face of his brutal abductor.

'You're gonna pay for this,' snarled the thug, gesturing to the white bandage covering his left eye. 'You can forget about an eye for an eye. I'm gonna take both of yours and present them to that witch sister of yours on a plate.'

Recalling Suzy's fate, Hamish felt his blood boil. He stepped forward, thrusting his face within an inch of the abductor's nose. 'Does hitting girls make you feel big?' he spat, resisting a strong urge to head-butt him.

The abductor's lone eye turned into a slit and his knife-thin mouth into a sneer. 'I hope the smell wasn't too offensive,' he chuckled, waving the sack at him. 'I made sure you got the executioner's head bag. You've been keeping good company. We carry the festering heads of executed criminals to London Bridge in that sack to be impaled on spikes for all to see . . .'

Hamish blanched, revulsion replacing anger.

The abductor laughed contemptuously. 'Now, turn around!' he snarled, withdrawing a dagger from his doublet.

But Hamish didn't move. He had no intention of turning his back on him. Nothing would have pleased him more than to have his hands untied, but he wasn't going to risk it with this animal. For all he knew, it was just as likely he'd end up with the knife in his back. Or even worse, an arm around his neck and his eyes gouged out.

'I said turn around!' bellowed the thug, grabbing his shoulder and throwing him to the ground.

'That's enough, Mr Standish!' boomed a voice from behind.

Gratefully, Hamish saw one of the other black-uniformed kidnappers striding purposefully towards them. This one was tall and sinewy with closely cropped white hair. And judging from his set jaw and stern demeanour, he was very much in command. 'Mr Standish, go and help the others now!' he barked.

Glancing impatiently at the approaching man, Standish cursed under his breath. 'Next time, you won't be so lucky,' he growled, standing over Hamish. 'I'm gonna make your life a living hell before I kill you . . .'

'Mr Standish, that's an order!' bawled the man, his shrill tone an octave higher.

'Yes, sir,' Standish muttered resentfully. He began backing away, his glowering gaze locked on to Hamish. Then, with a cruel smirk, he sniffed the sack, feigned vomiting and guffawed loudly.

'You've made yourself a dangerous enemy there,' cautioned the officer, helping Hamish to his feet and freeing his hands. 'You'd better watch your back from now on.'

Rubbing his wrists, Hamish looked at the officer and recognition dawned on him. 'You were with him last night, weren't you?' he said.

'Aye,' he replied, 'and after what you did to him, both you and your sister should be dead now. Mark my words, he's a mean one, that one. And he's not going to rest until he's had his revenge.'

Hamish nodded. 'Thanks,' he said, 'that was pretty much what he was just explaining to me.'

'All right, fall in with the others,' instructed the officer brusquely, signalling an end to their conversation. But just as Hamish was about to go, the officer reached out and stopped him. 'And a word of advice,' he said grimly: 'be prepared, because the next time he comes for you, it'll be when you're alone.'

Hamish felt a knot of cold inevitability in the pit of his stomach. 'Thanks,' he said, 'I'll remember that.'

'Now fall in!' snapped the officer, releasing his arm.

Turning away, Hamish took in his new surroundings. Feeling uncomfortably vulnerable, he breathed in deeply, calming his nerves, savouring the crisp early morning air.

The dewy forest glade sparkled in bright sunlight. Cobwebs glistened in the damp grass and birdsong filled the air. Ahead, he could see several guards marshalling his bewildered fellow captives into rows and it struck him as incongruous that such a beautiful forest clearing should also be their prison. Joining the back of a line, he counted twenty-four captives. But bizarrely, he noted only six kidnappers. Then it occurred to him: apart from the knives used to cut their bonds, he hadn't seen any weapons. Surely, he mused, their chance of escape was good. If they acted together, twenty-four boys could overpower six lightly armed guards. Looking around him, he could tell that some of the others were having similar thoughts, their darting eyes appraising the opposition and weighing up the odds.

'Escape would be foolish!' boomed the tall officer from the front. 'The forest around you stretches for dozens of miles in every direction. It's full of animal traps that will bring down a man. To risk life and limb would be foolhardy because I can assure you, you're about to begin a better life . . .'

Noting the confusion and uncertainty in the grimy faces around him, Hamish had to concede it was a clever ploy. There had been no need for weapons or more guards to ensure their compliance. A few well-chosen words had done the job. True or not, the combination of threat and hope was enough to persuade this motley group where their best interests lay.

'You'll be better off here than where we found you, that's for sure,' continued the officer, 'so follow me and all will become clear.' Then turning on his heel, he headed straight for a narrow path leading into the light-dappled forest.

Barking encouragement, the other guards quickly marshalled the prisoners into a single file and they all set off in rapid pursuit. Walking at the back of the snaking procession, Hamish breathed a sigh of relief when he saw Standish peel off towards the ox-drawn, canvas-roofed cart that had brought them to this place. It wasn't long before the path widened and Hamish, determined to put as much distance as possible between himself and his would-be executioner, hurried to the head of the group. Less than ten minutes later the path turned sharply to the right and, as one, they all stopped dead in their tracks.

'Dear God,' breathed Hamish incredulously.

The officer looked at him and grinned. 'It's a spectacular sight, isn't it?'

What Hamish saw boggled his imagination. They were standing at the edge of the tree line, looking down at a vast circular plain, like a giant volcanic crater carved into the middle of the forest. The scale of it was extraordinary. But what it contained took their breath away. For rising from its centre, cathedral-like, was the largest stately house that Hamish had ever seen. And surrounding it in every direction, like a sprawling township, was a sea of white canvas interspersed by an elaborate network of alleyways, thoroughfares and open squares.

Hamish stepped forward for a better view, and when he did, his eyes were drawn to the hundreds of black specks milling about inside it. 'How many people are down there?' he asked, transfixed.

Amused by the awed faces around him, the officer laughed. 'We've rescued thousands,' he said.

Hamish frowned. 'Rescued?' he repeated quizzically, looking up at him.

'Aye, rescued!' chuckled the officer, setting off down the steep slope, waving for them to follow.

'What do you mean, rescued?' called Hamish, stumbling after him.

'Like I said, all will be revealed soon enough,' yelled the officer over his shoulder. 'Now, come on!'

Enthralled by the spectacle below, the group descended, careful not to lose their footing on the steep grassy slope. In moments the black specks became people and Hamish realised they were all wearing the same uniform as their captors. He also noticed that they were all boys, similar in age to him or older. Reaching the flat plain, they entered the canvas township, grateful for its shade, and marvelled at the bustling activity around them. With one eye on the officer ahead, Hamish surveyed the open-sided tents, taken aback by the scope of work underway inside. Everywhere he looked, he could see groups of boys being tutored in trades, from pottery and woodworking to metal forging, building and leather tanning. It was like a huge factory, he mused. But what struck him most were the boys themselves. Compared to the malnourished and bedraggled group he was with, they all appeared to be healthy. And judging by the concentration etched into many of their faces, it was clear that they were willing students. From time to time, boys stopped what they were doing and waved across at the new arrivals. And what he saw in those faces was not the haunted look of captivity; it was contentment and camaraderie.

Reaching stone steps leading up to the imposing facade of the grand house, Hamish whistled softly. It was like no other building he had ever seen. Peering up at it, he guessed it had evolved over the centuries from castellated fortress to stately home. The differing architectural styles suggested that it had either been destroyed and rebuilt multiple times or been continually extended. If its immense size was anything to go by, he suspected it was the latter.

'Notice the height of the doors and windows,' said the officer, pointing to their placement more than sixty feet above the ground. 'This house has always been susceptible to attacks because of its sunken elevation, so the builders compensated by elevating their architecture into the air.'

'It's amazing!' admitted Hamish. 'Nobody could look at this house and doubt its owner's wealth and power.'

Waiting for the rest of the group to catch up, the officer eyed him suspiciously, predicting his next question.

Hamish didn't disappoint. 'Who owns it?' he asked curiously.

But the officer ignored him, waving for the group to follow him up the terraced steps towards the enormous double doors that were the main entrance.

Watching him go, Hamish turned towards the canvas township, recalling a quotation from Winston Churchill. 'It's a riddle wrapped in a mystery inside an enigma,' he murmured thoughtfully to himself.

When they entered, the great hall was bathed in brilliant sunlight. Diagonal rays streamed in through the arched windows set high into the whitewashed walls, reflecting off the tall surfaces and making the square room seem larger than it actually was. Looking around, Hamish noted the simple zigzag designs chiselled into the masonry around the arched windows and he calculated that this part of the building must have been the original Norman keep. Dating back to the eleventh century, this strong tower would have been the castle's main living area and its most heavily defended area. Five hundred years later it was crammed with long rows of wooden tables and benches. Skulls and antlers decorated the walls, adding to the room's imposing appearance. At the far end, opposite the grand entrance they'd just passed through, was a raised platform and Hamish wondered what kind of entertainment was offered.

Directing them to a table in front of the stage, the officer instructed them to sit.

Compliantly they took their seats. Nobody uttered a word.

Looking along the table, Hamish had his first chance to study his fellow captives. What he saw unsettled him. Most of them were clothed in filthy rags. They were also chronically malnourished. The boy sitting opposite him was positively skeletal. The vertebrae in his neck jutted out and Hamish wondered how it managed to prop up his dome-like head. Bald patches dotted his cranium and the outline of his teeth was clearly visible through the translucent parchment of his sunken cheeks. Sensing scrutiny, he looked up through vacant eyes and Hamish shuddered, forcing a smile. But the boy didn't react. He simply lowered his head.

Turning his attention to a heavy-set figure sitting diagonally opposite him at the far end of the table, Hamish noted his broad shoulders and muscular arms and wondered how he'd been captured. With a thick neck and square, shaven head, he didn't look like someone who would have succumbed easily. He must have put up a hell of a fight, mused Hamish, watching him closely. Hunched forward with his arms folded, he too had his head bowed. But unlike the others, he was avoiding eye contact. The muscle in his jaw twitched as he clenched and unclenched his teeth, and Hamish sensed defiance. His clothes, filthy but intact, set him apart from the others. He also wore sturdy boots while the other boys walked barefoot. Exuding menace, he resembled a dangerous rottweiler impatient to be unleashed and Hamish made a mental note to avoid him.

The clunk of a metal bolt broke the silence and a door in the corner of the hall swung slowly open. Hamish noticed the officer and guards shooting nervous glances at each other before snapping to attention as a portly figure strode in, flanked by two guards. Hamish's heart sank. One of them was Standish. And judging by his malevolent smirk, he was relishing the moment.

'Welcome,' intoned the portly figure, coming to a halt at the head of the table. 'I'm pleased to make your acquaintance.'

Guessing him to be in his mid-sixties, Hamish was struck by his ordinariness. Dressed modestly in a plain brown doublet and matching breeches, there was nothing regal or imposing about him. Bald, with a long jowly face, his most prominent features were his eyebrows: two spiky silver tufts above small grey eyes. His expression was inscrutable and he reminded Hamish of a polite shopkeeper. Yet judging by the tall officer's nervousness, there was obviously something about him that elicited fear.

Reaching into his doublet, the man withdrew a candle. Intrigued, they watched him light it and spill a few drops of molten wax onto the table. Then, setting the candle into the rapidly drying pool, he continued. 'Allow me to introduce myself,' he said, smiling thinly at the bemused faces looking up at him. 'I am the Lord Protector and I am offering you a new life. This candle will burn for precisely one hour. During that time, all I ask is that you listen to what I have to say. If, after the candle has gone out, you wish to leave this place, then you have my solemn word that you will be free to return to wherever we found you ...'

Noting the surprised faces around him, Hamish watched the hunched rottweiler staring at the flame inches from his nose, an expression of studied indifference on his broad features. He looked bored, reflected Hamish, as if the situation he found himself in was an irrelevance. The guards had noticed too and were glaring at him, angered by his lack of respect.

'... But first, you must be hungry after your journey,' said the Lord Protector with a clap of his hands.

Immediately, a procession of six maids came bustling in. Carrying trays, they circled the table placing steaming bowls in front of them. It wasn't until the delicious aroma reached his nostrils that Hamish realised how hungry he was. Picking up a spoon, he stirred the thick broth and almost laughed when he saw the tender chunks of meat and vegetables in the rich sauce. Like the others, he launched himself at it, eating ravenously.

Watching dispassionately, the Lord Protector waited until they'd drained their bowls and had begun tearing at the warm, freshly baked loaves before he continued. 'I know it's been a long time since you last had a meal like that,' he said gravely. 'In fact, I stand corrected. Some of you have *never* had a meal like that ...'

Hamish reached for a leather tankard and slaked his thirst on the tepid liquid, then refilled it from a large earthenware jug. The bitter ale tasted like nectar and he reflected that Genin had been right; he *had* developed a taste for it. Bread in one hand, ale in the other, he looked up at the Lord Protector and experienced a profound pang of gratitude.

'Like you, countless thousands of people in this country are starving,' intoned the Lord Protector solemnly. 'Like you, countless thousands of people are destitute and homeless. And like you, countless thousands of people are losing family and friends to the plague every day. Now ask yourselves, what's being done to alleviate your suffering?' After a momentary pause, he answered his own question. 'Nothing. Nobody is doing anything to help you. And nobody has any intention of helping. Not the Queen. Not the Church. Nobody. As far as they're concerned, you're vermin. But to me, you are all victims. Victims of an unjust and unfair society, a society in which there are only two groups: the "haves" and the "have-nots". A society in which the wealthy few focus only on enriching themselves while the poor majority are left to rot.' He paused again, scanning his audience. 'My friends, injustice and inequality triumph in England where justice and equality should rule. Each day I hear appalling stories about life in England from people just like you. And it only serves to stiffen my resolve to do something about it. But there's one story I'd like to share with you, because I think it sums up everything that's wrong with modern England.' He nodded towards Standish, who hustled out and returned a moment later escorting a pale, anxious-looking boy, dressed in regulation black. Hamish guessed him to be slightly younger than himself.

'Come in, Daniels,' said the Lord Protector, with a welcoming smile. 'As I explained to you earlier, I'd like you to tell us your story and how you came to be here.'

Daniels climbed onto the stage and began in a clear and measured voice. 'Two years ago I lived in the village of Shene, eight miles south-west of London. I lived with my parents and my younger sister in a small but happy house. We were poor but somehow my parents always managed to put food on the table. They were very religious – good Catholics – and they always thanked God for our good fortune. But my father refused to renounce his faith when Catholicism was banned. He didn't agree with the Queen's religious settlement and he wouldn't accept her as the head of the Church in England. He also hated the way the new services were in English rather than Latin. So he refused to attend church and was fined and threatened with prison. We couldn't afford the fines. My mother begged him for all of our sakes to go. She pleaded with him to keep his true faith hidden in his heart and finally he agreed. But what we didn't know was that he'd also started attending Catholic mass illegally at a friend's house. And one day he never returned. We found out later that he'd been betrayed. He was executed as a lesson to others.' Shaking his head at the memory, he paused and took several deep breaths before continuing, his voice sounding increasingly strained. 'My mother had to get a job, so she began working as a cook in the local magistrate's household. He was a miser. She came home one day saying he'd threatened to sack her for throwing away rotten meat. He accused her of wasting food. Soon afterwards, he and his family fell ill. The daughter died. My mother was accused of poisoning them. Of course, she protested her innocence saying she'd been forced to cook with unfit meat.' His chin trembled as he fought back his tears. His words came out in short staccato bursts. 'She was tried and found guilty ... by the same magistrate who accused her ...' Tears began rolling down his cheeks and his voice became an anguished cry. 'She was convicted and given a poisoner's sentence ... to be boiled alive ... It was a public execution ... My sister and I were forced to watch ... She was plunged naked into boiling water ... then hoisted up on chains so that the crowd could see her skin peeling off and hear her screaming ...' Overwhelmed, he broke down, burying his face in his hands.

Appalled, Hamish put down his bread, his appetite gone.

Composing himself quickly, the boy sniffed loudly and wiped his tears with his sleeve. 'After that, my sister and I were forced from our home,' he croaked. 'We couldn't pay the rent because nobody in Shene would employ the children of a Catholic poisoner. So we went to London to find work but ended up living on the streets. My sister died of plague. I was starving when the Lord Protector rescued me and brought me here. That was a year ago. He fed and clothed me. He's taught us new skills and he's preparing us for a return to a fairer society. I may have lost my own family but at least I'm part of a bigger one now ...'

Raising a hand, the Lord Protector signalled for him to stop, then nodded towards Standish. He waited until the boy had been escorted from the hall before he spoke again.

'Gentlemen, what you have just heard may not be uncommon, but there's an important lesson to be drawn from it: that there really is hope. Hope for a better life. And, gentlemen, that hope begins here.' Pausing, he looked down at the dying candle and smiled thinly. 'An hour ago, I asked you to listen to what I had to say, and I thank you for listening. But now you have an important decision to make, a decision that will affect the rest of your lives. You can either return to the life you know or you can begin a new one here. If you choose to stay, all I require is that you swear an oath of allegiance to me for the next two years. During that time, we shall strive together to bring justice and equality to this great nation of ours.' He pointed towards Standish and the tall officer, who were now sitting at a table at the far side of the hall. 'Those of you who wish to leave, please go and see Mr Standish over there ...'

Turning in his seat, Hamish saw the thug leering back at him, a cruel smile playing on his thin lips.

'... And those of you who wish to stay, please make your pledge of allegiance with senior officer Captain Long.' Then, bidding a curt farewell, he departed the hall as abruptly as he had entered it.

For a long moment the group sat in silence, glancing at each other uncertainly. Then slowly, one by one, they began to get up.

Watching them line up in front of the officer, Hamish wondered what they were really signing up for. And why two years? Granted, the Lord Protector had made a compelling case for reform in England and he'd filled their stomachs. But it all sounded too good. Hamish's sixth sense urged caution. There had to be a catch. But try as he might, he couldn't identify it. Anxieties and apprehensions sluiced through his mind. He had to decide soon. The queue was shrinking and the other boys were leaving the hall. There were only two of them left. The rottweiler hadn't moved. He was still hunched over the table. Suddenly, Hamish thought of Suzy and his heart lurched. Alone without him, she'd be out of her mind with worry. Then he recalled his promise to her and his decision was made.

He got up and crossed the hall, sensing Standish's malevolent gaze boring into him. Like a one-eyed rattlesnake hypnotising a mouse, he was watching Hamish's every move, drawing his prey in.

Steeling himself for a final confrontation, Hamish had just taken a deep breath and fixed him with a defiant glare when suddenly a powerful hand grabbed him by the arm, stopping him in his tracks.

'Go there and you're a dead man,' hissed a voice from behind, causing him to spin around. It was the rottweiler, glowering an inch from his face. Hamish smelt his breath and grimaced. 'Trust me,' he rasped, 'if you sign out, you sign your own death warrant.'

Shocked, Hamish stared at him, lost for words.

Then without warning the rottweiler shoved him in the chest, propelling him into the nearby queue.

Time seemed to slow as he slammed into the skeletal boy who was signing his pledge and sent him flying. An explosion of air erupted from the boy's lungs as he sprawled backwards, knocking over an inkpot and scattering scrolls onto the floor.

Outraged, the officer sprang out of his seat. 'What's going on?' he roared, his eyes flashing fury at Hamish.

Dazed, Hamish swayed on his feet and it took him a moment to find his voice. 'I ... I ...' he stammered, but the rottweiler interrupted him.

'What he's trying to say is, he wants to sign in,' he snarled, clamping Hamish's arm, holding him steady.

Silently, the officer studied them both, his hostile gaze moving from one to the other and back again. Then he dipped the tip of the quill into the spreading ink pool and held it out to Hamish.

His heart pounding, Hamish took it.

'Make your mark on this,' murmured the officer, unfurling a scroll and holding it open.

The clamp around his bicep was released and Hamish glanced at the rottweiler uncertainly. It was then that he realised he didn't have a choice. With a deep foreboding, he leant forward and scratched his name at the bottom of the parchment. Then, moving aside, he watched as the rottweiler signed and began to walk away without a backward glance. Quickly, Hamish went after him. 'Excuse me, but I need to know something,' he said, tapping him on the shoulder.

The rottweiler turned around and Hamish noticed a curious mixture of impatience and sorrow in his dark eyes. Confused, he was about to start quizzing him when the beast lashed out, driving a massive fist into his solar plexus.

An explosion of pain drove the wind from his lungs and

Hamish fell to his knees, then collapsed to the floor, writhing in agony. Unable to inhale, his lungs screamed for oxygen and he started to panic, clutching his throat. Suddenly the spasms subsided and he gasped loudly. As his senses slowly returned to normal, he curled up in a foetal position, awaiting the next blow. But none came, only laughter. Baffled, he opened his eyes and looked up. His heart sank. Standish was clapping the rottweiler on the back. And in that moment he knew; the attack dog had found himself a new master.

CHAPTER SIX

'What's that?' screeched the curator furiously, jabbing a finger at Suzy's painting.

Startled, she looked up at him, her cheeks flushing. Everyone was watching.

'It's not right!' he exclaimed angrily. 'It's not right! I told you, you must copy the portrait in front of you exactly. It's got to be a perfect reproduction. What don't you understand about that?'

'I . . . I . . . just felt he should look more . . . more human,' she replied quietly.

'What?' he yelped. 'You're not being paid for your artistic interpretation! You're being paid to copy that portrait!' Turning to the semi-circle of twelve artists sitting in the ramshackle studio, he went on, his voice shrill with indignation. 'I won't tolerate this. I won't tolerate any deviation from the approved portrait in front of you. Is that clear? Is it? This creature here seems to think she can break the rules. But she can't. She can't. I won't have it. I won't . . .'

Embarrassed, Suzy thought he was going to explode. His ferret-like face with its long pointy nose was the colour of beetroot and he was shaking violently.

'Is that clear? Is it? Is it?' he cried hysterically.

Silently, everybody nodded.

'Good,' he snapped. 'Now get back to work!'

Breathing heavily, he waited until they'd all resumed painting before he fixed Suzy with his small beady eyes. 'I'll take this,' he hissed, snatching her canvas from its easel. 'I'll keep it as proof of your insubordination. And mark my words, if you try anything like this again, you'll be out. Now get another canvas and start again.'

Shaken, she watched the tiny figure scuttle to his office, a converted stall in the corner of the ancient barn, and slam the door. Then, with a heavy sigh, she got up from her stool and crossed the earthen floor to fetch another canvas. Setting it on her easel, she picked up some charcoal and began sketching the unremarkable figure for the sixth time in less than two weeks. It was repetitive work, she reflected miserably but what made it worse was the subject himself. Like the world's most nondescript bureaucrat, his blandness was exceptional. From his pallid complexion to his expressionless face, everything about him was grey and unimpressive. Even his clothes – a frilled white collar above a black tunic – complemented his greyness perfectly. Outlining the shiny oversized head, she sketched the loose folds of skin hanging below a weak chin and decided he led a sedentary life.

Picking up her paintbrush and palette, she began mixing several shades of grey and smiled inwardly, recalling what had so infuriated the curator. Bored, she had added a touch of rouge to the sallow cheeks and slightly enlarged the small hawkish eyes, introducing a glint of amusement. She'd also made the mean, slash-like mouth marginally fuller, adding a trace of a smile and bestowing on him an air of gentle benevolence.

Applying the paint in small neat strokes, she wondered who he was. Nobody seemed to know. According to the others, anyone who'd shown an interest in him had disappeared, never to be seen again. Taken aback by the fear in their eyes, Suzy had resolved never to ask the curator.

Noticing the shadows falling on her canvas, she looked up at the nearest window set high into the barn's timber wall. Red clouds streaked the dusk sky. Any minute now the curator would emerge from his office to conduct his rounds before sending them home. He was a creature of habit; it was always the same, she reflected. As if on cue, his door was flung open and he shuffled out, moving among them, inspecting their work and issuing instructions for the following day. Watching his animated gestures, she could tell that he was tenser than normal, slightly manic even. His head twitched as he spoke and his words came out in short breathless bursts. His eyes too were wild and a sheen of sweat glistened on his forehead. At first she wondered if he was sick, but as she continued watching him it suddenly dawned on her. He wasn't ill. He was terrified.

Disconcerted, she watched him approach the girl beside her. Sweating profusely, he had just begun appraising her work when there was a loud bang on the door. Gasping, he spun around. 'They're early!' he yelped, his eyes wide with fear. Then stumbling across the uneven ground, he approached the door tremulously.

'Who's there?' he cried out, peering through a crack in the weathered timber.

Intrigued, Suzy and the others watched him unbolt the door and open it hurriedly. Although they were unable to see who he was talking to, they could tell from his twitching that he was panic-stricken.

'Yes, Master,' he jabbered, 'but ... but ... I wasn't expecting you until after dark ... The painters are still ... still here ... I was just about to send them home ...'

Suzy felt a pang of pity for him. Even from where she was sitting at the far end of the barn, she could see him quivering beneath his grey smock. His spindly legs in their russet breeches and pale stockings were trembling, and she wondered who could instil such fear in a man. But no sooner had the thought crossed her mind than in burst three powerfully-built men, brushing him aside and heading straight for his office. Like archangels of the Apocalypse, their features obscured by long, hooded black cloaks, they swept past Suzy and she shivered involuntarily. An air of menace trailed in their wake and for the first time in her life, she sensed evil.

Terrified, the curator scuttled after them, slamming the door behind him.

'Who was *that*?' whispered Suzy, glancing at the girl beside her.

But the girl didn't reply. She just stood there, rigid with fear.

Tense seconds turned into interminable minutes and all they could hear was the curator's unintelligible whine. Pleading and pitiful, he sounded like a tortured soul negotiating with the devil himself. Then suddenly, his door flew open and he staggered out, his face twisted with rage.

'You!' he screamed, pointing at Suzy. 'Come here, now!'

Suzy's blood ran cold. She glanced at the others, hoping

desperately he was addressing somebody else. But their shocked stares confirmed her worst fears.

'Come here!' he wailed, incensed by her hesitation. 'Now!'

Her legs like jelly, she climbed to her feet and stumbled towards him, a familiar tide of panic threatening to overwhelm her.

'Get in there!' he snarled, grabbing her arm painfully and flinging her inside.

With a groan, she ricocheted off the doorframe, lost her footing and fell to the ground heavily. Disorientated, she got to her knees and shook her head, clearing her vision when three pairs of black boots loomed into view. Slowly, she looked up and her breath caught in her throat. 'You ...' she gasped.

Gazing down at her from behind a rough table, the grey man smiled thinly. 'Come in,' he said, a hint of amusement in his voice. 'I've been looking forward to meeting you.'

Watching him warily, she had just clambered to her feet, smoothing her apron, when she saw what he was holding and her heart sank.

'I'd like you to explain this,' he said, tapping her painting.

Her mind raced and the seconds it took her to find her voice seemed like an eternity. 'I ... I ... just felt ...' she stuttered. 'I just felt that your portrait should look more ...' Desperately, she groped for the right words. More than anything, she wanted to avoid offending him. But try as she might, the words wouldn't come and she realised that honesty was her only option. She swallowed hard and took a deep breath. '... I just felt that your portrait should look more *human*,' she said, wincing.

Behind her, the curator gasped.

The grey man's eyes narrowed. 'I see,' he murmured ominously.

Suzy felt a cold sense of foreboding in the pit of her stomach. Thinking about the painters who'd disappeared for simply showing an interest in his identity, she guessed she was about to join them. Wherever that might be, she thought, fearing the worst.

But as the seconds ticked slowly by, irritation began to supplant fear. His silent appraisal had been intimidating at first but now it was beginning to annoy her. She wondered if it was an interrogation technique. If so, it wasn't going to work, she decided. She'd already confessed to her crime and she had no intention of incriminating herself any further. Suddenly emboldened, she looked up at his hooded guards and smiled.

The grey man frowned. 'And what do you find so amusing?' he snapped indignantly.

Suzy's half-smile met his stare and she almost laughed. Not only did he look pompous but he sounded it too. Her impatience roused, she regarded him defiantly. 'Your guards,' she retorted; 'they look like grim reapers. And if you don't mind me saying, I think my painting flatters you.' The moment the words left her mouth she realised her insult and groaned inwardly as she watched him bridle.

'I *do* mind you saying it,' he growled irritably, 'but I must admit I prefer it to the original ...'

His words struck her like a thunderbolt and she stared at him, lost for words.

The grey man laughed softly, amused by her shock. 'Don't worry, you heard me correctly,' he said. 'I prefer your version to the original.'

If Suzy was surprised then the curator was stunned. 'But ... but ... my lord, you approved your portrait months ago and we've produced dozens!' he exclaimed, aghast. 'It will take considerable work and time to alter them all ...'

The grey man sat back in his chair and pushed himself to his feet by leaning heavily on the table with both hands. 'I'll pretend I didn't hear that,' he muttered darkly. Then, thrusting the painting at the curator, he turned back to Suzy. 'I've got an important commission for you, so collect your belongings because you're coming with me.'

A chill ran up Suzy's spine. 'Coming ... with ... you?' she repeated hesitantly.

The grey man nodded. 'You're a talented artist,' he replied. 'I can put your skills to good use.' Then without another word, he pulled up his hood and turned away, motioning for her to follow.

*

The messenger was exhausted. He'd been travelling for three days and he ached all over. But his destination was now in sight and he consoled himself that nobody in all of England could have made the journey faster. Watching the gulls wheeling overhead, their shrill screams becoming more frantic the closer they got to land, he inhaled deeply, savouring the fresh salty air. High clouds scudded across the blue sky and the ship's great white sails flapped loudly in the strong breeze. Behind him, the captain bellowed an order and he watched all hands rush to lower the sails and prepare to dock. The messenger smiled. Life was good, he mused, but if today was a success it was going to become much sweeter. Pressing a hand to his breast, he felt the scroll concealed inside his doublet and a warm surge of excitement coursed through his veins.

The first to disembark, he strode down the gangplank scanning the crowded dockside, searching for his contact. With one hand on his purse, he pushed past the throng of porters and waved away the pedlars jostling for his custom. Ahead, he could see a gang of ragged but tough young men watching a haughty-looking man dressed in a red silk doublet getting off a nearby ship. A pampered French aristocrat foolishly parading his wealth, he guessed. Had it been dusk, he wouldn't have given much for his chances.

Warily, he reached a dilapidated warehouse at the far end of the jetty, its barn doors wedged wide open. Entering cautiously, he expected to find somebody there but apart from a mountain of lobster pots stacked against the far wall and rows of small, upturned wooden boats, the place was deserted. He frowned. That was strange, he thought. This was definitely the rendezvous point. But where were they? He stepped forward, about to call out when suddenly he heard movement behind him and felt something sharp press into the small of his back.

'Don't move, Anglais!' came a heavily accented growl. 'One false move and I'll skewer you like a chicken. Now, give me your purse!'

With a sharp intake of breath, he snapped to attention, reaching for the leather pouch attached to his belt. If it was money he wanted, he could take it, he thought to himself. Compared to the main prize, the contents of his purse were an irrelevance.

'Nice and slow,' came the growl. 'Now, drop it on the ground in front of you and give me the scroll.'

The messenger froze. 'Scroll?' he repeated casually, trying desperately to conceal his alarm.

'The scroll, Anglais!' came the growl. 'Don't make me ask again.'

Wincing, he felt the sharp tip prod his back. His mind raced. How could this be happening? He hadn't told anyone. Then recalling his oath, he knew he had only two choices. *Succeed or die.* Slowly, he slipped his hand into the breast of his doublet, his fingers brushing past the scroll, probing instead for the intricately carved handle. He found it. Visualising his next move, he began withdrawing it, assessing his assailant's height from the rasp of his breathing. He closed his eyes and inhaled deeply, filling his lungs with oxygen. Then without warning he spun around, his liberated blade an extension of his right arm, arcing upwards, closing in on his assailant's throat. In a blur, their eyes locked and the messenger recoiled. 'Ramirez!' he cried, his dagger coming to a halt an inch from its target. 'What in God's name are you doing?'

The Spaniard grinned. 'Welcome to Calais, my enemy friend!' he laughed, clapping him on the shoulder. 'I've been tracking you since you landed. I'm glad to see you've still got some fight left in you!'

The messenger laughed, shaking his head at the swarthy figure stooping down to retrieve his purse. 'Ramirez, you have a sick sense of humour,' he said, noting how his beard was still as thick and black as his long, tied-back curls. 'But next time, I might not be so forgiving.'

With a sarcastic guffaw, the Spaniard handed him the leather pouch.

The messenger grew serious. 'So will he see me?' he asked, slipping his dagger back into his doublet.

Ramirez narrowed his eyes and replied gruffly, 'Si, senor, at dusk.' He paused, with a mischievous smile. 'Now come, let us find somewhere to drink and you can tell me all about life in England with your devil queen.'

*

'Fire!' bellowed the tutor.

With a loud *thwump*, eleven arrows soared high into the morning air: sixteenth-century missiles locked on to a large circular target some thirty yards in front of the twelve novice archers. With a simultaneous thud, the arrowheads embedded themselves deep into the straw-weave target and the tutor cried, 'Good work! We'll make crack shots out of you yet!' Then he turned to Hamish, his smile fading, and shook his head slowly. 'Well, perhaps not all of you.'

Bending down to retrieve the arrow lying on the scorched grass between his feet, Hamish felt his cheeks burn as sniggers broke out around him.

'Never mind, Hamilton,' laughed Blakey, clapping him on the back. 'You'll get the hang of it eventually. Here, let me show you.'

Watching the tall, good-looking boy with the natural authority of a born leader take another arrow, Hamish felt a pang of gratitude for his stewardship. It had come as quite a surprise but Blakey had sought him out on his first day. He'd been eager to congratulate him for maiming Standish. While Hamish would never boast about it, he couldn't help enjoying the notoriety it had brought him. It had certainly helped him to establish himself within this new community. He watched Blakey score another effortless bulls-eye, then loaded his own bow and pulled back the twine. What struck him again was how tight it was. Holding his breath, he summoned up every ounce of strength he could muster and hauled back the trigger string. His extended anchor arm began to tremble under the pressure and he struggled to grip the bow and control the arrowhead at the same time. Quickly, he aimed and fired. The arrow sped from its launcher, rose high into the air and landed short of the target.

'Never mind, let's see what you can do with this,' chortled the tutor, handing him a wooden sword.

It was Blakey who noticed the flash of irritation that passed across Hamish's face. 'Don't worry,' he murmured, leaning forward, 'we're using wooden swords for our own protection. Steel swords are only issued to the fully trained.'

Turning the sword over in his hand, Hamish noted the intricately decorated handle and perfect weight balance and realised it wasn't a toy at all; it had clearly been made by a master craftsman for the safe teaching of a most deadly art.

Urging restraint, the tutor handed a similar sword to another boy. 'Be gentle with him,' he said. 'Remember, you've had three months of training, he's had none.'

Stepping sideways, Hamish locked his eyes on to those of his smirking opponent. He could tell from his swagger that he was already revelling in certain victory. His heart pounded and he felt adrenaline surging through him. *Trust your instincts,* he told himself. *Be patient and wait for the right moment.* His senses on full alert, he circled around, his gaze never leaving his opponent's face. Suddenly, the boy lunged, thrusting his blade forward. Instantly, Hamish sidestepped and blocked him with a loud crack of wood on wood. Moving apart, they continued to circle, each appraising the other. His replica blade gripped tightly, Hamish slipped into a world of his own in which only he and his opponent existed. His muscles coiled, he knew that he had to let the more experienced boy carry the fight to him. *Block and wait, block and wait* became his silent mantra. Then he saw it, in his eyes. The boy was growing impatient. He wanted a swift victory and he was about to launch his charge. As if on cue, he made his move: darting forward, his blade swinging in from the side. With a loud crack, Hamish blocked and retreated. Pressing on, the boy committed himself and lunged forward. And as he did so, Hamish acted instinctively. Timing his move to perfection, he sidestepped and rushed forward, catching his over-extended opponent off guard. Bringing his arm down hard, he crashed the base of his sword's handle into the boy's shoulder blades, sending him sprawling to the ground. Quickly, he pressed his blade into the back of the boy's neck and the outside world came crashing back into his consciousness as loud cheers erupted around him.

'Where did you learn that?' laughed Blakey, clapping him on the back.

'I've no idea,' he replied weakly. 'No idea at all.' The effects of the adrenaline were wearing off and suddenly he felt exhausted.

'Good work, everyone!' yelled the tutor. 'You've earned your dinner!'

Chattering excitedly, the group began drifting off towards the stately building rising up from the canvas township.

'You're full of surprises, aren't you, Hamilton?' observed Blakey, walking beside him. 'First you maim Standish, then you prove yourself to be a skilled swordsman in your first training session. But to look at you, nobody would ever guess it.'

Hamish smiled at the backhanded compliment. 'Thanks, but there's one thing you're forgetting,' he said. 'I'll never be a decent archer.'

'Yes, and that's another surprise,' replied Blakey pensively, looking up at the group ahead. 'We've all grown up using the bow and arrow to hunt for food. We had to in order to survive. But it's obvious you didn't ...' Pausing, he gestured towards a long tent set apart from the main complex. Hamish knew it to be the infirmary where the most seriously malnourished boys were sent to convalesce. '... and yet you didn't need to spend time in the fattening tent either ...'

Hamish could tell what he was thinking. 'So why am I here?' he interjected.

Blakey stopped and looked at him curiously. 'Yes,' he said.

'It's a long story,' replied Hamish, thinking of Suzy and sighing heavily. 'And one I find hard to believe myself. Perhaps one day I'll share it with you. But right now, let's eat.'

Hesitating, Blakey saw the sorrow in his eyes and decided not to press him further. 'Fair enough; you can tell me in your own good time,' he said, falling into step beside him.

Together, they climbed the stone steps leading up to the building's grand entrance and joined a queue of boys waiting for their main meal of the day. Looking back across the sea of white canvas to the grassy slopes encircling the township, Hamish marvelled at its vastness. Reflecting on the monumental planning and organisation that must have gone into its construction, he had to admit it was a perfect hideout for a clandestine army. The cost of it too must be astronomical and he wondered who was funding it. Was it really all the work of one man, the self-proclaimed Lord Protector?

A sudden commotion from inside the hall broke his thoughts and he turned to see the guards marshalling everyone inside. 'What's happening?' he asked as they bustled through the doors.

Peering over the heads in front of him, Blakey gestured to the far end of the hall. 'It looks like the Lord Protector's preparing to speak,' he said.

Intrigued, Hamish counted six people on stage standing in a semi-circle around a square, knee-high wooden block. Three of the faces he recognised and three he didn't. With a sonorous boom, the doors closed behind them and the Lord Protector stepped forward. An expectant hush descended over the packed hall.

'It is with a heavy heart that I interrupt your dinner today,' he announced gravely. 'But something troublesome has occurred that I feel I must share with you all. When I invited you to join me in this venture, you did so by signing an oath of allegiance to me. In signing that oath, you also agreed to a set of conditions governing your conduct here. Every society requires rules that must be obeyed to ensure a harmonious existence. And when those rules are broken, it is only right that the perpetrators are punished in order to deter others from committing similar crimes. The same principles hold true within our society, our *family*. So it is with great regret that I stand before you today to announce that two of your brothers have been found guilty of committing heinous crimes against our family.' Pausing, he pointed towards a slightly-built, fair-haired boy trembling beside Standish. His face was ashen. 'Mr Peacock here has been found guilty of theft! He was caught stealing five eggs from the chicken coop. As you know, the normal punishment for such a crime in England is death by hanging ...'

Hamish gasped.

'... But I am merciful. As I rescued you all from a hopeless existence and gave you a new life, so too will I show leniency towards Mr Peacock here. Instead of his life, he will forfeit only his left hand ...'

Exhaling noisily, Hamish grimaced.

'What's wrong?' hissed Blakey.

'This is barbaric!' he whispered, watching Standish grab the whimpering boy's shoulders, forcing him to kneel.

'*Barbaric?*' repeated Blakey, aghast. 'Hamilton, where in God's name have you been living all these years? The lad's lucky. At least he'll still be breathing and able to wield a sword . . .'

But Hamish didn't respond. Transfixed by the horror show, he felt his stomach turn as Standish wrestled the boy's arm onto the block and reached for an axe. Raising it high above his head, the sneering brute looked across at the Lord Protector, who nodded once, and the blade descended.

With a dull thud, the axe severed hand from wrist and a red mist exploded from the stump.

Fighting back a strong urge to retch, Hamish groaned as the lifeless hand dropped to the stage and the boy fainted.

Blakey nudged the boy in front of him. 'Now for the main event,' he whispered conspiratorially.

Looking around, the boy smirked.

Hamish frowned. 'Main event?' he asked, perplexed.

Blakey smiled. 'Just watch!' he said, staring straight ahead.

Following his gaze, Hamish saw Standish shoving the rottweiler towards the block. 'What the . . . ?' he began to say, but his words petered out the moment he saw the cruel leer on Standish's face. It told him everything he needed to know. Somehow, the attack dog had fallen out of favour with his master. And they were about to find out why.

'Look at him squirm,' sneered Blakey. 'He thinks he's such the big man. This'll teach him.'

'Another theft!' roared the Lord Protector, pointing an accusing finger at the rottweiler. 'Mr Chimes here was discovered with a hammer and chisel concealed under his bed . . .'

The name struck Hamish like a bombshell and he gasped, studying the heavy-set figure being forced to kneel. His mind whirred, searching for *that* name. Then he saw it, in another lifetime, emblazoned across a high-sided lorry. 'Discreet removals!' he breathed incredulously. 'It can't be!'

But the bulldog resemblance was unmistakable.

'. . . stolen from the blacksmith,' cried the Lord Protector, 'and once again I'll show mercy by taking only his left hand!'

Blakey sniggered. 'Payback time!'

Cold realisation slapped Hamish across the face and he gasped. *It's a set-up! The hammer and chisel were planted!* His pulse raced and panic began to rise up inside him. Time ticked by in slow thudding seconds as the axe rose high into the air, about to begin its terrible descent. Then, as if having an out-of-body experience, he heard an anguished voice cry out, '*Stop!*'

The hall froze. Stunned silence filled the air and astonished faces gawped at him.

The Lord Protector stepped forward. His face was like thunder. 'Who said that?' he bellowed, scanning the crowd.

Swallowing hard, Hamish raised his hand. 'I did!' he called out weakly.

'Come here, now!'

Like a parting sea, the crowd in front of him moved aside and he approached the stage nervously. Sensing hostility, he clambered up the steps and saw that Standish had lowered his axe and was smirking at him evilly.

'What's your name?' snapped the Lord Protector.

'Hamilton, sir. Hamish Hamilton,' he replied, concentrating on keeping his voice steady.

'Well, Mr Hamilton, perhaps you would be good enough to explain what you mean by this interruption.'

Holding his gaze, Hamish took a deep breath. When he spoke, his tone was emphatic. 'He's innocent, sir.'

'And how exactly do you know that?' scoffed the Lord Protector dismissively.

'Because he didn't do it, sir.'

'Well, if he didn't do it then perhaps you'd be good enough to explain to us who did.'

Hamish hesitated and looked out into the crowd. Blakey's face had paled and there was alarm in his wide eyes.

Hamish's pulse quickened. 'I did it!' he replied firmly.

Instantly, uproar broke out in the hall and the Lord Protector raised his hands, calling for silence. When the din had finally subsided, he turned back to Hamish. 'Well, Mr Hamilton. That was certainly a noble, if not foolhardy, admission. But why should we believe you? What proof do you have?'

'What proof do you have that it was Chimes?' he countered.

A flicker of surprise passed across the Lord Protector's face and he smiled thinly. 'Very clever, Mr Hamilton. Very clever indeed,' he said quietly. Then, turning to the hall, he continued. 'In light of Mr Hamilton's extraordinary intervention, I have decided to adjourn today's proceedings. Clearly, I need to investigate this matter further. Enjoy your dinner.'

He waited until the hall's great doors had swung open and orderly queues had formed before turning back to Hamish. 'I think we need to have a proper conversation, young man,' he said, brushing past him. 'Come with me!'

*

'Does anyone know he's in France?' asked the messenger, walking quickly.

'No,' replied Ramirez, cursing as he stumbled on the cobbles. 'He's staying hidden on board.'

Turning a corner, they reached the harbour and saw the galleon anchored at the far end of the jetty, silhouetted against a vermillion sky.

'I see you Spanish still think big is beautiful!' quipped the messenger, laughing softly. 'I thought you'd have learnt your lesson in 1588!'

Ramirez's face darkened and he grabbed the messenger's arm. 'Whatever you do,' he growled, bringing him to a halt, 'never mention 1588 to him or Cadiz! Or you'll end up with a blade in your belly!'

Taken aback, the messenger realised that the scars still ran deep after all these years. 'Don't worry,' he replied, patting him on the shoulder. 'I'm here to make a delivery, not to give him a history lesson.'

Ramirez released him and they approached the warship. Its three masts cast long shadows over the still water. Looking up at the massive hull, the messenger saw weathered faces with hard gimlet eyes watching him suspiciously through the open canon hatches. His pulse quickened as he followed Ramirez up the gangplank and stepped on board the enemy vessel. Two soldiers snapped to attention, their metal breastplates and curved helmets reflecting the sky's fiery glow. Surveying his surroundings, the messenger whistled softly. If ever the term 'shipshape' required illustration, he thought, this was it. Everything about the ship was spotlessly clean, from the polished deck and carved railings to the gleaming brass fittings. Even the ropes were perfectly coiled and cotton clean.

He followed Ramirez up the ladder to the bridge and together they walked over to the ship's giant wheel. From here he could see to the bow and beyond, to the small town of Calais readying itself for nightfall. Apart from the two soldiers guarding the ship's entry point, nobody else was on deck, but he knew there would be a full contingent of 180 men billeted below.

'Wait here,' instructed Ramirez gruffly. 'I'll come back for you when he's ready.'

The messenger watched him disappear inside, and stood for a moment admiring the intricately carved royal coat of arms on the door. Pressing his hand to his breast, he contemplated the potential historic ramifications of his dispatch and felt excitement stir within him. Not only could it change *his* life, he reflected, but it could also chart a new beginning for England. Suddenly, the gentle click of a door-latch broke his thoughts and Ramirez appeared, motioning for him to enter. The time was upon him. Taking a deep breath, he withdrew the scroll, smoothed down his doublet and stepped inside.

The Great Cabin was breathtaking. No stranger to luxury himself, the messenger surveyed the oak-panelled room spanning the entire width of the ship and marvelled at its opulence. Crimson and gold silk drapes framed a floor-to-ceiling window running the length of the room, affording panoramic views of the ship's aft. Two crystal chandeliers hung from the ceiling, their flickering candles bathing the sumptuous stateroom in a warm golden glow. Vivid tapestries depicting hunting scenes graced the walls while deep-pile Persian rugs covered the floor. Highly polished mahogany furniture abounded, from a gleaming long table and chairs to a great sideboard, its sturdy shelves showcasing an array of gold and silverware, encrusted with precious jewels. Then his eyes fell upon a large oak chest, its heavy lid propped open, and the breath caught in his throat. It was filled with gold doubloons, a Spanish treasure of dazzling value.

Suddenly, out of the corner of his eye, he detected movement and turned as a small figure stepped out from behind a tall wing-backed armchair. 'Your Majesty,' he breathed, bowing to one knee. 'I am truly honoured.'

The response was gracious but firm. 'Arise, sir. You have come far.'

The messenger rose and looked down at the most powerful ruler on earth. At just over four feet tall with closely cropped mousy hair, a pale round face and neat pointed beard, what King Philip II of Spain lacked in physical stature he made up for with his flamboyant clothing. Resplendent in a rich golden doublet, its exquisite embroidery shimmering in the candlelight, he was wearing matching breeches and cream silk tights that accentuated his stick-thin legs. Tiny golden velvet slippers cosseted his feet. He might be a bird of a man, the messenger reflected, but nobody could fail to be impressed by his plumage.

The King's demeanour was courteous and cultivated. Smiling serenely, he waved his guest to an armchair facing his own and sat.

Sinking gratefully into the soft upholstery, the messenger watched the King's face grow serious. When he spoke, his voice was solemn, his accent strong.

'I have been awaiting your terms eagerly, Protestant,' he said. 'As God is my witness, I have long prayed for the day when I will finally crush your heretic Queen and restore England to the Holy Roman Church. By uniting our nations, I will fulfil my pledge to His Holiness the Pope and create a Catholic empire that will rule the world for eternity.'

'Then perhaps this will atone for past failures,' said the messenger, leaning forward and offering the scroll.

The King's eyes flashed with fury and he snatched the document. 'Damn you to hell!' he snarled, breaking the wax seal and unfurling the parchment.

Watching him read, the messenger smiled, recalling the cause of his ire. It had begun nine years ago in 1588, a year still seared into England's collective memory. A seemingly invincible Spanish Armada of a hundred and thirty towering galleons carrying thirty thousand men had been sent to rendezvous with the Duke of Parma's army at Calais before launching their invasion of England. At least, that had been the plan. But what they hadn't counted on was English guile. A Tudor fleet, under the command of Sir Francis Drake, had sailed from Plymouth to intercept them and at midnight on the 28th of July, five fire-ships packed with wood and pitch had been set ablaze and sailed into the heart of the Spanish fleet's protective crescent formation. The resulting inferno, fanned by high 'Protestant' winds, had caused panic, scattering the fleet, allowing the smaller, nimbler English vessels to pick them off at will.

It was the most humiliating defeat in Spanish naval history. Twenty thousand men were killed and a third of its fleet destroyed. By contrast, the English lost only a hundred men with no ships sunk, sparking wild celebrations and ushering in a new era of national confidence.

Savouring the memory, the messenger smiled and noted that the King was reading the terms again. And well he might, he mused, for the price was high. But that hadn't deterred him before. And it was unlikely to deter him now.

Devastated by his navy's defeat, the King had sworn revenge and set about rebuilding his Armada. Eight years later in 1596, final preparations were being drawn up for the conquest of England when his plans were thwarted again. An English fleet of one hundred and fifty ships under the command of a brilliant young officer had carried out a daring raid on the Spanish port of Cadiz. For two weeks, English troops had ransacked the town, destroying a large proportion of the Spanish fleet and upsetting King Philip's plans indefinitely. Or so England had believed. But what nobody had anticipated was the King's obsession. And now, almost two years on with his Armada rebuilt, England once again braced itself for invasion.

The King lowered the document. Deep in thought, he was silent for a long moment. 'I will not rest until I have achieved my Great Enterprise of England and claimed the crown for my daughter,' he said. Then, pausing, he leaned over and set the parchment alight on a nearby candle.

Suddenly anxious, the messenger watched it blacken and curl as the flame licked up towards the King's fingers.

'No record must ever exist that such an exchange took place,' he continued, dropping it to the floor. 'History will recall that I and I alone fulfilled my pledge to God and Rome. The conquest of England will be my greatest triumph. And mine alone.' He paused, gazing deep into the messenger's eyes and beyond, as if into his very soul. 'I assent,' he said. 'Now go!'

CHAPTER SEVEN

'Come in and sit down,' instructed the Lord Protector, directing Hamish towards two wooden chairs facing an unlit fireplace at the far end of the high-ceilinged stateroom.

His footsteps echoing on the dusty floorboards, Hamish was immediately struck by the immense room's austere appearance. Although bathed in bright sunlight from three floor-to-ceiling mullioned windows, affording panoramic views of the canvas township outside, it felt cold and soulless like an empty warehouse. Stark whitewashed walls gave way to what he guessed was an elaborately carved oak-panelled frieze housing a walk-in stone fireplace, but that too had been whitewashed over. Even the furniture was simple and sparse. Sitting down, he looked back to where he'd entered and noticed that the Lord Protector had taken a seat behind the only other item of furniture gracing the room: a rickety wooden table piled high with books. Silence hung over them as Hamish waited nervously, watching the Lord Protector hunched over the biggest book he'd ever seen. But as the seconds turned into minutes, his apprehension began to dissipate. For here, at study, the man no longer exuded stern authority. His gaunt face, pale and drawn, had lost its hard frown. Now, he appeared more relaxed, reflective and altogether less intimidating, like a learned scholar ruminating over a complex conundrum. It was as if he'd removed a burdensome robe on entering the privacy of his own quarters. Engrossed in the book, he seemed oblivious to everything around him.

Hamish coughed quietly.

Distracted, the Lord Protector looked up. 'Ah, Mr Hamilton, I'm sorry to have kept you waiting,' he said softly, closing the heavy tome and climbing to his feet.

It wasn't until he rounded the table that Hamish noticed he was walking with a slight limp.

Grimacing, the Lord Protector sat down beside him. 'Now, what is it we need to talk about?' he asked distractedly.

Hamish frowned.

'Ah yes, that performance of yours just now,' the Lord Protector said. 'I'd like you to explain why you felt compelled to intervene.'

Hamish took a deep breath and spoke quietly. 'As I said, sir. Chimes is innocent.'

'And how precisely do you know that?' he replied curtly.

Hamish swallowed hard. 'He was set up, sir. The things you found under his mattress had been planted there.'

The Lord Protector leaned back in his chair, pursed his lips and ran a hand across his domed head. 'Is that so?' he said thoughtfully. 'And what evidence do you have to support that theory?'

'I don't have any evidence, sir,' he said, recalling the look of horror on Blakey's face. 'It's just a feeling I have.'

'A *feeling*?' exclaimed the Lord Protector. 'You halted proceedings because of a *feeling*?'

Hamish nodded. 'Yes, sir,' he said quietly.

The Lord Protector's face darkened. 'I deal in facts, not feelings,' he snapped, but he broke off as the sound of singing began drifting in from outside. Wearily, he climbed to his feet and limped over to the window.

Hamish watched him craning his neck, scanning the township beyond.

'Standish!' the Lord Protector yelled. 'Standish!'

Suddenly, the door flew open and in burst the scowling brute, fixing Hamish with his lone eye. 'Yes, my lord?' he growled.

'That song! Where's it coming from?' he barked, without turning.

Standish's cold stare shifted to his master's back. 'My lord, I don't know but I'll silence it immediately.'

'Good,' he snapped. Then, turning around, he glanced at Hamish and paused. 'On second thoughts, no,' he said pensively. 'Instead, go and commend them for the fairness of their song.'

Standish's mouth fell open. 'Commend them?' he repeated aghast.

The Lord Protector smiled thinly. 'Don't you see?' he said. 'It's a testament to what we've achieved here that boys who'd once lost all hope can celebrate their new lives through song.'

Hamish smirked, revelling in Standish's discomfort. It was no wonder he looked agitated. He was used to meting out punishment, not praise.

The Lord Protector waited until he'd closed the door before continuing. 'Mr Hamilton, I notice from that accent of yours, you come from up north.'

Hamish nodded. 'That's right, sir. Northumberland.'

'Well, tell me about yourself and how you ended up here.'

Hamish's pulse quickened. For a moment, he wondered how he'd react if he told him the truth, but he dismissed the notion as soon as it had entered his head.

The Lord Protector sat down again. 'Don't worry,' he said, noting his hesitancy. 'Nothing you tell me will shock me. I've heard the most terrible tales of injustice and inhumanity. I doubt your story is any more remarkable.'

Hamish decided to keep it as brief and as close to the truth as possible. 'Sir, to be honest, there isn't a lot to tell. My family were forced from our smallholding a few months ago. We came south in search of a new life and were staying with friends in Islington when your black shirts abducted me and brought me here.'

Listening expectantly, the Lord Protector raised his eyebrows. 'Mr Hamilton, you're economical with words,' he observed. 'But tell me something. You say you halted today's proceedings because you had a feeling that Mr Chimes had been set up. So why did you confess to the crime?'

'Sir, because I thought it was the only way I could stop the miscarriage of justice,' he replied quietly.

The Lord Protector smiled. 'So, Mr Hamilton, you're a man of principle and compassion,' he said. 'And honesty too!'

Unsure whether he was being complimented or mocked, Hamish held his breath.

'Those are unusual traits in this day and age,' he continued earnestly. 'And especially in someone who's experienced the harsh realities of life.'

Hamish exhaled softly.

'You're intelligent too,' the Lord Protector observed. 'It's a shame you can't read and write . . .'

'But of course I can!' he exclaimed, frowning.

The Lord Protector's eyes narrowed. 'Only those of noble birth receive education,' he said suspiciously.

Groaning inwardly, Hamish berated himself. How could he have been so stupid? Compulsory education for everyone hadn't been introduced until the late nineteenth century. Until then, it had been the preserve of only the rich. Desperately, he scrabbled for a plausible explanation. 'My uncle taught me,' he explained quickly, recalling the ruined abbey where he and Suzy had played as children. 'He was a lay brother at Hulne Priory . . .' He let his words trail off, hoping his interrogator wouldn't probe him further.

His luck was in. The Lord Protector had become distracted by the singing, which was growing steadily louder. Frowning, he climbed to his feet and limped over to the window, then froze as a thunderous roar erupted.

Intrigued, Hamish hurried over. The sight that greeted him took him aback. Staring up was a sea of faces, their rapt attention focused on the figure standing in front of him.

Laughing softly, the Lord Protector raised a hand and the crowd cheered, like delirious football fans celebrating a goal. 'See how they love me!' he murmured.

Hamish smiled. 'Sir, nobody could doubt the respect and affection you command here.'

The crowd burst into song again and the Lord Protector stood watching, his hands clasped behind his back. 'Mr Hamilton, I have a proposition for you!' he said after a long moment.

Startled, Hamish stared at the back of his head.

'Young man, I need a recorder,' he continued. 'A recorder to chronicle events here such that history will recall accurately our forthcoming crusade. A new chapter in our nation's glorious history is about to begin and I'd like you to help me chronicle it.'

Hamish was lost for words.

Turning away from the window, the Lord Protector noticed his surprise and gestured for him to sit. Then he crossed over to his desk and opened the giant leather-bound book. 'Mr

Hamilton, have you ever heard of the Magna Carta?' he asked.

'Erm, yes, I've heard of it,' he replied slowly, 'but I don't know what it's about.'

'The Magna Carta was originally drawn up in 1215,' explained the Lord Protector. 'Also known as the Great Charter of Freedoms, it was designed to resolve a dispute between the English barons and King John about the rights of the monarchy. Essentially, it required the King to accept that he was no longer above the law. It limited his power. It meant that if he disobeyed the laws of the land, he could lose his crown and possibly even his head. It also granted certain rights to the people, such as the right not to be imprisoned unfairly. The Magna Carta has been updated periodically over the years to put right various wrongs, but its core purpose has never changed – to protect the people from the tyranny of monarchs.'

Hamish listened intently.

'As you can imagine, the Magna Carta's never been popular with the monarchy. Even today, over three hundred and fifty years later, Queen Elizabeth views it as an evil document. She believes it was forced upon her forefathers using brute force. But she also fears it. So much so that she recently stopped a bill from going to Parliament seeking to reaffirm its legitimacy. As far as she's concerned, she's been ordained by God to rule this kingdom. She believes she's answerable to God alone. But the Magna Carta denies her the unlimited powers she covets. Instead, it binds her to the same earthly laws that govern all her subjects.

'When you consider the injustice, corruption, starvation and pestilence blighting our society, can you imagine what else she would have wreaked upon our nation were it not for the Magna Carta? Queen Elizabeth's forty-year reign has brought this country two things, Mr Hamilton: hopelessness and suffering.' Pausing, he gestured for Hamish to approach and waited until he'd crossed the room before continuing.

'This document is the culmination of five years' work,' he said, tapping the huge tome lying open on the table. 'The Lord Protector's Grand Charter here enshrines a fundamental truth: that all people should be free and equal without distinction of class or status. I have revised and updated the Magna Carta such that the people of this country should no longer have to look to the next life for salvation. They should have it in this one.'

Listening spellbound, Hamish looked down at the black spidery handwriting and realised he couldn't fault anything he was hearing. How was it possible that the Queen believed she had a divine right to rule? And how could she and her court be so blind and unsympathetic to the chronic suffering taking place outside their gilded cages? Perhaps it *was* time for a compassionate thinker like the Lord Protector to replace the ruling minority. After all, they owned and ran the country through no other qualification than their birthright. What was more, their priorities lay not with the people but with their own self-interest. Suddenly, it all made sense to him. The Lord Protector *really was* building a salvation army of highly trained and loyal soldiers to create a new society based on fairness, equality and liberty. Surely, he reasoned, that could only be a good thing, not just for sixteenth-century England but for future generations as well. If the nation's history was based on fairer foundations then perhaps centuries of social conflict could be avoided. After all, he reasoned, why should the country have to wait until the industrial revolution for greater social justice when something positive could be done about it now?

'Mr Hamilton, the Great Salvation begins here,' continued the Lord Protector. 'Will you help me record it for posterity?'

It was then that Hamish knew what he must do.

*

Suzy awoke with a start and sat bolt upright. It took her a moment to remember where she was. Then, sighing contentedly, she fell back into the soft luxury of her warm bed. Pulling up the blanket, she gazed at the tiny room's low ceiling and yawned, unable to recall the last time she'd slept so soundly.

A knock on the door broke her thoughts and she smiled as a girl's voice called out, 'Mistress Suzy, are you awake yet? It's time to get up.'

'Come in, Rosie,' she called, watching the door open and a young maid enter. Wearing a floor-length russet dress, rolled up at the sleeves, and a white linen apron, the pretty girl was carrying a large earthenware jug. Setting it down on a table, she crossed over to the window and pulled back the curtain.

Bright early morning sunlight streamed in, causing Suzy to squint as she threw back the covers and hurried over, eager to check out her new surroundings. 'Dear Lord, where are we?' she gasped, taken aback by the vast circular plain surrounded by a steep hill and what appeared to be a sea of canvas far below.

'I'm not rightly sure, miss,' the maid said, laughing softly. 'The camp's location is a closely guarded secret.'

Suzy frowned. 'Rosie, is this a prison camp?' she asked anxiously, noting the regimented network of narrow lanes and open squares intersecting the canvas below.

'No! Don't you remember what I told you last night?' she replied, sensing her disquiet.

Suzy racked her brain. Although she recalled the maid's kindness she remembered little of their conversation. After hours on horseback, most of it in darkness, she'd been dead on her feet when she'd finally arrived. Accompanied by two guards, she'd been helped to the kitchen and entrusted to Rosie's care. Her recollection was hazy. She remembered eating a bowl of hot stew and bread. Then there was a seemingly endless trek through a warren of dark corridors and up interminable stairs before she'd collapsed on the bed, exhausted. Beyond that, she remembered nothing.

Rosie opened the window and pointed to a large clearing at the foot of the hill. 'Look over there,' she said. 'You can see the lads practising their archery and sword fighting.'

In the distance, Suzy saw dozens of figures milling about in carefully choreographed patterns and the penny dropped. 'Of course, it's a training camp!' she breathed, transfixed.

'And I'm to show you around before you meet the Lord Protector later today,' the maid reminded her.

Suzy frowned. 'Lord Protector?' she repeated, puzzled.

The maid rolled her eyes. 'Didn't you listen to anything I said last night?' she said, feigning indignation. Then, smiling, she gestured to the view outside. 'This is all his doing,' she explained. 'He's the one who rescued everybody. And he's the one preparing us for a better life.'

Suzy met her gaze and a flower of hope bloomed inside her. 'How many people are down there?' she asked quietly.

'I'm not rightly sure,' replied the maid, 'but we cater for thousands.'

Suzy's pulse quickened. She almost didn't dare to ask the question. 'Rosie, where did all those lads come from?'

'Why, from all over the country,' she replied. 'Like us, they were rescued from the streets and given new lives here.'

*

'Not bad, not bad at all, Mr Hamilton,' murmured the Lord Protector, closing the leather-bound notebook. Standing in front of the fireplace, he looked across at Hamish, who sat at the rickety desk. 'Your prose is certainly more succinct than is customary, and some of your spellings are incorrect, but on the whole, your handwriting is legible and I think you've summarised today's proceedings quite well. I particularly like your summary of the mercy I showed Mr Chimes.'

Relieved, Hamish watched him limp over to the window.

'Mr Hamilton, you're going to hear some disturbing rumours about my last recorder,' he said without turning.

Hamish frowned.

'I understand that some of the boys believe I had him murdered,' he continued gravely. 'But I can assure you there was nothing sinister about his sudden departure from camp. He simply went home to care for his wealthy uncle, that's all.'

Hamish stared at him. Something didn't add up. Unsettled, he took a deep breath, about to question him when there was a rap at the door.

*

'Don't worry, we're nearly there,' Rosie murmured, sensing Suzy's unease as they turned down another long, dark passageway. The stone tunnel-like walls were lined with occasional candles, casting small pools of flickering yellow light onto the cold, dank surfaces. Their footsteps echoed as they followed a guard who seemed to vanish between light pools, melding in and out of the darkness like a ghostly apparition.

Suzy shivered again, but only partly because of the cold. What threatened her composure was anxiety. And fear – brought on

125

by the extraordinary sights and stories she'd been exposed to during her tour that day. Intuitively, she knew she'd arrived at the centre of a potentially catastrophic universal storm.

The sheer scale of the assembled force was worrying enough, she reflected, but what she found profoundly disturbing, beyond even the boys' eagerness to fight, was their slavish devotion to their cause. It was as if they'd all been brainwashed. The same mantra tumbled from their mouths. They'd been doomed to lives of despair and premature deaths. But they'd been rescued. Now they had food and shelter, a home and extended family. They'd regained their strength and learnt new skills. They spoke of hope, for a new and better life. They viewed themselves as a collective key to unlocking the unjust shackles binding society. They were going to create a new social order based on liberty, equality and compassion. And the overriding objective of what they called this Great Salvation was simple: to rid the country of the ruling elite. Furthermore, they owed their lives to just one person: the feared and revered Lord Protector.

Suzy shuddered. The fact that the camp was being dismantled meant only one thing. This army of well-intentioned but misguided zealots was about to march. And although they didn't know it, they'd been programmed to provoke a conflict that could devastate the foundations upon which her world was built. Her mind raced. At any moment now she would be coming face to face with the architect of calamity. Uncertainty and unease congealed into panic, swelling in the pit of her stomach. Prickling beads of perspiration broke out across her forehead and her legs felt suddenly weak. Pausing, she leaned against the wall, her head bowed, breathing deeply, willing herself to calm down.

'Poor love, you must be ailing!' exclaimed Rosie, rushing over, placing an arm around her shoulders. 'You've hardly eaten a thing all day.'

Slowly, Suzy's mind began to clear and the debilitating tide receded.

Ahead of them, the guard's ghostly figure appeared out of the darkness. 'Get moving!' he barked. 'We haven't got time to stand around talking.'

Looking up, Suzy smiled at him apologetically. 'I'm sorry,' she said weakly. 'I don't know what came over me.' Then, taking a deep breath, she started down the passageway again, grateful for Rosie's support.

Within moments they arrived at a door and the guard knocked.

Suzy's hands trembled and the sound of her pulse in her ears was like a beating drum. Concentrating on breathing steadily, willing herself to remain calm, she heard a voice approaching the door. She frowned. It sounded familiar. Quickly, she scoured her memory, trying to place it. Then she saw it and gasped. 'It can't be...' she whispered as the door opened and there he stood, a thin smile playing on even thinner lips.

'*You?* The *Lord Protector?*' she exclaimed in surprise.

The grey man laughed softly. 'Come in, Suzy,' he said, gesturing for her to enter. 'I've been looking forward to your arrival.' He waited until she'd stepped past him before issuing murmured instructions to the guard.

The scene that greeted her stopped Suzy in her tracks. A wave of shock and disorientation tore through her body, spinning her internal compass upside-down. She blinked several times, unsure whether her eyes were playing tricks on her. But they weren't. It really was Hamish and he was rushing towards her, his arms outstretched, his face lit up in astonished delight. And then the euphoria and relief arrived, overwhelming her, causing her to choke back both laughter and tears. Instinctively she went to embrace him, but no sooner had she moved forward than she halted, her sixth sense urging caution. Quickly, she glanced over her shoulder. The grey man was closing the door, about to turn around. There was little time. She had to warn him fast.

Instantly, Hamish noticed the hard, forbidding look in her eyes and he stopped abruptly, his smile fading rapidly.

Suzy spoke in an urgent, barely audible voice. 'You don't know me!' she hissed, glaring at him ominously. She could sense his confusion and saw a momentary look of pain pass across his face. But he nodded anyway.

Conflicting thoughts and emotions swirled through them as

they stood like strangers, waiting for the Lord Protector to break the silence.

'Mr Hamilton, I'd like you to meet Suzy,' he said, joining them in the centre of the room. 'She's a talented artist who's going to produce a visual record of our Great Salvation ...'

Inwardly, Suzy groaned at the news. The irony of having to chronicle the very enterprise that could destroy their world was as sick as it was twisted.

Hamish acknowledged her with a curt nod.

'... and Suzy, Mr Hamilton here is my recorder,' he continued. 'He's responsible for chronicling our Great Salvation, so you'll both be working together for the foreseeable future.'

When Suzy reciprocated, her tone was detached and formal. 'Mr Hamilton, I'm pleased to make your acquaintance,' she said.

She was very aware of the grey man looking at her curiously. 'That accent,' he said, 'it's similar to Mr Hamilton's. Where do you come from?'

Suzy felt her pulse quicken. 'From the north-east of England,' she replied evenly.

The Lord Protector's gaze shifted from one to the other, then back again to Suzy. 'You don't happen to know each other, by any chance, do you?' he asked.

Simultaneously, their insides churned with anxiety, but they shook their heads, looking at him blankly.

'Suzy, what's your family name?' he asked, frowning.

Cold fear gripped her and she thought she might falter. But her words when they came were instinctive and firm. And the unequivocal way they fell from her lips surprised even her. 'Why, it's *McLeod*, sir. My name is Suzy McLeod.'

Impressed by her quick thinking, Hamish sighed softly. If he hadn't known better, he'd have believed her himself. But most importantly of all, he could tell that the Lord Protector was convinced.

'Mr Hamilton, is there anything else we should be talking about?' asked the Lord Protector.

'Er, no, sir. I don't think so, sir.'

'Then please leave us. Miss McLeod and I have much to discuss.'

With a perfunctory glance at Suzy, Hamish departed, relieved to escape the charade. Why she'd insisted on playing such games was a mystery to him. What could she possibly know that he didn't? He needed to find out. And he needed to find out fast. Slipping into the passageway, he closed the door quietly and crept off, hugging the darkest shadows, eager to elude Standish, who rarely strayed far from his master's side.

Just then a door creaked open and bright light flooded the far end of the passageway. Hamish's heart sank. Silhouetted in the doorway was his arch-nemesis. Hurriedly, he pressed his back to the wall and inched forward, probing the cold stone for the recessed doorway he knew would lead him to a storeroom. Like several other hiding places around the vast building, he'd used it before. His fingers found the latch.

With the light behind him, Standish held his breath, listening for movement. 'What's taking them so long?' he muttered to himself, stepping forward, squinting into the darkness.

Leaving the storeroom's door slightly ajar, Hamish waited until he heard Standish retreat to his quarters before reaching into his pocket for the candle he'd started carrying around for just this type of occasion. After checking the coast was clear, he darted into the passageway, lit it on the wall-mounted candle opposite and returned to illuminate the storeroom and wait for Suzy. Positioning a wooden crate next to the door, he sat down and surveyed the windowless chamber in the flickering yellow glow. An array of furniture was set around the bare brick walls, dark oak mainly and most of it elaborately decorated. Tall-backed dining chairs featuring intricate floral carvings sat atop a highly polished long table, while broad cupboards and side-boards of various shapes and sizes provided rests for piles of colourful tapestries, drapes and floor coverings, all of which would have looked at home in a baronial hall. A hall such as the Lord Protector's office, he thought. And not for the first time, he wondered why the leader of the Great Salvation eschewed such finery. Perhaps it was a distraction, he speculated, glancing through the small gap between door and doorframe into the passageway beyond.

There was still no sign of Suzy. He wondered how long he'd

have to wait. It was chilly and seemed to be getting colder. He began buttoning up his doublet and felt the chain around his neck. Quickly, he withdrew the precious timepiece from under his shirt and pressed the metal clasp. The circular lid sprang open. Examining the complex face, he ignored the time and compass, focusing instead on the barometer. What he saw startled him. The pointer had swung markedly since yesterday. Until now, order had been the dominant force. But in the past twenty-four hours, somewhere and somehow, chaos had ascended.

Suddenly the heavy clunk of a metal bolt broke his thoughts and he whipped round, peering through the gap. His heart leapt. It was Suzy. She was leaving the Lord Protector's office. And she was alone. Quickly, he stood up and leaned into the passageway, pressing his finger to his lips, gesturing for her to enter.

Suzy beamed at him and hurried over. 'Oh, Hamish,' she whispered, grabbing his hand.

Pulling her in, Hamish closed the door silently and turned to face her. She was smiling, but there were tears in her eyes and when she spoke there was a catch in her voice. 'Oh, Hamish, I was so frightened that night.'

'I know,' he whispered, embracing her tightly. 'It's okay.' Swallowing hard, he sensed that the warmth suffusing him was also suffusing her, cheering and rejuvenating them both. 'Tell me,' he whispered, prising her away, 'how did you get here?'

'It's a long story,' she replied, then she recounted what had happened since that fateful night at Jeremiah's house.

Hamish whistled softly as her story came to an end. 'Wow, that's certainly some journey!' he conceded. 'But you're wrong about one thing.'

Suzy frowned. 'What do you mean?' she asked.

Hamish took a step back. 'The Lord Protector, or "grey man" as you call him, he's a good man. And I support his Great Salvation.'

Suzy stared at him. 'Not you as well!' she groaned, recalling the well-rehearsed mantra of the others.

'Listen, we have the chance of a lifetime!' he countered, irritated by her dismissive tone. 'We're going to be part of something that'll improve the lives of millions, not just in this time but for centuries to come—'

'Oh, spare me the speech!' she interrupted angrily. 'I've heard it all before!'

'Then how can you be so dismissive?'

'Because, brother of mine, that's not why we're here!' she snapped. 'Or have you forgotten?' Then without waiting for a response, she recited the advice given to them what seemed a lifetime ago. 'Your task here is to restore the harmony between chaos and order. To do so, it's vital you disregard any concepts of good and evil or right and wrong. You're not here to act as your conscience dictates. Imbalance is the only enemy. It's imperative you remain ruthlessly impartial.'

Hamish considered her words for a long time. 'But surely we can do something positive in the process as well?' he ventured finally.

'Oh, don't be so naïve!' she sighed in exasperation. 'Don't you see? The world we know is based on Queen Elizabeth ruling England for forty-five years until she dies in 1603. It's 1597 now, which means she's still got six years left. Therefore any challenge to her position before that is a direct attack on the twenty-first century we know. And it's your benevolent Lord Protector who's posing the biggest threat.'

Hamish gave a resigned sigh. 'So what do we do?' he asked quietly.

Relieved, Suzy regarded him for a long moment. 'For harmony to be restored,' she said, 'the threat must be neutralised.' She reached into her apron, withdrew a small cloth bundle and handed it to him. 'Here, you left this behind the night you were abducted.'

Hamish unfurled the wrapping and held up the ivory-handled dagger in its leather scabbard. Taking hold of the carved lion's head, he slipped it out of its sheath and saw the sign of Equilibrium etched into each side of the glinting blade. Then, frowning, he looked up at her and spoke uneasily. 'Sis, what are you suggesting?'

When Suzy replied, her words chilled him to the bone. 'Assassination!' she said. 'The Lord Protector must be assassinated.'

'But we're not assassins!' he protested.

'We are *whatever* it takes to restore harmony!' she snapped harshly. And for the first time, she understood precisely what drove Jeremiah Graves.

Just then a creak at the door made them both jump and they whirled around to see it swing slowly open.

Suzy gave a startled gasp.

Cold fear entered Hamish's heart and he snarled to conceal it. 'What do you want?' he demanded, hiding the blade behind his back.

Standish's face twisted into a sneer. 'Well, looky, looky,' he chuckled, his voice grating like iron on stone. 'What have we got here?'

'Leave us and return to your quarters!' growled Hamish, taking a step forward. 'As recorders of the Great Salvation we have business to attend to!'

Standish stepped up to him. 'Hamilton, I think our time has finally come!' he sneered, slowly removing the bandage from his left eye.

Hamish recoiled at the bloody black hole.

Standish laughed softly. 'If you think this is gruesome, just wait 'til you see what I'm going to do to you.'

Suzy closed her eyes and pressed a hand to her chest. She felt sick and her heart was pounding against her rib cage. It all seemed so insane. She couldn't believe that history was about to repeat itself. But this time she feared Hamish would be taken from her forever unless she could stop it. Taking a deep breath, she opened her eyes and grabbed Standish by the wrist. 'Leave him alone!' she screamed.

Both would-be combatants froze, staring at her in surprise.

Then Standish began to laugh, softly at first, then harder until he was howling hysterically.

Hamish and Suzy glanced at each other uncertainly. Each could see the fear and confusion in the other's eyes.

Without warning, Standish slammed a fist into the side of her face, launching her off her feet, sending her crashing into the wall and crumpling to the floor with a low concussed moan.

Time seemed to slow and it took Hamish a moment for the

sickening reality of what had happened to sink in. Disbelief and horror congealed into fear, splashing the back of his throat like acid. But overwhelming his fear was the one emotion that was even more powerful: rage. Fuelled by adrenaline, he was primed to kill. With a roar, he flew at the leering brute. Clutching the knife behind him, he rammed his shoulder up into Standish's solar plexus, knocking him off balance and twisting his body to unleash the blade. But Standish saw the flash of steel and, falling backwards, grabbed Hamish's wrist and slammed it against the heavy table, knocking the knife out of his grasp. Hamish flinched as pain shot up his arm and he staggered backwards, searching for the weapon. But it was no use. It was gone.

'Not so brave now, Hamilton!' sneered Standish, charging at him like a bull. They collided head-on, crashing to the floor heavily.

Pinioned under Standish's crushing weight, Hamish twisted and writhed, wincing at the stench of his opponent's breath. He was trapped. Desperately, he jerked his head up and sank his teeth into a cauliflower ear. He tasted blood.

Standish howled, grabbing his hair, trying to prise him away. But Hamish gripped on. Frenzied blows began raining down on him and he knew he couldn't hold on for much longer. He was tiring and the hits were taking their toll. With one last effort, he ground his teeth into the cartilage, and wrenched at it with all his might. A guttural roar erupted and Standish rolled away, clutching the side of his head, blood oozing between his gloved fingers.

Dazed, Hamish got to his knees wearily and spat out the gristle, praying that Standish had lost the will to fight. He couldn't have been more wrong.

Enraged, the wounded beast sprang at him, grabbing his throat with both hands, knocking him to the ground heavily. 'Now you've had it!' he snarled, squeezing down hard.

The wind knocked from his lungs, Hamish clawed at the vice starving him of oxygen. His legs pedalled frantically and he twisted and writhed. His eyes grew wide as panic gripped his screaming lungs. His mind began to cloud and he knew that unconsciousness was just moments away. Desperately, he changed tack and thrust forward, scratching wildly at the face above him, his fingers groping for the soft tissue of that lone eye. It was just enough.

Standish reared up and released his grip. 'Oh, no you don't!' he spat. Then climbing to his feet, he chuckled malevolently, watching Hamish gasp and cough, filling his lungs with air.

Weak and disorientated, Hamish lay there, looking up at him, wondering why he'd called off the attack. He could see blood trickling down the side of Standish's face, dripping on to his tunic.

'Get up!' he barked, reaching down and offering him his hand.

Startled, Hamish pulled himself up on to one elbow, eying the outstretched glove suspiciously.

Standish laughed softly. 'Go on, take it!'

Cautiously, Hamish reached out.

It was then that Standish kicked him square in the face.

*

Suzy regained consciousness, blood trickling from her nose. She blinked a few times, trying to focus on the figures in front of her. Fog blanketed everything. Her vision. Her memory. Her hearing. The muffled sound of talking filled her head like an echo. A heated conversation was taking place above her. She blinked again, pushing herself upright, trying to decipher who it was.

'What in God's name are you doing?' yelled Chimes, grabbing Standish by the shoulder and spinning him around. Blanching at the grisly remains of his bloody ear and empty eye socket, he dragged him away from the motionless figure lying prostrate on the flagstones, haloed in a pool of blood. 'Have you gone mad? Do you have any idea what the Lord Protector will do if he discovers you've tried to kill his new recorder?'

Standish glared at him, wild-eyed. 'What are you doing here?' he snarled, wiping his mouth with the back of his glove, smearing blood across his chin.

Chimes gestured towards the open door, to a terrified-looking girl standing in the passageway. 'Rosie was concerned her mistress hadn't returned to the kitchen after meeting the

Lord Protector. She came looking for her when she heard a scream.'

Standish grunted. 'Well, now you're here, do something useful and shut the door,' he said. 'I haven't finished yet. Keep guard and don't let anyone in.'

An icy chill ran down Suzy's spine. 'No!' she sobbed. 'Please, no!'

Chimes looked down at her propped against the wall and hesitated. Her face was streaked with blood and there was an angry weal on her left cheek.

'Chimes, if you want to atone for your misdemeanour and work for me again then shut the door ... *now!*' pressed Standish impatiently.

Holding his gaze, Suzy shook her head. 'No! Please!' she implored. 'You must stop this!'

To her horror Chimes smiled the cruellest smile she'd ever seen. Then dismissing the maid, he slammed the door and turned back to the fray.

'Welcome back, Chimes!' Standish laughed softly, turning to the unconscious figure sprawled on the floor. 'Now, where were we?' he sneered. 'Ah, yes, an eye for an eye ...'

Suzy gave a horrified gasp, watching him kick her brother, trying to rouse him. The room seemed to sway. Time was running out. Her mind raced. She couldn't just sit by and let Hamish die without a fight. Anguish and hate twined together like strands of a rope, threatening to strangle her. She had to act and she had to act now. Climbing to her feet unsteadily, she reached into her apron and withdrew the small cloth parcel. Unfurling it nervously, her fingers closed around the ivory handle. The time that had once seemed impossible to imagine had finally arrived.

As if in a trance, she slipped the blade from its sheath and stepped forward, calmly and silently appraising her target's back. She was almost upon him. Her mind was numb. Mechanically, she raised her arm, about to bring the blade crashing down when her wrist became trapped. Startled, she glanced at Chimes. He was shaking his head. She frowned, tugging at his grip, imploring him with her eyes to let go. But he shook his head and wrested the dagger from her grasp. Hopelessness and desolation washed over her and she felt like her heart would break. All was lost. There was nothing more she could do. As if she were a rag doll, Chimes pulled her away. And in a single fluid movement, he swung around and plunged the blade into Standish's neck.

Slow, thudding seconds ticked by as a fountain of blood erupted from the severed artery and Standish wheeled round, grasping helplessly at the handle sticking out of his neck, an expression of wide-eyed disbelief on his face. As he fell to his knees, his eye rolled up and he seemed to mouth something, but no words came out, only a gargled wheeze. Then he crashed to the ground like a felled oak. His legs twitched and were finally still.

The ensuing silence seemed to last an eternity.

Suzy took her hands away from her mouth and spoke in a small, bewildered voice: 'You didn't have to do that.'

'Yes, I did,' replied Chimes. 'I couldn't let you do it.'

'But why?'

'Because it was obvious you've never stabbed anyone before. And believe me, you never should because it'll haunt you for the rest of your life.'

Suzy smiled at him. 'Thank you,' she whispered, her voice thickening. 'Thank you.'

'Besides,' he added with a grim smile, 'a glancing blow to the shoulder blade wasn't going to stop him!'

Hamish stirred and groaned. Raising his head off the ground, he blinked a few times, flinching at the candlelight. His vision was blurred and his hearing muffled but he recognised the voices talking. 'Chimes? Suzy?' he called out, but he regretted it instantly. The pain was excruciating. His head felt as if a bomb had exploded in it. Suddenly a wave of nausea washed over him and he rolled on to his side, vomiting wretchedly.

Suzy and Chimes waited until he'd finished before hauling him up to his feet. It was then he saw the glutinous red lake and the island corpse. 'Dear God!' he croaked. 'What happened?'

Chimes laughed softly. 'All in good time, my friend,' he said. 'But first we need to get you fixed up.'

Suzy glanced at him anxiously. 'What are we going to do with the body?' she asked.

'Don't worry, leave it to me,' he replied. '"Discreet removals" are a speciality of mine.'

Hamish and Suzy coughed in unison, glancing at each other in amazement.

Carefully, they began making their way towards the door, avoiding the red slick, when Chimes stopped abruptly, staring at the floor.

'What's the matter?' hissed Suzy.

His eyes were like saucers.

'Look!' he exclaimed, pointing.

'Oh, my God!' she breathed.

Standish's corpse was fading. Its solid form was dissolving slowly into thin air. Even the lake of blood was receding, evaporating before their eyes, vanishing like a mist of breath on a mirror.

Within moments it had gone. Standish had been erased. And all that remained on the decontaminated flagstones was an ivory-handled dagger, the Sign of Equilibrium glowing blood-red.

CHAPTER EIGHT

The messenger groaned and turned over in his bed. 'What is it?' he croaked resentfully, blinking at the fluttering candle hovering above him.

'My Lord, you must come at once!' insisted a cultured voice from the darkness. 'The Queen requests your presence immediately.'

'For the love of God, Cecil, it's the middle of the night!' sighed the messenger wearily. 'What's so important that it can't wait until morning?'

When he replied, Robert Cecil, Secretary of State and right-hand man to Queen Elizabeth, couldn't hide his impatience. 'Like you, my Lord Essex, I would give anything for a full night's sleep. But as Her Majesty's servants with apartments in the Royal Palace we are duty-bound to attend to her every whim, day or night. And believe me, in her current mood, you dare not delay.'

Reluctantly, he reached for his robe. 'What's vexing her at this hour?' he asked sourly.

'In short, your absence from court these past three days,' replied Cecil, stepping aside. 'When she learned of your return she demanded to see you immediately.'

Essex shook his head in exasperation. 'For pity's sake, *Pygmy*, I can't be in two places at once!'

The Queen's chief political adviser bridled. 'By God, I'll ask you not to use that name,' he spat bitterly. 'It's enough that I have to endure it from Her Majesty. I won't tolerate it from others. And especially not you!'

Essex smirked, pulling his heavy robe tightly around him against the cold. It never failed to amuse him that his rival felt so sensitive about his short, stunted stature and deformed back. 'My apologies,' he said with a sardonic laugh, gesturing towards the door. 'Shall we?'

Robert Cecil regarded the arrogant courtier with loathing.

'Damn you to hell, Essex!' he said, turning his back on him. And without another word, they set off along the dark warren of oak-panelled corridors towards the Royal Privy Chamber.

A mile later, they arrived at a polished door bearing the royal coat of arms and both men paused, breathing deeply, preparing themselves for the fearsome onslaught they knew awaited within. It was then that Essex had a sudden thought. 'Her Majesty's foul temper wouldn't have anything to do with my proposed raid on the Spanish fleet, would it?' he asked quietly.

Cecil was silent for a long moment. Then, sighing heavily, he nodded. 'Aye, it weighs heavy on her mind,' he conceded softly. 'But you know what she's like. One minute she supports it, the next she's tortured by indecision and doubt.'

Essex shook his head, holding his rival's gaze. 'Damn it, Cecil, her kingdom's on the brink of invasion,' he hissed. 'The Armada's at harbour in northern Spain waiting for the weather to improve. If they sail, all will be lost. A pre-emptive strike is our only hope. It worked at Cadiz. And by God, I can do it again at Ferrol.'

Cecil's features clouded over and suddenly he looked much older than his thirty-four years. 'Always war,' he murmured, sounding exhausted. 'It's the only thing that you and your supporters pursue ...'

Essex felt the anger and frustration rising up within him. 'Oh, spare me your lecture about diplomacy,' he snapped, interrupting him. 'War might be barbaric and expensive, but it's necessary.'

To his surprise Cecil held up his hands in mock surrender. 'Please allow me to finish what I was about to say,' he said patiently. 'While I abhor your voracious lust for military glory, Lord Essex, I must concede that we've exhausted all diplomatic and political options. It's clear that the Spanish won't rest until they've overthrown Her Majesty and restored the Catholic Church to England. It's therefore a matter of surprise to me that I find myself agreeing with you for once. A military solution is indeed our only option.'

Essex stared at him, lost for words.

'I should also tell you that I have made my position clear to

Her Majesty,' Cecil continued, amused by the athletic lord's surprise. 'And if I didn't know her better, I'd suggest that the dilemma causing her the most anguish is not whether we should go to war but who will lead it.'

Essex frowned. 'But I will, of course!'

'And therein lies the issue,' replied Cecil, stroking his mousy beard thoughtfully. 'Her Majesty can't bear the idea of being parted from you. Worse still, she's resisting putting you in harm's way for fear of losing you forever.'

Essex grimaced. 'But that's madness!' he complained. 'Her realm's more important than I am.' But he knew that Cecil was right. He *was* the Queen's favourite. He'd spent years cultivating her affection, lavishing upon her his devotion and generosity. And it had served him well, for he was now one of the two most powerful men in the land. If tragedy ever befell Cecil, his influence over her would be total. But what he hadn't counted on, and what concerned him now, was that the very dependence he'd nurtured risked thwarting his ambitions irrevocably. 'What do you suggest we do?' he asked.

Cecil smiled thinly. 'Why, Lord Essex, you should continue doing what you always do,' he said, a hint of sarcasm entering his voice. 'Flatter and charm her!'

Marshalling his resolve, Essex took a deep breath and knocked. Immediately, the door swung open and the two men entered purposefully, brushing past a terrified-looking lady-in-waiting and bowing to one knee as they reached the centre of the richly furnished room.

'Ah, my Lord Essex! It's so good of you to grace us with your presence!' trilled the Queen, contemptuously.

His head bowed, averting his gaze respectfully, Essex focused on the gleaming floorboards, awaiting the Queen's command. The atmosphere in the sumptuous chamber was oppressive and he could sense her staring at him with unusual hostility.

'Pygmy, you may stand!' she muttered coldly. 'But Essex, you remain on bended knee.'

Suddenly nervous, Essex heard his stunted rival lever himself awkwardly to his feet.

'Lord Essex, can you begin to conceive how offensive I found your sudden departure from court?' she shrilled indignantly. 'Despite my bestowing great favours on you, you had the barefaced effrontery to take your leave without so much as a backward glance or farewell. I don't mind telling you, Essex, that I'm minded to call in my loans and rescind your tax on sweet wines...'

Her words struck him like a bombshell and his bowels turned to water.

Cecil smirked. Her ability to skewer opponents where it hurt most was one of the Queen's great strengths and he knew this would scare the living daylights out of Essex. For despite his status, he lived beyond his means. For almost ten years now he'd been the sole beneficiary of the customs tax paid on all sweet wines imported into England. Yet despite such riches, he still relied on the Queen's charity to avoid bankruptcy. And if she chose to withdraw her patronage, he would be ruined.

'What say you, my lord?' she snapped icily.

Essex took another deep breath, fighting back his anxiety, but when he replied, his tone was confident and sincere. 'Your Majesty, I say please allow this most unworthy servant to look upon his Queen and humbly seek her forgiveness. It wounds me deeply that my thoughtlessness could cause such distress to my one true love.'

Cecil groaned, rolling his eyes as the Queen's pursed lips broke into a delighted smile.

'Oh, my lord, you are too much!' she laughed, feigning annoyance. 'What am I to do with you? Pray stand and account for your most unhappy absence!'

Breathing a huge sigh of relief, Essex got up, smiling dazzlingly, regarding her with absolute devotion. 'The depth of Her Majesty's forgiveness is matched only by her beauty,' he said graciously.

Shaking his head, Cecil watched the sixty-four-year-old monarch swoon, smiling coquettishly at the handsome lord some thirty-three years her junior.

Grudgingly, he had to hand it to Essex: he was a skilled manipulator of the highest order. Suave and debonair, his ability to melt the hardest of ladies' hearts was legendary. But to stir in an old woman the flutter of youthful love and make her feel vital, attractive and desirable was astonishing.

Flanked by two tall candelabras, the Queen's gown of silver silk and gold lace shimmered in the flickering yellow light as she gazed adoringly at Essex from a raised dais. On her head she wore a great red wig topped with a garland of rubies and pearls, with two curls hanging down to her shoulders. Cecil could see she was enthralled. Engaged in flirtatious discourse, her severe, whitened face with its little hooked nose and small, jet-black eyes had softened and she cackled uproariously, revealing irregular blackened teeth. Distastefully, he watched the courting ritual for several minutes. Then, when he could bear it no more, he cleared his throat loudly.

Immediately, they broke off and looked at him impatiently.

'My apologies for the interruption, Your Majesty,' he said quickly, noting her displeasure, 'but Lord Essex and I must press you urgently on the subject of the Spanish and their enterprise of England.'

Sighing wearily, Queen Elizabeth pressed the back of a hand to her forehead. 'Must we really discuss it now, Pygmy?' she groaned. 'I feel a terrible headache coming on.'

It was typical of her, he reflected acidly; any excuse to avoid making a decision. 'I'm sorry, Your Majesty, but to delay any longer would put your throne and kingdom in great peril,' he pressed, glancing at Essex pointedly.

'He's right, Your Majesty,' said Essex quickly. 'Only the weather stands between the safety of your realm and the Spanish. Right now, the Armada is awaiting calmer seas at Ferrol. If we don't act now before it sails, you may as well bid farewell to all that you hold dear.' He paused, noting her pained expression, and moved closer, reaching for her hand. 'Your Majesty, I implore you to grant me leave of absence to lead an expeditionary force.'

She held his gaze for a long moment. Then, reaching out, she cupped his cheek affectionately and spoke with sadness, bordering on despair. 'My dear, dear Essex,' she said. 'Sometimes I wonder, who is the fool?'

Essex frowned uncomprehendingly.

'Is it me, for allowing you to risk life and limb?' she continued softly. 'And then to return home as a national hero. Or are you the fool? Young, impetuous and gloriously indulgent of an old woman.'

Listening closely, Cecil knew exactly what she meant and he admired her all the more for it, recalling how two years ago, Essex had defeated the Spanish at Cadiz and returned to England as the nation's hero. Understandably, Her Majesty had been envious, jealous even, for she wanted no rivals for her people's affections. And now she was being asked again to risk losing him or elevating his reputation further. Cecil often worried about Essex's ambitions and the tricks he might pull if he wasn't around to protect her. But in his heart, he knew there was no need to fret.

Essex's reply was forthright. 'Your Majesty, to sit by and do nothing would make fools of us all.'

Smiling thinly, she patted his cheek. 'Of course, you're right, dear Essex,' she sighed resignedly. 'Run along and save my crown. And may God protect you.'

Essex grinned broadly. 'Your Majesty won't be sorry,' he assured her excitedly. He bowed low, and was about to take his leave when she raised a hand and his heart sank. Surely, he thought, she couldn't change her mind now. 'Your Majesty?' he enquired uneasily.

Disconcerted, he watched her face darken and when she addressed him, her tone was as cold and bleak as death itself. 'Lord Essex, mark my words well,' she muttered, savagely. 'Don't you ever forget who is the prince and who relies on the prince's favours.'

*

'It's eerie, isn't it?' called Rosie, climbing the steps to the medieval hall's grand entrance, where Suzy was absent-mindedly sketching the early afternoon view.

'It's very strange,' she conceded morosely, watching the maid approach with a jug and two leather beakers.

'I thought you could do with a drink,' she said, pouring some cloudy liquid into a cup and handing it to her. 'This heat saps the energy, all right.'

Suzy put down her charcoal and drank thirstily, thinking of Genin. At least he'd been right about one thing, she reflected gloomily. Even if all else failed, she'd successfully developed a taste for ale.

'It's the silence that gets me,' said Rosie, sitting down beside her on the top step, looking out across the sun-kissed plateau. 'Normally this place is bustling, but today it's like a ghost town. It's sad to think our time here's coming to an end.'

Suzy's insides turned over and she thought of Hamish. Her pulse raced and she prayed with all her heart that he'd find the strength and courage to do what he had to do. Picking up the piece of charcoal, she forced herself not to dwell on it, concentrating instead on sketching the barren plain where once had been a sea of canvas workshops and sixteenth-century production lines. All that remained now was the expansive swathe of accommodation tents in the distance and the armoury to her right, where a team of workers were busily loading a column of high-sided carts. It had been a strange day, she reflected, tracing the outline of the marquee from which crossbows, pikes and other weapons were being hoisted onto the transporters. After an unusually generous meal at eleven o'clock in the morning, the troops had been consigned to their tents and ordered to rest. No explanation had been given. And none was needed. Everyone knew that the big day had finally arrived.

*

'It's an arresting sight, Mr Hamilton, wouldn't you agree?' intoned the Lord Protector, standing at the window, surveying the moonlit view outside.

Hamish stopped writing and looked up from his chronicle. Relieved, he set down his quill, got up from the desk and walked over. The sight that greeted him blew him away. 'Dear God!' he exclaimed, astonished by the scale of the massed ranks below. For as far as the eye could see, bathed in the silvery light of a full moon, thousands upon thousands of black figures stood in geometric rows, the majority of their faces glowing from the torches they held, the vigorous flames dancing and licking the cool night air.

The Lord Protector laughed softly. 'Together on parade at last,' he murmured. 'A new model army of six thousand soldiers. Fully trained and ready to march.'

Just then there was a knock at the door. It was Mr Long. 'My lord, your army's fully assembled and awaiting your command.'

'Any sign of Mr Standish?' he enquired, turning away from the window.

Hamish's pulse quickened. Instinctively, he touched his nose and flinched.

'I'm afraid not, my lord. We've turned the camp upside-down and there's been no sign of him anywhere.'

The Lord Protector shook his head, at a loss. 'I just don't understand it,' he murmured.

'My lord, we know who saw him last,' continued Mr Long. 'Apparently, Standish got drunk the other night and let slip he was going to leave. Seems he'd become disillusioned with the Great Salvation.'

'I find that hard to believe! Who was it?'

'Chimes, my lord.'

'Chimes?' he repeated, looking at Hamish in surprise. 'The thief we granted mercy to?'

Hamish nodded. 'Yes, sir. Chimes and Standish were close.'

The Lord Protector paused, frowning. 'What happened to your face, Mr Hamilton? How did you get those cuts and bruises?'

Hamish's heart skipped a beat but when he replied, he did so unequivocally and without hesitation. 'Standish, sir. In revenge for me blinding him in one eye. And to tell you the truth, sir, I don't mind if I never see him again.'

The Lord Protector's eyes narrowed and Hamish held his gaze.

'My lord, your recorder's speaking the truth,' interjected Mr Long. 'I was there the night we took him and I've had to protect him from Standish on several occasions since. I think Standish probably waited until he'd taken care of unfinished business before leaving.'

Hamish exhaled softly and made a mental note to thank Mr Long.

'Mind you,' he added, thoughtfully, 'I'm surprised he didn't kill you ...'

'Thank you, Mr Long. That will be all!' barked the Lord

Protector, cutting him off. 'I'll be addressing the troops shortly, so fetch me my speech, Mr Hamilton.'

As the officer departed, Hamish crossed to the desk quickly and rummaged through the piles of loose papers and notebooks, searching for the document they'd been working on the day before.

'Come on, come on!' the Lord Protector snapped irritably. 'We haven't got all night!'

Hamish found it and hurried over.

Impatiently, the Lord Protector snatched it from his grasp and turned to the window, reviewing the text in the moonlight.

It was then that Hamish realised the moment he'd been waiting for had finally arrived. Silently, he reached for the dagger tucked inside the waistband of his breeches. Lifting his doublet, he slipped his hand inside, his fingers closing around the familiar ivory handle. His mouth was dry and his heart thumped so loudly he feared the Lord Protector might hear it. But he didn't need to worry. Engrossed in his oration, the leader of the Great Salvation was oblivious to everything around him. Adrenaline surged through Hamish's veins, fortifying and bracing him for what he must do. Gripping the dagger tightly, he stepped forward, appraising his target, feeling strangely calm and dispassionate. Suzy was right, he thought. They had no choice. Imbalance *was* the only enemy, restoration of harmony their sole objective. Nothing else mattered. Morality was irrelevant, as was their conscience. Resolutely, he took a deep breath and raised the blade high above his head, about to lunge, when suddenly he glimpsed his reflection in the window and recoiled. Appalled, he staggered backwards, staring in horror at the instrument in his palm. What he'd seen was grotesque. It was the face of a cold-blooded killer, a ruthless, cowardly murderer. Self-defence was one thing, he reflected bitterly, but murder was a different matter entirely. And he wanted none of it. No matter how worthy their cause, nothing would drive him to that. Hastily, he slipped the knife back into his waistband as the Lord Protector turned around.

'Are you all right?' the Lord Protector asked, noting his recorder's harrowed expression.

Hamish nodded, running a hand through his hair.

'Good. Then come with me. And bring your notebook. To London we go.'

*

Gripping the rail with both hands, Essex smiled and threw back his head, inhaling deeply, filling his lungs with the salt air. At the same moment, the ship's rolling bow crunched into another mountainous wave, spraying icy droplets over his face, stinging him and making him feel more alive than he'd felt in a long time. Exhilarated, the Lieutenant General and Admiral of England's army and navy surveyed his fleet, one hundred and fifty warships carrying ten thousand soldiers, thundering south, their ballooning white sails pitching and tossing them through the treacherous waters of the Bay of Biscay and on to northern Spain. Peering up at the ominous sky, he studied the low blanket of grey cloud and prayed to God for a safe passage. These waters weren't for the faint-hearted, he reflected determinedly, but fortune favours the brave and he had a deal to honour. A warm glow of excitement stirred within him as he contemplated his return to England, safe in the knowledge that if all went well, this mission would be his crowning glory.

A sudden yell broke his thoughts and he spun around to see the helmsman fighting to control the wheel. 'Admiral! I can't keep her steady!' he cried. 'The wind's too strong!'

'Maintain course and speed!' he shouted back, bracing himself against the rail as the ship crested another wave and nosed down into a deep trough.

The wooden hull juddered and the masts groaned as the ship ploughed into an arcing wall, water crashing over the bow, streaming across the deck and knocking several men off their feet. Essex reconsidered. Speed was of the essence but he had to be mindful of the conditions. And the helmsman was right. The weather was turning ugly. Releasing the rail, he staggered across the bridge and gave the order to slow.

In the next instant, a screamed warning chilled him to the bone.

'Storm ho! Storm ho!'

Wheeling around, he saw a drenched crewman leaning out

over the starboard side, gripping the rigging with one hand and pointing to the horizon with his other.

What he saw turned his blood cold. 'Jesus, Mary and Joseph!' he murmured, staring wide-eyed at a scene of apocalyptic horror. From port to starboard, the sky had turned black and a roiling bank of sinister clouds was rolling inexorably towards them, lightning flashes illuminating the raging foam-capped seas. The buffeting wind howled, clanking and whipping the sails against their yards. Low rumbles of thunder grew steadily louder and raindrops began assaulting the deck. Quickly, Essex weighed up their options, but in his heart he knew they had little choice. They couldn't outrun it.

'Batten down the hatches and brace yourselves!' he bellowed. 'Steer a course into it!'

Bitterly, he realised their only chance was to try to ride it out. Squinting through the rainsqualls, he stared into the gnashing jaws of hell and shuddered. His fleet was about to be swallowed whole.

*

The first grey light of dawn was seeping across the sky when the order was given to halt. Around him, relieved sighs mingled with exhausted groans as weary soldiers slumped to the forest floor while Hamish looked on guiltily.

'It's all right for some!' Blakey said with a smirk, sitting propped against a tree, nudging Chimes conspiratorially.

Smiling sheepishly, Hamish shrugged, raising his notebook aloft by way of explanation, and glanced at Suzy sitting beside him on the cart's bench. Sandwiched between him and their driver, she'd hardly said a word all night and he could tell by her scowl that she was still furious with him. Morosely, he supposed she had every right to be. They shouldn't have got this far. After all, if he'd had the nerve to assassinate the Lord Protector then perhaps their mission would be over and they would be able to return home. But murder was murder, he'd insisted, and he wanted no hand in it. His only regret – and he had to concede it was a major one – was that the outcome of the Lord Protector's Great Salvation was now out of their hands. He just hoped and prayed that the Queen was prepared.

But something puzzled him, an anomaly about their nocturnal journey he didn't understand. Throughout the night, they'd been met with scenes of jubilation in every town and village they'd passed through. From cottages and hovels, dishevelled and malnourished men, women and children had spilled out onto the road, waving and cheering their progress south, their grimy faces lighting up at the loaves of bread tossed from the heavy carts trundling past. It was evident that their route had been prepared in advance. The Great Salvation was being carried along on a wave of euphoria and goodwill. But if the Lord Protector's propaganda had been designed to whip up popular support, he reasoned, surely it meant they'd also lost the element of surprise. Word was bound to have reached London by now, and therein lay his dilemma. Why hadn't the Queen sent an army to intercept them?

Watching their driver clamber down, he had just decided to stick his head into the lion's mouth and ask Suzy when the Lord Protector came galloping around a bend in the track, his dappled grey horse snorting and rearing up as he reined it in. Hastily, he dismounted and Hamish noticed that he was walking without a limp.

'Mr Hamilton, Miss McLeod, come with me!' he barked. 'We proceed on foot from here!' His tone was officious and he had about him the air of a general, energised and resolute, ready to commence battle.

Wordlessly, they climbed down as he ordered Mr Long to rally the troops and fan out, left and right. There was a buzz of expectation in the air. Weary legs suddenly had a spring in their step and like shadows six thousand soldiers began moving stealthily through the trees, their swords drawn, crossbows loaded and senses on full alert. Within minutes, they reached the edge of the wood and like a black tide they spilled from the trees, surging into a patchwork of grassy meadows, their dewy slopes running gently down to a walled city less than half a mile away.

The Lord Protector signalled a halt, but for most of his troops it was unnecessary. They were already standing motionless, staring in stunned awe at the fabled capital of England, a place that all of them had heard about but few had ever seen. Never in their wildest imaginations had any of them expected to be where they were now, on the brink of invading the greatest city on earth, ready to liberate a nation.

'This is a truly momentous occasion!' called the Lord Protector, his hands raised, summing up what most of them were thinking. 'History will recall this day until the end of time ...'

Hamish and Suzy were also marvelling at the spectacle, wide-eyed, but for very different reasons. Never in *their* wildest dreams had they envisaged witnessing the actual city destroyed by the Great Fire of London in 1666. Nor could they reconcile it with the vast, sprawling concrete metropolis of its twenty-first century guise. It was too small and surreal for words. Silently, they surveyed the square mile of densely packed timber houses with their steeply-pitched roofs and tall chimneys disgorging thin plumes of white smoke into the pale, early-morning sky. Ringed by a high castellated wall, the city's skyline was dominated by two buildings; the foursquare Tower of London and the biggest church they'd ever seen. It took them a moment to realise that the hulking stone edifice was St Paul's Cathedral, which would be rebuilt by Sir Christopher Wren after the Great Fire and crowned with his elegant dome. Intersecting the city, the Thames flowed so wide in places that its south bank slipped into marshes. A solitary bridge spanned its narrowest point, but it was the strangest-looking bridge they'd ever seen. It appeared to be designed not for traffic but trade because it was crammed with tall, dilapidated, multi-storey timber buildings, many of them hanging precariously over the river, supported only by the flimsiest of struts and buttresses, prompting Hamish to wonder if London Bridge really was going to fall down.

With one ear on the rallying call, he realised he should be taking notes and was opening his notebook when the Lord Protector's words struck him like a sucker punch to the solar plexus, forcing him to take a step backwards.

'London's ready to rise up and the Queen's terrified!' he bellowed. 'England's army has sailed for Spain, leaving her defenceless and unable to resist our Great Salvation ...'

Tremulously, Hamish met Suzy's gaze and a cold knot of fear

entered his stomach. No words were necessary. He could see the anger and despair in her eyes and he knew she was right. The game was over. Their mission had failed. And what was more, he was to blame. Nervously, he pressed a hand to his chest, clutching the hidden timepiece. With all eyes on the city, now was his chance to confirm their worst fears. And suddenly he felt very afraid.

*

'Admiral, we lost twelve ships!' announced the young Commodore sombrely. 'Eight hundred and sixty-four men are dead or missing. Nine hundred and thirty-two men are injured and forty-eight vessels require major repairs ...'

Essex flinched, stung by the status report. 'Sweet Jesus!' he muttered, gripping the rail with white knuckles, surveying what was left of his battered fleet, pitching and yawing on the high sea. Even without his telescope, he could see broken masts and smashed hulls and it was clear to him that every vessel had sustained damage. Most of their sails were shredded and torn, as if they'd been clawed by a giant cat, and long strips of canvas trailed and flapped pitifully in the stiff breeze. In all his years at sea he had never experienced such diabolical fury, and his heart went out to the poor souls who'd perished. He closed his eyes, inhaling deeply, thankful to be alive.

He sensed the Commodore watching him expectantly.

'Fetch me my chart,' he muttered coldly, and he waited for the young officer to lay out the map before he released the rail.

Deep in thought, he plotted the fleet's position and weighed up their options. Returning to England was out of the question. It was too soon. And turning east towards Spain would be futile given their current condition. He smiled thinly. There was only one thing they *could* do. He'd have to abort stage one of the plan and move on to stage two. Destroying King Philip's contingent of decoy ships at Ferrol was no longer a viable option. It had only ever been a charade designed to enhance his reputation and convince his army that victory was theirs. It was ironic, he thought, but the storm had presented him with the perfect excuse to move on to the most important part of the plan.

'Set a course for the Azores,' he snapped brusquely. 'We'll continue heading west.'

The Commodore frowned. 'My Lord, the Azores?' he repeated in surprise.

Essex regarded him coldly. 'Must I repeat myself,' he growled menacingly, 'or do you require a geography lesson?'

The Commodore blanched and it took him a moment to find his voice. 'Admiral, my ... my apologies,' he stuttered. 'I know where the Azores are but ... but I don't understand why you wish to take us there, because they're under Spanish control.'

Sensing his fear, Essex smiled, clapping him on the back. 'It's a fair question, Commodore,' he conceded, graciously, 'and one that I too would have asked at your age ...'

Exhaling, the Commodore smiled tightly. 'Thank you, Admiral,' he murmured.

Essex pointed to the chart and when he spoke, his tone was patient but firm. 'Look, we're in the Atlantic Ocean here, heading west. The Azores lie dead ahead here and are made up of nine islands spread across three hundred and seventy miles. Importantly, the smaller islands are uninhabited, making them perfect hiding places for us to carry out repairs and tend to the wounded.' He paused, looking at the young officer pointedly. 'Everything clear so far?'

The Commodore nodded earnestly.

'Good. Now consider their location,' he said, tapping the chart. 'The Azores lie nine hundred and fifty miles off the Spanish coast in the mid-Atlantic. That makes them ideal transit ports for Spanish treasure ships sailing from their territories in the West Indies and South America en route to mainland Spain. If we can intercept the West Indies treasure fleet, then not only will we cut off Spain's ability to finance its war against England but we'll also boost our own coffers in the process.' Pausing again, he glanced at his officer, who was smiling now, clearly impressed.

'Admiral, I bow to your superior wisdom and experience,' he said. 'If I sounded doubtful before, I apologise most profusely.'

Essex nodded curtly. 'Then make haste, Commodore!' he snapped impatiently. 'We haven't a moment to lose.'

It was only when the young officer had saluted him and turned away briskly that Essex allowed himself the indulgence of a broad, self-satisfied grin.

CHAPTER NINE

Suzy cringed, groaning in revulsion at a row of severed heads grinning ghoulishly down at her from the fortified gatehouse. Impaled on poles and crawling with maggots and flies, the defiled faces looked like those of mutilated zombies, their disintegrating features and rotting flesh exposing greyish bone and blackened teeth to the elements. But worst of all were the birds. Unperturbed by the soldiers passing below, dozens of burly ravens squabbled for positions on the matted hair, pecking frenziedly at eye sockets, ripping out moist tendrils and devouring them hungrily.

'It's not a pleasant sight,' conceded Chimes, walking beside her, noting her disgust. 'But it's not supposed to be. The rest of their body parts will be hung over London's other gates as a warning to all who enter.'

'Who are they?' she asked, her words echoing under the stone archway.

'Traitors and criminals,' he replied. 'It's easy to lose your head in London these days, but thankfully I didn't recognise any of them.'

Suzy looked at him in surprise. 'Are you from London, then?'

Chimes hesitated. He wasn't used to being questioned about himself and he felt uncomfortable. The less people knew about him, the better. It was what had kept him alive so far.

'Well, are you?' she pressed.

Emerging into a narrow street, he recalled their final clash with Standish and decided to break the habit of a lifetime. After all, he reflected, they shared a remarkable secret and inexplicably, he sensed he could trust her. 'Yes,' he said finally. 'I come from London.'

'Which part?'

'What?'

'Which part of London do you come from?' she repeated patiently. 'It's a perfectly reasonable question!'

'All of it!' he muttered, gruffly. But intuitively he knew it wouldn't satisfy her, so he elaborated, gesturing to the Lord Protector marching three rows ahead. 'Before I got involved in all of this, I was homeless, living on the streets. If I'd been caught, I'd have been whipped and thrown out of the city. So I lived in the shadows and occasionally, I'd see the severed head of someone I knew. Generally, they'd been caught stealing food. End of story.'

But Suzy was intrigued. 'How did you survive?'

His eyes narrowed and he looked at her suspiciously. 'Look, what is this? The Spanish Inquisition?'

'I'm interested, that's all,' she said with a shrug. 'I promise I won't tell anyone.'

Chimes sighed. 'Like I told you before,' he relented, 'my speciality's discreet removals, so surviving wasn't a problem as long as I didn't get caught. And I know the city well, so if someone wanted something, I could usually get it for them without leaving a trace. For a fee, of course.'

Suzy frowned. 'But if you were so invisible, how did the Lord Protector catch you?'

Chimes flinched as if he'd just been slapped across the face and snapped, 'That's enough!'

Disconcerted, Suzy noted his bitter scowl and decided not to pursue it, turning her attention instead to the medieval street ahead. Once again, she was struck by how cramped and claustrophobic it was. On each side was a terrace of irregular, half-timbered buildings, their upper floors extending out over the lane, almost touching, and restricting the daylight to create a gloomy corridor along which people were moving aside to watch them march past, three abreast. As ever, the stench was abhorrent, but her reflex to retch at the sludge underfoot had vanished. She'd become immune to it and it no longer bothered her that her shoes and the hem of her long skirt were caked in it. Her only fear was of the windows above, and she prayed that people would wait until they'd passed before emptying any chamber pots into the street.

It was then she noticed the faces observing them. Far from rejoicing, people stared in silence, their wary, watchful gazes concealing whatever emotions they were feeling. If they supported them, they weren't showing it, and she guessed they were awaiting the outcome because to do otherwise on the Queen's doorstep would probably risk retribution if the Great Salvation failed.

Turning left, the procession entered a broad thoroughfare flanked on each side by tall, elegant town houses and she noticed a bustling street market grinding to a halt as everybody suspended trading to observe the black column snaking west. Once again, the atmosphere was subdued and apart from the occasional squawk of a chicken, the only sound to fill the air was the rhythmic squelching of their marching boots.

'Where are we?' she hissed, glancing at Chimes.

'Cheapside,' he said, smiling thinly. 'I used to do good business here. See those houses over there? They're owned by wealthy merchants. This is London's main produce market. Everything sold here comes from the streets around: Honey Lane, Milk Street, Bread Street, Poultry, Pudding Lane ...'

'Pudding Lane!' she gasped, without thinking. 'The Great Fire of London!' Then instantly, she realised her error and glanced at him in alarm, praying he hadn't heard.

'What did you just say?' he demanded, eyeing her with a mixture of suspicion and hostility.

Suzy shook her head quickly. 'Nothing, I was just talking to myself.'

'Oh, don't give me that!' he rasped, leaning towards her. 'I heard you. Great Fire of London! What are you talking about?'

Her heart sank and she looked at him desperately, imploring him with her eyes to drop it.

But he was having none of it. 'Tell me!' he pressed darkly. 'Because if you don't, I'll turn you in as a witch!'

Swallowing hard, she realised she had no choice. He wasn't going to accept 'no' for an answer and she could hardly bluff her way out. She gave a resigned sigh. 'Look, please don't ask me how I know,' she half-whispered, moving closer, making sure nobody else could hear. 'But you must make sure that your family and friends are out of London on the night of Sunday, 2nd September 1666. That's when a fire will break out at

Thomas Farynor's bakery in Pudding Lane, which will devastate London. Please, you must believe me.'

Chimes held her gaze for a long moment and for the first time in his life, he felt genuinely unnerved. Normally, nothing much fazed him, but his stomach was performing somersaults. Then he realised why. He could see it in her eyes. This girl wasn't a witch. She was speaking the truth. And what was more, he actually trusted and believed her, like he'd known her for years. It took him a minute to collect his thoughts and when finally he spoke, he sounded as flabbergasted as he felt. 'Un ... bloody ... believable!' he breathed, shaking his head. Then, noticing her fearful expression, he smiled and murmured, 'Don't worry, your secret's safe with me.'

Suzy exhaled softly. 'Thank you,' she whispered. 'Thank you.'

'Mind you,' he added with a mischievous grin, 'the next time I get you and your *brother* Hamilton alone I want some answers ...'

'How did you know?' she gasped, staring at him wide-eyed.

Chimes chuckled. 'I might not be the sharpest arrow in the quiver,' he said, tapping his nose, 'but I know. You may have fooled his nibs over there, but I've seen enough of the two of you together by now to know.'

*

'I expected cheering, not silence,' murmured Hamish as he and Blakey turned left, following the Lord Protector into an immense square, dominated by the mammoth Cathedral of St Paul. Far bigger than the domed version that would one day replace it, this church was like a city within a city, its cloisters and massive precinct doubling as a cemetery and busy market-place. Marching through a shantytown of flimsy stalls, Hamish saw booksellers, stationers and printers all fall silent and he deduced that this was the main market for writing and publish-ing materials. Suddenly an unsettling thought struck him and he peered into the thronging crowd, praying that William Shake-speare wasn't one of the faces staring back at them, because the last thing in the world he and Suzy needed was for England's greatest playwright to immortalise the Great Salvation.

Ahead of him, the Lord Protector slowed, taking a handkerchief from his pocket and wiping his forehead. He was limping again and Hamish could tell he was tiring. Looking up at the clear blue sky, Hamish felt the warm sun on his face and, not for the first time that day, he wondered what was going through their leader's mind so close to his moment of destiny.

As they turned right into another narrow lane, a tall red-brick gatehouse loomed into view and Hamish frowned, surprised to be leaving the walled city. Then he recalled their destination and glanced at Blakey in confusion. 'Wouldn't it have been quicker to head straight for Westminster?' he whispered, peering up at the forbidding archway, festooned with grisly body parts.

Blakey shook his head. 'I don't think speed's the priority,' he replied, leaning closer. 'My guess is our route through the city's been a show of force to reassure people and galvanise their support.'

Hamish raised his eyebrows. 'They don't look impressed to me!'

'That's because they know what's waiting for us at the top of the Strand there.'

'The *Strand*?' he repeated, aghast, peering along a wide earthen avenue of higgledy-piggledy houses. Bathed in glorious sunshine, the rural landscape was so far removed from what he knew of modern London that all he could do was shake his head. To his right, grassy meadows stretched for as far as the eye could see and to his left, beyond elegant townhouses, formal gardens swept down to the river. The entire area that would one day become Oxford Street, Piccadilly Circus, Regent Street and the rest of the West End was nothing more than fields, trees and grazing livestock.

Then it dawned on him that the imposing square he expected to find at the top of the Strand wouldn't be there either. For the Battle of Trafalgar and Nelson's victory over Napoleon still lay hundreds of years into the future.

Just then a sonorous bell began tolling and the Lord Protector stiffened, peering up at the church to their left. 'That's the warning!' he called out over his shoulder. 'Draw your weapons and be prepared.'

Hamish felt his pulse quicken and fear stirred in the pit of his stomach.

'This is it,' his friend murmured, drawing his sword and gesturing to a tiered stone spire rising missile-like from the centre of the rough ground ahead.

Hamish frowned at the ornate hexagonal roundabout. 'What is it?' he whispered hoarsely.

'The Eleanor Cross,' replied Blakey flatly. 'It marks the entrance to Whitehall, the main road into Westminster. King Edward built it in 1290 as a memorial to his wife.'

Behind them, the tension in the ranks was palpable and Hamish noticed the Lord Protector walking with renewed vigour. His limp had gone and once again he exuded purpose and resolve in steely measure. His shoulders were back, chest out and jaw set firm, and Hamish suspected that what was fortifying him was also firing up his troops: adrenaline.

Turning left into Whitehall, they finally saw it. Resistance. A tall barricade of ploughs, carts, tree trunks and even barges dragged up from the river had been piled high across the wide road, blocking access to the City of Westminster and the Royal Palace beyond. And standing to attention in front of it, the blades of their pikes glinting in the sunlight, a column of sixty soldiers glared at them, their grim, foreboding expressions signalling that the only way past would be over their dead bodies.

Hamish breathed a sigh of relief. Although the odds were still stacked squarely in the Lord Protector's favour, at least the Queen wasn't going to go down without a fight. It had unsettled him that they'd managed to pass through London unchecked, but the more he thought about it, the more sense it made that her one and only line of defence should be here. Looming up behind the barricade, he could see Westminster's heavily fortified gatehouse, its portcullis closed and its battlements teeming with archers.

Raising a hand, the Lord Protector signalled a halt some fifty yards from the giant hurdle and turned around. 'Mr Long, you wait here,' he ordered. 'Mr Hamilton, you come with me and be ready to take notes. Mr Blake, you protect me.' Pausing, he scanned the troops behind. 'Miss McLeod, come here,' he barked, spotting Suzy several rows back.

Protectively, Chimes helped her to push her way through.

'McLeod, I want you to stay here and sketch the scene ahead,' he instructed her solemnly. 'History must recall this moment accurately.'

His tone seemed so grave and serious to her that he sounded like he was carrying the weight of the world on his shoulders. And then she realised he *was*. He was carrying the weight of *her* world on them and, if everything went to plan, he was going to destroy it forever. Resignedly, she reached for her sketchbook, watching him set off towards the barricade with Hamish and Blakey in tow.

'Gentlemen, come and join our Great Salvation!' he called out, halting twenty yards from the Queen's soldiers. 'The time for suffering is over. Like the rest of the nation, you are just as much victims of the heinous regime you seek to protect . . .'

Making notes, Hamish glanced up and saw straight away that the Lord Protector's normally persuasive oratory was failing to have the desired effect. Far from winning them over, he seemed to be alienating them with every word. Their gimlet eyes bored into him contemptuously and, from time to time, they smirked evilly as if relishing the prospect of garrotting him. Hamish was pleased, but he was also deeply apprehensive. Anxiously, he glanced over his shoulder at the massed ranks of the Great Salvation and wondered why the Queen's forces appeared so unmoved. They were hopelessly outnumbered. Whitehall was a sea of black, thousands of armed soldiers ready for combat. It was a sight that shouldn't just have intimidated them; it should have struck fear into their very hearts. And yet, for some reason, they seemed impervious to it.

A sudden commotion at the side of the barricade startled him and the Lord Protector's words trailed off as two soldiers emerged through a hastily-made gap.

Intrigued, Hamish could tell that whatever was happening wasn't planned because the soldiers ahead were exchanging uncertain glances. Then, moments later, another figure appeared, so spectacularly dazzling in the bright sunlight that, at first, he thought he was hallucinating. But one look at the astonished faces beside him confirmed he wasn't imagining things. It really *was* her. And she was striding straight towards them, accompanied by a small bird of a man with a hunched back. 'I don't believe it,' he whispered, struggling to take in the enormity of what he was witnessing.

Mesmerised, Suzy stopped sketching and stepped forward. 'It can't be!' she breathed incredulously.

'On whose authority do you dare covet my crown?' trilled Queen Elizabeth I indignantly, her small jet-black eyes appraising the Lord Protector distastefully.

Lost for words, Hamish could see that the blood had drained from the Lord Protector's face and he too was struggling to find his voice.

'Your ... Your ... Majesty, I covet no crown!' he stammered, fighting to regain his composure.

'In that case, why are you here?' she snapped angrily.

Spellbound and overawed, Hamish felt his knees trembling and his heart pounding. He couldn't believe it. He was actually standing within an arm's length of England's greatest Queen. Resplendent in a glittering gown of gold and silver silk with a matching ermine-trimmed cloak, she wore a great white wig topped with a golden crown encrusted with diamonds and rubies. In one hand she held a sceptre and he wondered if the outfit she was wearing was her coronation dress. It was certainly over-the-top enough, he reasoned, and such an occasion would warrant such exalted grandstanding. If today was going to be her last as Queen then it was only fitting that she'd choose to wear the same imperial robes she wore on her first.

There was one thing about her that disturbed him, though. Her face. Accentuated by the harsh sunlight, her pinched, wizened features were caked white, contrasting starkly with her blackened teeth.

'It matters not who I am, but what I stand for,' countered the Lord Protector, rediscovering his equanimity. 'The people of this country have lost hope. They have suffered for too long. You and your corrupt court have forsaken them. I represent change and salvation. In future, the people's welfare will be king, not the greed and self-interest of your ruling elite—'

'Oh, spare me your righteous but hollow rhetoric!' shrilled the Queen dismissively, cutting him off. 'You speak words worthy of praise in any man's heart. But from your mouth, that's all they are – words, empty words!'

The Lord Protector bridled and Hamish wondered what was going on in that oversized dome of his. No doubt its whirring computer was processing and analysing her defiance at incredible speeds. But for the first time, Hamish looked at him and wondered if he really had the charisma to deliver his praiseworthy vision. Planning and execution had got him this far. Rational logic had won over people's minds. But he still had to translate his noble words into heroic deeds. And to win the people's hearts, he'd need to engage with them on an emotional level. And watching him compute, Hamish very much doubted he'd been programmed for empathy.

'Order your soldiers to stand aside, woman!' the Lord Protector demanded. 'Your wretched reign is over.'

The Queen smiled, but Hamish saw the flash of anger in her eyes. 'Do your troops know to whom they've sworn their allegiance?' she enquired, casually.

'To justice, equality and compassion,' he snapped. 'Now order your soldiers to stand aside.'

'Just as I suspected,' she muttered, shooting a knowing glance at the stunted man beside her. Then, pausing, she turned her gaze on Hamish. 'Young man, kindly explain to me what you are doing.'

The world slowed and for a moment Hamish didn't know who she was speaking to. His heart skipped a beat and instinctively, he looked around him. Then realisation dawned on him and he stared into her amused eyes, his mouth open, too stunned to speak.

'He's my recorder,' snapped the Lord Protector, impatiently.

'Damn you to hell, man!' she exploded. 'Was I not addressing the boy? Has he not a voice?' Her anger dissipated as quickly as it had flared. 'Well, boy?'

Hamish swallowed hard and took a deep breath. 'Erm . . . Your

Majesty ... I'm ... I'm recording the Lord Protector's Great Salvation,' he stammered self-consciously.

'Lord Protector's Great Salvation, indeed!' she scoffed, as if rolling the words around her mouth and finding them not to her taste. 'Well, my young recorder, listen carefully and record well.'

Hamish frowned, watching her step to one side, preparing to address the assembled army.

'Henry Cuffe!' she cried, pointing at the Lord Protector. 'You have all sworn an oath of allegiance to Henry Cuffe, a competent but unimaginative civil servant who was passed over for promotion by my Secretary of State here, Robert Cecil. From what I hear, he left office an embittered man for a new career elsewhere ...'

Hamish was stunned. And so too was Suzy.

'Enough of this!' bellowed the Lord Protector, interrupting her. 'Order your soldiers to stand aside, now!' His voice cracked, the first real signs of stress beginning to show. 'I said now!'

But the Queen stood firm, glaring at him. 'Tell me, Cuffe, do you enjoy the theatre?' she asked pointedly.

Surprised by the question, Hamish glanced at him and saw that his hands were trembling and beads of sweat were trickling down his face.

'What's that got to do with anything?' he replied, bemused.

'By God, answer my question!' she cried.

He hesitated, eyeing her suspiciously. 'I loathe the theatre,' he growled.

'And what about music and dancing, do you enjoy those?' she pressed.

His eyes narrowed and he pulled a handkerchief from his pocket, dabbing his forehead impatiently. 'This is irrelevant!' he snapped.

'Damn you, you graceless little man,' she spat contemptuously. 'If today's going to be my last as Queen, the least I'd expect is for you to answer my questions. But I can see that you're nothing but a coward and a cuss!'

It was too much. She'd goaded him too far and he yelled, 'By God, woman, they're nothing but immoral and degenerate time wasters!'

The Queen laughed softly. 'So speaketh a Puritan!' she cackled, gesturing for Hamish to write it down. 'There's your answer, recorder. You've all signed your allegiance to a fanatical Protestant who'd ban all forms of human enjoyment so he can shackle you to his bleak interpretation of the Bible.' Then turning to the crowd, she pointed an accusing finger at him and cried, 'Mark my words well: this so-called Lord Protector of yours will protect you from spending your own free time as you choose. He'll create new laws banning all sports and entertainment. Arts and culture will be forbidden. He'll strip your churches of all ornaments and decoration and create cheerless cells, where you'll be forced to spend more time at prayer. He'll even make swearing a criminal offence. In my view, whether a man swears or not is a matter for his own conscience, not a matter for law ...'

Hamish stopped writing and looked at him, recalling the storeroom in which he'd waited for Suzy the night Standish had died. He had wondered at the time why the Lord Protector eschewed such fine furniture, preferring instead a stark, soulless office. But the more he thought about it, the more sense it began to make. And what about the singing that had drifted in that day? The Lord Protector's initial reaction had been one of fury. He'd wanted it silenced. But for some reason he'd changed his mind and instructed Standish to go and commend the singers. Then it dawned on him. No wonder Standish had been surprised. The Lord Protector had been tolerating it for his own ends. And then Hamish knew. That tolerance would surely cease the moment he ruled.

'You've been too weak for too long!' roared the Lord Protector furiously. 'You had an opportunity to finish what your father started. The dissolution of the Roman Catholic Church in England was his dream. But you, you were so frightened of offending your Catholic allies in Europe that you compromised. Instead of being true to Protestants like me, you abandoned us. By treading the middle ground, you've ended up keeping much of Catholicism in your so-called Protestant Anglican Church.'

'You pathetic, blinkered fool!' cried the Queen, jabbing a

gnarled finger at him. 'I had to unite the people of this country under a single church. I had to appease everyone with my religious settlement. Today, people are free to believe in many ideas, provided they obey the law and live in peace. It was the only way I could avoid unnecessary bloodshed. But you, Cuffe, you would create civil war between Protestants and Catholics if you had your way. Unlike you, Cuffe, I believe in harmony.'

Startled by her comment, Hamish looked at her, wondering if her prescient words were a sign. But regardless, he'd heard enough to be sure of one thing. They'd all been duped. The so-called Great Salvation was nothing more than a cynical ruse to grab power.

'Order your men to step aside,' snapped the Lord Protector. 'I won't ask again.' Then peering over his shoulder, he called out, 'On my command, Mr Long. Prepare to storm the barricade!'

Hamish's heart leapt. Time was running out. Quickly, he stepped back and caught Blakey's eye, noting that he too was having grave misgivings. His forehead was furrowed and when Hamish shook his head imperceptibly, it was clear from his relieved nod that he accepted what must be done.

Slowly, Blakey raised his sword and looked across at Chimes.

The Queen's face was an implacable mask. 'I'll never submit my crown,' she hissed, 'not to you or anyone else.'

'Then you leave me with no choice,' uttered Cuffe, raising his arm.

Alarmed, Hamish wheeled around, his laser-like stare seeking out Chimes, imploring him to act. But he didn't need to worry. The rottweiler had already exchanged knowing glances with Blakey and was drawing his sword.

'What's happening?' whispered Suzy anxiously.

'Things are just about to get interesting,' replied Chimes through gritted teeth. Then moving swiftly, he crept up behind Mr Long and pressed his blade to the back of his neck. 'Don't make a move,' he snarled. 'Don't even breathe. It's the end of the road for you and your fraudulent chief over there. He's tricked us all. He cares not for the people, only for power.'

With a sharp intake of breath, the Lord Protector's second in command froze, but before he could react further, Chimes clubbed him over the head with the base of his sword and he slumped to the ground unconscious.

A low rumble of consternation broke out as Chimes briefed the troops nearest to him, exhorting them to rise up against Cuffe. Word spread through the ranks like wildfire and it was with growing relief that Suzy watched doubt and disbelief turn rapidly to anger.

'Mr Long, attack, attack!' bellowed the Lord Protector, dropping his arm, leering triumphantly at the old woman standing defiantly before him.

But instead of the bloodcurdling roar of a stampeding horde, a restless clamour filled the air.

Imagining the alarm bells ringing inside Cuffe's head, Hamish reflected it was like watching a train wreck in slow motion. Unable to compute the shattering turn of events, it was only a matter of time before he crashed and burned. The warning signs were written all over his gaunt, rapidly paling face. Bewildered confusion appeared first, followed almost immediately by panicked alarm. Then the moment of sickening realisation arrived when he twisted around and gasped in horror, paralysed by Blakey's sword pressed to his throat and the sight of his motionless army beyond.

'No!' he choked, pushing aside the blade with his gloved hand. 'This can't be happening!' And then his fury exploded, overwhelming him and filling the air with his strangulated scream. 'Attack! Attack! I order you all to attack!'

But nobody moved. They just stood there, bitter in betrayal, condemning him with their hostile stares.

Suddenly, his legs buckled and he crumpled to his knees, mumbling incoherently, a seemingly broken man.

'Guards, arrest this man for high treason!' yelled the Queen pitilessly.

But before they could move, he sprang to his feet clutching a dagger and lunged towards her with surprising agility.

'Leave him!' shrieked the Queen, waving back her troops as he skidded to a halt, the blade raised high above his head.

Berating himself for being caught unawares, Blakey stepped forward, his sword extended, determined to make amends.

'By God, I said leave him!' screeched the Queen furiously, stopping him in his tracks. Then, to everyone's astonishment, she unfastened her cloak and dropped it to the ground beside her. 'So you want to rid England of her prince, do you?' she snarled, clasping her hands behind her back, thrusting out her chest. 'Well, now's your chance. But I suggest you aim well, for the heart you strike beats only for the love of its people. And until it stops, that love will never die.'

Watching transfixed, Hamish and Suzy held their breath, marvelling at her bravery but also fearing the worst. This was it, they thought. It had all boiled down to this. The fate of their world rested on this moment.

Astounded, Cuffe hesitated, glancing anxiously at the blade trembling in his hand.

'Do it!' she cried. 'By God, smite down this prince and be done with it!'

But again he hesitated and although he was sweating profusely, Hamish could see he was shivering.

The Queen smiled coldly. 'You haven't got the guts!' she snorted. 'You never wanted my blood on your hands. I suspected as much.' Then pausing, she held out her hand. 'Pray, hand me the knife and I'll grant you a swift death.'

Ashen and suddenly looking old beyond his years, Cuffe dropped the dagger and slumped to his knees, sobbing.

'You pathetic, weak fool!' she sneered derisively. Then turning to her Secretary of State, she muttered, 'Take him away, Pygmy, and throw him in the Tower!'

CHAPTER TEN

'What's your name, recorder?' snapped the Queen brusquely.

'Hamilton, Your Majesty. Hamish Hamilton,' he replied quickly, his nerves still jangling.

'Well, Hamish Hamilton, I suggest you hand over your chronicles to my Secretary of State here,' she said. 'The court will require evidence of Cuffe's treason and I want to ensure the prosecution receives the full facts.' Pausing, she looked up at the thousands of timorous faces watching and laughed softly. 'As for witnesses, I don't think we'll be short of those,' she cackled, turning her beady gaze on Blakey. 'And you, sir, I am indebted to you. You have a good face and you didn't disappoint me.'

Behind her, Hamish saw the shackled figure of Cuffe being led away and it suddenly dawned on him that their mission was over. He and Suzy had achieved what they'd set out to do and they could now go home safe in the knowledge that the world they came from still existed. A frisson of excitement stirred within him and he peered over his shoulder, seeking out Suzy. As he did so, a thought occurred to him. Emboldened, he took a deep breath and cleared his throat. 'Your Majesty, my sister also has evidence of Cuffe's treason,' he said.

The Queen fixed him with a quizzical frown. 'Your sister?' she enquired. 'Pray explain, boy!'

'My sister Suzy's an artist,' he said, pointing her out and noticing Blakey's surprise. 'Her task was to capture a visual record of the Great Salvation. She has sketchbooks full of drawings. Cuffe wanted to create a permanent exhibition marking his rise to power and Suzy's drawings were going to be turned into a series of paintings.'

'What unbelievable vainglory!' scoffed the Queen, peering across at the dishevelled girl fidgeting nervously.

Unsettled by her gaze, Suzy frowned. 'Who's she looking at?' she whispered anxiously, glancing at Chimes.

'You, I think,' he murmured out of the corner of his mouth.

'You, girl, come here!' trilled the Queen. 'And bring your sketchbook.'

Suzy shot Chimes a look of alarm.

'Go on, don't worry,' he said, sensing her panic. 'You'll be all right.'

Taking a deep breath, Suzy steeled herself and was just about to step forward when she saw a sudden look of incredulity pass across the Queen's face.

'That symbol!' gasped the Queen. 'I've seen it somewhere before!'

Startled, Hamish twisted around, following her gaze, and saw it immediately: the Sign of Equilibrium. Painted in black on a giant white flag, it was fluttering in the warm breeze, held aloft behind the silent horde at the side of Whitehall.

'Standard bearer! Come forth and identify yourself!' yelled the Queen's Secretary of State.

Automatically, the crowd parted and a tall figure stepped forward, his identity obscured by a long hooded black robe.

Chimes bristled. 'I wondered when he'd show up,' he muttered under his breath.

Suzy looked at him in surprise. 'You know him?'

'Aye,' he muttered, with a bitter scowl. 'He's the son of a bitch who blackmailed me.'

'Blackmailed you?' she repeated quizzically.

But he didn't respond. He just stood there glaring at the hooded figure walking slowly towards them, his black robe billowing in the breeze.

'Reveal yourself!' barked Robert Cecil, stepping forward, placing himself between the Queen and the mystery interloper.

Hamish smiled, watching him approach. All he needed to do was swap his standard for a scythe, he reflected, and he'd be the spitting image of the angel of death.

'I command you to reveal yourself!' repeated Cecil, motioning for Blakey to draw his sword.

'That won't be necessary ...' Hamish began to say, but his words petered out as the Reaper pulled back his hood and Cecil recoiled as if he'd just been shot.

'No!' he gasped, staggering backwards, clutching his chest. 'It can't be! You're dead! Executed in France ...'

'Now why would you think that, Robert?' asked Jeremiah Graves.

Cecil's face had paled and his eyes were almost popping out of his head. 'My ... my ... father told me!' he stammered incredulously. 'A year ago ... he said ... you'd been executed! By the French ... for ... for ... spying!'

'Your father's a wily old fox,' responded Jeremiah flatly.

'Pygmy, who is this man?' shrilled the Queen indignantly, bustling forward, regarding Jeremiah coldly. 'And what's that symbol?' she snapped. 'I'm sure I've seen it before.'

'Your ... Your ... Majesty, th ... this ... is Jeremiah Graves,' stuttered Cecil hoarsely. 'He ... he's ... he's one of my father's ... agents.'

The Queen frowned. 'What do you mean, one of your father's agents?'

But Cecil was too stunned to reply. His eyes were like saucers staring at a ghost.

Jeremiah smiled knowingly. 'Your Majesty, you have indeed seen this symbol before,' he said. 'Robert's father William Cecil, Lord Burghley has worn it virtually every day for the last fifty years.'

Reflexively, Queen Elizabeth pressed a hand to her chest, a shadow of pain in her eyes. 'Lord Burghley?' she whispered falteringly. 'My Spirit?'

Jeremiah nodded and reached into his robe, withdrawing what appeared to be a gold signet ring. 'Your closest adviser, the man you refer to as your Spirit, he's worn it every day, Your Majesty,' he said, holding it up to her.

Intrigued, Hamish saw the familiar sun-like symbol glint in the sunlight and he guessed from her sharp intake of breath that the Queen recognised it too.

'Where did you get this?' she whispered, reaching out and taking it from him, examining it closely.

To Hamish's surprise, Jeremiah's shoulders sagged and he looked suddenly tired. 'Lord Burghley gave it to me last night, Your Majesty,' he said, sadly. 'I'm afraid death is almost upon him. He requested that I give it to Robert here.'

Slipping it on to her finger as if trying it out for size, the Queen stared at it for a long moment. 'But what does it represent?' she whispered.

'Your Majesty, it's the symbol of universal harmony.'

'Of course,' she breathed, smiling wistfully. 'Harmony has always been my Spirit's watchword. For over fifty years, he's counselled me about the unpredictable forces of chaos and order. And how each of them in their extreme manifestations can lead to unholy ruin. That's why I've always pursued the middle ground. "*Never deviate from harmony's path,*" he's always said. And, of course, he's right. It has served England well.' She paused, wiping a tear from her eye, and sighed, 'Never has a prince had a truer friend.'

With a heavy heart, Robert Cecil listened to the Queen's words and reflected that such was her affection for his father, she'd taken to feeding him herself these past few weeks. Lord Burghley was like a father to her and he shuddered to think how she'd cope without him because he truly was a remarkable man. Or so he'd thought. Until now, that is, until the re-emergence of Jeremiah Graves into his life. Because something was troubling him, something about his father he didn't understand. 'Why did Lord Burghley tell me you were dead?' he asked.

Jeremiah looked at him for a long moment and when he replied there was a hint of regret in his voice. 'Robert, we'll talk about it later,' he said quietly. 'Right now, we have far more pressing matters to discuss.'

Cecil felt anger and frustration bubble up inside him. 'God damn it, tell me, I need to know,' he snapped. 'After all, you're my father's ward and he's always treated us like we were brothers. So why would he do such a thing?'

Jeremiah hesitated.

'Answer him, man!' trilled the Queen impatiently. 'It's a fair question and he has a right to know! And besides, I didn't think my Spirit kept secrets from me, so I'm curious to know exactly who you are.'

Jeremiah sighed, regarding Cecil sadly. 'Robert, you must believe me, it concerned your father greatly,' he said. 'But unfortunately, he didn't have a choice. It was a necessary deception.

Your father has trained me in the dark arts of espionage for the same reason he's trained you to take his place at the Queen's side – to protect and advance Her Majesty's interests, you within her court and me beyond it, in the shadows where plots and rebellion foment ...'

'Yes, yes, I know that,' interjected Cecil testily, 'but why the need to tell *me* you'd been killed?'

'Because, Robert, Lord Burghley discovered several plots within the very heart of Her Majesty's court to have you both assassinated.'

The Queen and her Secretary of State stared at him, stunned.

'Robert, the last thing in the world your father wanted was to mislead you,' he continued. 'But the plotters and schemers are some of the very same people you deal with on a daily basis. I was sent undercover to gather intelligence and build a case against them. We couldn't involve you for fear of alerting them, so we had to invent a cover story to explain my sudden and protracted disappearance. It was imperative for our success that you and the Queen continued conducting business as usual, oblivious to the threats surrounding you—'

'By God, tell us their names and I'll have them hung, drawn and quartered!' exploded the Queen furiously.

Jeremiah shook his head. 'I'm afraid it's not as simple as that, Your Majesty,' he said.

'And why not?' she snapped indignantly.

'Because the Spanish flag is already flying in England, Your Majesty.'

Hamish gasped and his blood ran cold.

'But that's impossible!' cried the Queen, staring at him in disbelief. 'England's forces are at this very moment destroying the Spanish fleet before it sets sail!'

'England's forces are currently in the Azores, Your Majesty,' he corrected her patiently. 'And this morning an advance Spanish raiding party landed in Cornwall, destroying the village of Mousehole. They're now heading north to Penzance, preparing the ground for the arrival of the main invasion force, which lands in three days' time. Your Majesty, one hundred and forty

Spanish galleons carrying twenty-four thousand troops are currently sailing for England.'

'Dear God!' exclaimed Cecil. 'England's defenceless!'

Horrified, Hamish clutched the timepiece hidden under his shirt, shuddering to imagine what he might find. But whatever it was, he reflected bitterly, it was academic now, because one thing was certain. Their nightmare was only beginning. And suddenly he felt very afraid.

'By God, I'll have Essex's head for this!' muttered the Queen savagely. Then turning to Cecil, she snapped, 'Well, Pygmy, what do you suggest?'

When he replied, his tone was bitter but resigned. 'I'm afraid we have no choice, Your Majesty. We must gather what forces remain and make haste to Penzance. If we can prevent the Spanish ships from making port then perhaps we can prevent the invasion. It's our only hope.'

Jeremiah nodded but the Queen regarded him doubtfully. 'That's all well and good,' she snapped, 'but our remaining forces amount to less than a thousand men, certainly not enough to secure Penzance and defend London as well.'

'Your Majesty, take a look behind me,' interjected Jeremiah quickly. 'There are six thousand soldiers standing there, highly trained, with no appetite for Spanish occupation.'

The Queen looked at him as if he'd gone mad. 'Don't be so absurd! Less than an hour ago, that army was all ready to depose me! How could I possibly place my trust and realm in the hands of those who would seek ill for me?'

Suddenly infuriated, Hamish threw caution to the wind. 'This army bears you no malice!' he protested.

The Queen's face darkened and she rounded on him. 'How dare you!' she shrilled. 'How dare you address me without proper decorum! Have you lost your senses, boy? I'm in no mood to take counsel from a lowly pipsqueak! In fact, at this very moment in time, I'm minded to throw you to the wolves!'

Hamish reeled, taken aback by her ferocity, but he pressed on regardless, his sense of injustice overcoming his fear. 'But Your Majesty, it's true!' he insisted. 'This army bears you no ill feelings. As far as they're concerned, the Lord Protector's Great

Salvation was all about creating a fairer society. They're all patriots who want only what's best for the people of England. When Cuffe showed his true colours, you saw their reaction. They were appalled. Because for them, the Great Salvation wasn't about power or religion – it was about making the lives of ordinary people better. If these soldiers are guilty of anything, it's that the person they placed their trust in wasn't worthy of it.' His heart was pounding and he could see her eyes growing wider. 'Your Majesty, if you can inspire hope in them again – hope for a better life – then they'll support you and sing your praises for years to come. And so will future generations.' The record finally set straight, he swallowed hard, preparing for another tirade.

But the Queen didn't respond. She just glared at him for what seemed like an eternity and, finally, when he thought he could bear it no longer, he noticed the hint of a smile creeping over her lips. 'Well, well, well,' she muttered, 'I don't know whether you are brave or reckless, young man, but never before have I experienced such brazen audacity. So the question is, do I flog you or commend you? That's my dilemma. I'll say this for you, though: your argument is well said. I grant you that. So let's see if what you say is true, shall we? Let's find out if this righteous army of yours really is prepared to ride to *my* salvation.' Then, after turning to her Secretary of State to issue solicitous instructions, she stepped forward to address the crowd.

'My loving people,' she cried, 'though I have the body of a feeble woman, I have the heart and stomach of a king, and a king of England too. I think it foul scorn that anyone should dare to threaten the crown of a king, so pity not Cuffe, for he betrayed you just as surely as he did England. But it is clear to me now that you took up arms against me under false pretences and for that I will not condemn you. However, you must know this: the causes that you champion are just as dear to my heart as they are to yours. I can assure you that there is no king in all the world who loves his people as I do mine. So rest assured that I count my people's suffering as my own. And I swear to you that while there is breath in this feeble body, I will pursue reforms to remedy the ills blighting this great nation of ours.

'And to the abusers of my people I say this: there is no jewel or treasure in this entire world as valuable to me as my people's love and wellbeing. So beware – for any injustice you inflict on them, you also inflict on me. And God help you then, for I swear to you, your fate will be bloody and bleak.'

Listening spellbound, Hamish saw the anxiety and fear rise from the crowd as relieved faces lit up, buoyed once more with hope.

'Of myself, I must say this: I never was nor ever will be a greedy, scraping grasper, nor a waster. My heart was never set on worldly goods, but only for my people's good. What you do bestow on me, I will not hoard up, but rather receive to bestow on you again.' She paused, catching her breath, and was about to continue when a joyous cheer shattered the air. Hurriedly, she raised her palms, motioning for quiet.

'My dear people, it grieves me to inform you that England is facing its darkest hour. I have just learnt that the Spanish flag is flying in Cornwall.'

Instantly, the atmosphere turned febrile, bitterness and anger crackling in the air like electricity.

'With England's army and navy in the Azores, England is virtually defenceless. You are all that stands between England's freedom and Spanish tyranny ...'

Jeremiah smiled thinly. He'd seen and heard enough. 'They're with us, Robert,' he murmured softly. 'But our chances of success remain slim at best.'

Cecil nodded solemnly. 'Follow me,' he said, turning towards the barricade, 'and bring whomever you need. We have much to do and Her Majesty's granting us whatever resources we need. Westminster Palace is at our full disposal.'

*

Essex raised the telescope to his eye and smirked. 'Now there's a sight for sore eyes,' he murmured, studying the lone galleon moored in the sleepy harbour of Ponta Delgada. The water sparkled like silver glitter and high clouds rolled across the huge blue sky as he scanned the volcanic island of San Miguel, marvelling at the lush green hills rising steeply from the azure sea. Sighing contentedly, he trained his lens on the rows of low, whitewashed buildings surrounding the bay and he began to laugh, imagining the locals' alarm when they awoke from their siestas to discover England's navy berthed outside.

Lowering his eyeglass, he turned to his Commodore. 'Bring us broadside to the harbour mouth,' he snapped, 'and prepare for action. We fire on my command.'

The young officer smiled. 'Yes, sir!' he barked, saluting him and turning away briskly.

'And Commodore!' he called out, halting him. 'Instruct the rest of the fleet to remain a mile offshore and to await further orders.'

Suppressing a smile, Essex crossed the bridge and gripped the rail as the helmsman swung the wheel hard to port, bringing the ship slowly around. Below him, he could see all hands rushing about, readying the vessel for war, lowering the sails, priming the cannons and hauling open the gun hatches.

Within a minute, the Commodore had returned. 'Admiral, we await your command,' he said, snapping to attention.

Essex smiled thinly. 'Good work, Commodore!' he said, as the ship slowed, swinging into position at the harbour entrance. Then to the gun crews below, he yelled, 'Gunner one, fire a shot across her bow!'

His order was met with a deafening roar and the deck shuddered as a cloud of white smoke billowed up from the recoiling barrel. Essex held his breath. The last thing in the world he wanted to do was hole the ship. Its cargo was far too precious for that. Suddenly, a thunderclap erupted from the quayside and a thick plume of dust and debris shot high into the air. Essex exhaled softly. 'Gunner two, same again and mind you don't hole her!' he called.

Once again, there was a sharp report and a second cannonball hurtled towards land, ripping through the wharf and erupting in a towering geyser of water and planking. Essex smiled, about to order a third, when a loud cheer went up, fingers pointing to a white flag being hoisted up the galleon's mast.

The Commodore gasped in astonishment. 'I don't believe it!' he exclaimed. 'They didn't even put up a fight!'

Essex regarded him coldly. 'And what would you have done,

had you been captain of the Spanish vessel?' he snapped.

Taken aback, the officer stared at him, momentarily lost for words.

'Bloodlust has no place in a commander's armoury!' he bellowed. 'And neither does taking unnecessary risks with the lives of your men.'

The Commodore blanched. 'My ... my apologies, Admiral,' he stammered weakly, aware of everybody watching.

Essex glared at him. 'Your apology's accepted, Commodore,' he growled, enjoying his discomfort. 'But it's abundantly clear that you still have much to learn. So I think the next three weeks will do you good!'

Startled, the young officer frowned. 'Three weeks?' he repeated uncertainly.

'That's right, Commodore,' he replied curtly. 'We'll be spending the next three weeks here carrying out repairs and tending to the wounded. And during that time, I'm putting you in command of hunting down and seizing Spanish treasure ships passing through these waters. Do I make myself clear?'

The Commodore's eyes gleamed and Essex noticed the colour returning to his cheeks. *That'll keep you out of my way,* he thought as the officer thanked him profusely.

'Oh, and one more thing, Commodore,' added Essex, pensively. 'It's always important to show graciousness in victory. So make arrangements for us to dine with the officers of that galleon tonight.'

Snapping to attention, the Commodore saluted him. 'Yes, sir!' he barked, turning away.

Watching him go, Essex grinned, relishing the prospect of dining with Ramirez again. It had been weeks since their rendezvous in Calais and he was eager to catch up on news and toast their success. After all, everything was going according to plan and the chests of treasure aboard the Spanish ship were about to make him the richest man in England. But it was a reasonable price for the King of Spain to pay, he mused. Because if he was going to marry King Philip's daughter Isabella and rule England in the King's name then a king's ransom was the least he could expect. And then he began to laugh, gently at first, then harder, until his face was buckled, much to the consternation of those around him.

*

'Look, there's Warfield!' exclaimed Hamish, pointing at the crude disproportionate map of Britain laid out on the table in front of them.

Leaning over it, Jeremiah nodded and regarded him grimly. 'And have you seen where it is in relation to Penzance?' he asked quietly.

Hamish frowned, tracing his finger along the black line south. 'Dear God,' he whispered in alarm, 'it's on the main route to London!'

'That's right,' replied Jeremiah, looking across at Suzy. 'In three days' time, Warfield could be under Spanish occupation, and you know what that means.'

Blakey and Chimes frowned at one another, at a loss.

'So what?' mumbled Chimes. 'What's so special about *that* place?'

Hamish and Suzy felt their hearts leap into their mouths and they stared at Jeremiah anxiously, unsure of what, if anything, to reveal.

But they didn't need to worry. Jeremiah sensed their trepidation and responded for them. 'It's very simple,' he said matter-of-factly. 'That's where these two come from. It's their home town.'

Relieved, Hamish and Suzy exhaled softly.

'I'd wager there's more to it than that,' muttered Chimes. 'And anyway, how do you know so much about them, Reaper?'

Jeremiah's eyes narrowed. 'Because, Chimes, Hamish and Suzy are my wards,' he replied, gruffly.

'Your wards!' exclaimed Cecil in astonishment. 'But how, why?'

'They were entrusted to my safekeeping by their guardians in Warfield,' he explained. 'They came to stay with my mother and me in Islington. Robert, that's where I've been living this past year—'

'So, Reaper, that's why you blackmailed me!' exploded Chimes furiously.

178

Jeremiah was silent for a long moment. 'Chimes, I had no choice,' he said finally. 'It was hard enough betraying them in the first place, but I couldn't risk them being abducted without some form of protection ...'

Intrigued, Hamish looked across at Chimes, who was clearly struggling to contain his fury, and recalled their first encounter. It had been an agonising experience, he reflected, but had the rottweiler not coerced him into signing Cuffe's oath, Hamish knew he'd be dead by now, murdered by Standish. Of that he had no doubt. It all was all beginning to make sense now. But something still niggled at him. 'Why did you befriend Standish?' he asked.

Chimes smirked at him pityingly. 'Hamilton, you were a dead man walking!' he scoffed. 'What you did to Standish was only ever going to have one outcome. So I figured I might as well become his lackey and enjoy some perks while keeping tabs on you.'

'And for that, Chimes, you have my sincerest thanks,' interjected Jeremiah. 'You have my word that our little arrangement is now settled.'

Chimes guffawed mirthlessly and Suzy asked the question on everyone's lips. 'What little arrangement?'

Chimes smiled, revelling in Jeremiah's sudden discomfort. 'Oh, it was a compelling arrangement, all right,' he sneered, 'for him, that is, not me. Basically, he gave me the choice of being abducted on the same night as your brother or he'd turn me in as a thief. And you've all seen what happens to thieves in London, so it wasn't much of a choice. And to make matters worse, most of the thieving I've ever done was for him anyway. Only he doesn't call stealing documents from people's houses "thieving". He calls it "discreet removals"!'

Hamish and Suzy glanced at each other, laughing softly.

Jeremiah's face darkened and he crossed over to the small room's only window, peering out at the troops below. 'Enough of this!' he growled impatiently. 'There's work to be done, so let's get down to business. The Spanish will be here within days, so this is what I suggest we do ...'

Listening intently as he outlined his plan, they watched him prowl the room like a caged tiger, his brow furrowed, tapping the map repeatedly to illustrate his points. Ten minutes later, he drew to a close, standing at the head of the table, regarding them gravely. 'Well?' he said, finally.

To everyone's surprise, Suzy spoke first. 'I don't think any of us can fault plan A,' she said, looking around the table. 'As you say, if we can blow up the harbour entrance at Penzance, we can prevent the Spanish ships from entering port and unloading their troops and supplies. But we must remember that Penzance is now behind enemy lines. That'll make it difficult but not impossible.' Pausing, she frowned and sighed heavily. 'But plan B's unworkable, in my opinion. I agree that our back-up plan has to be based on the worst-case scenario of twenty-four thousand Spanish troops landing successfully. But I think engaging them on the battlefield is doomed to failure, whether it's in Cornwall or Wiltshire ...'

Without exception, the five other occupants in the gloomy oak-panelled room stared at her through wide, disbelieving eyes.

'... We're hopelessly outnumbered,' she continued earnestly. 'And even ignoring the logistics for now, marching six thousand troops to a battlefield two hundred miles away in two days would leave them too exhausted to fight. It would also leave London dangerously exposed ...'

Chimes couldn't contain his frustration any longer. 'Since when do we listen to girls lecturing us about war?' he exclaimed, looking around the table.

It was a red rag to a bull and Hamish rushed to Suzy's defence. 'Wind your neck in, Chimes!' he shouted. 'That's my sister you're talking about.'

'I don't care whose sister she is,' he snarled; 'she's a girl. And girls don't lecture men about war. It's just plain wrong.'

'Then you're an idiot!' he yelled, shooting out of his chair, about to berate him further when Cecil raised his hands, motioning for calm.

'Gentlemen, gentlemen, let us not be diverted,' he said soothingly. 'I grant you it might not be conventional to discuss such matters with women, but let's not forget whom we all serve.

Given the current circumstances, I think it's prudent for us to explore all options and consider all opinions before deciding how best to proceed. So, Suzy, if I may ask, what do you suggest?'

Suzy smiled. 'The unconventional,' she said. 'We must adopt an alternative approach that terrifies the enemy into believing that every step he takes on English soil could be his last. I'm talking about guerrilla warfare, hitting them hard and evading capture ...'

'Guerrilla warfare?' repeated Cecil, frowning.

Suzy nodded. 'Take three hundred and sixty of our best soldiers and divide them into thirty groups of twelve men,' she explained. 'Each group, or cell, will be responsible for a specific stretch of the road running from Penzance to London. They'll dress like peasants and live in towns and villages along the way. Their job will be to lay explosives and ambush the enemy. That will give our main force enough time to prepare a proper welcoming party at, say, Windsor. Hopefully, by then, the Spanish will be so weakened and demoralised, they'll have no heart left to fight.'

'That's incredible!' exclaimed Cecil, glancing across at Jeremiah. 'I've never heard of such a thing but it's so simple, it could almost work!'

Jeremiah nodded. 'It would require huge quantities of gunpowder, though,' he said.

'No problem!' replied Cecil. 'I can organise that.'

'And fresh horses at regular intervals to carry them all that way without stopping.'

'Again, that can be arranged.'

'Then I see no reason why we shouldn't proceed on that basis,' concluded Jeremiah, looking at each of them in turn. 'All those in favour, raise a hand.'

One by one, their hands went up until only Chimes remained undecided.

'I'll only agree on one condition,' he muttered finally. 'That I accompany Hamilton and his sister in the defence of Warfield.'

Jeremiah smiled thinly. 'It's a deal,' he said. 'Cecil and I will organise the defence of London while the four of you lead the guerrilla campaign south-west.'

CHAPTER ELEVEN

It was Hamish who saw it first, a faint spot of yellow light penetrating the darkness like a pinhole in a black veil. 'That's *got* to be the inn,' he muttered, clenching his teeth to stop them from chattering, squinting at Chimes riding alongside.

But Chimes didn't respond. He just sat there, his head bowed, brooding silently.

High on the exposed moor, the temperature had plummeted and an icy wind howled mournfully, whipping at their rain-sodden clothes, hampering their already slow progress. Thick cloud blanketed the sky, compounding the blackness, rendering the muddy track even more treacherous for their horses stumbling blindly along it. Of the three hundred and sixty troops that had set off only twelve of them were left now and, to a man, they were colder, hungrier and more exhausted than any of them had ever been. 'Utter misery' was how Suzy had described it just one day into their journey. But now that a second night had fallen, Hamish wondered what double that was. Whatever it was, he thought ruefully, he never, ever wanted to go through it again. And the pain, excruciating pain the like of which he'd never known, only served to intensify his gloom. He was a novice rider, and there wasn't an inch of his body that didn't ache. It had been like sitting on a jackhammer for two days and he resolved that if he never rode a horse again, it would be too soon.

Dispirited, the group rode on, the wind wailing like a chorus of demons, taunting them, exacerbating their isolation and pushing them to the very brink of despair. They were travelling in silence now because words had long since become redundant. Comfort or complaint, nothing consoled, so they plodded on wordlessly, for mile after endless mile.

'That's it, that's the inn!' cried Hamish, jolting everyone from their reverie.

And sure enough, around the corner loomed a sight that warmed their hearts. A long, low thatched building with white-washed walls emerged through the blackness like a ghostly apparition. From its windows spilled light, a yellowy-orange glow that warmed and roused their spirits. Like a beacon at the end of a long tunnel, it drew them in, reviving them and re-igniting a spark of optimism.

'I don't think I've ever been so happy to see a pub in all my life,' laughed Suzy, noticing the sign hanging above the door.

Hamish had seen it too and the aptness wasn't lost on him either. 'The Rising Sun,' he read aloud, smiling at a picture of the dawn sun, emitting twelve golden rays.

'Hamilton, why don't you and your sister go in and make sure the innkeeper's expecting us?' called Blakey, dismounting. 'We'll see to the horses and join you in a few minutes.'

Needing no further encouragement, they clambered from their horses and staggered to the door, grimacing as they went, but any thoughts of their aches and pains vanished the moment they entered. Enveloped by warmth and the heady aroma of roasting meat, they laughed, marvelling at a snug bar room bathed in the orange glow of a roaring log fire and candles flick-ering on every table. With low beams, a rush-strewn floor and chickens roasting on a spit in the inglenook fireplace, the overall effect on their deprived senses was magical. Better still, the place was empty.

'We've got it all to ourselves!' Hamish said with a smile, crossing to the bar, calling for service.

But a minute passed and nobody appeared.

Frowning, they both turned, surveying the room again. Suzy heard a faint pulsating rumble coming from a high-backed wooden armchair facing the fire. Smiling, she gestured for Hamish to follow and crept over. There, much to their amusement, they discovered a great walrus of a man snoring peacefully, his fingers entwined atop a mountainous stomach. His hairless head lolled to one side, accentuating multiple chins, and his face glowed red from the heat of the fire.

'He must be the landlord,' whispered Suzy, noting his grimy white apron. Cautiously, she leant down and shook him gently by the shoulder, then stepped back as he stirred, mumbling incoherently.

'Here, let me try,' Hamish said with a grin, reaching down and taking hold of his bulbous nose between his thumb and forefinger.

Seconds later, a guttural snort erupted from the man's throat and his eyes popped open, blinking up at them in alarm. 'Oh, oh, begging your pardon!' he exclaimed, sitting bolt upright. 'I . . . I must have dozed off!'

'Don't worry, we could see that,' laughed Suzy. 'You should be expecting us. Jeremiah Graves should have sent word.'

The moment she mentioned his name, the landlord's face paled and he shot out of his chair. 'Aye . . . aye . . . I been . . . been expecting you,' he stuttered quickly. 'As he told me, the inn's closed to all my regulars. Place is yours for as long as you need it.' Then pausing, he looked at them anxiously and said, 'You . . . you won't tell him, will you?'

Hamish and Suzy frowned.

'Tell him what?' asked Hamish.

'About me falling asleep on duty,' he replied quickly.

'Why, of course not!' exclaimed Suzy, startled by the fear in his eyes. His relief was palpable and she wondered what on earth Jeremiah could have done to provoke such a reaction over something so trivial. But whatever it was, she knew what he was capable of and suddenly she felt a pang of pity for the rotund landlord thanking them so effusively.

'I'll get you some ale,' he said, smiling. 'And some food. You must be dog-tired after coming all the way from London.'

Just then the door burst open and in trudged Chimes, followed by the others.

'I think I've just died and gone to heaven!' laughed Blakey.

And heavenly it was too because an hour later, twelve contented customers sat around the fireplace, satiated, sipping tankards of ale, their cheeks glowing and their eyelids growing heavier by the second.

'That was, without doubt, the finest meal I've ever had,' sighed Blakey, stretching languidly.

Suzy smiled. It was true, she reflected. She'd never enjoyed a meal like it. The succulent roast chicken and thick rabbit stew had been out of this world and by the time she'd finished, she'd emptied her bowl three times and polished off a loaf of bread, much to the entertainment of everyone else.

'And it could be your last,' muttered Chimes flatly. His eyes were closed and nobody could tell from his deadpan delivery whether he was being serious or not. 'Warfield's still three miles down the road from here and we need to be on the other side of town by dawn. So the sooner you stop talking, the sooner the rest of us can sleep.'

Blakey's eyes flashed anger but before he could respond the landlord said, 'Before you all rest, I got something to show you. So if you wouldn't mind.'

Intrigued but reluctant to leave the warmth of the fire, they all got up and followed him out through the back of the inn, into a rough stony courtyard, flanked on each side by stable blocks. Shivering in the cold air, they crossed to the barn opposite and waited as he unbolted the door before following him in.

'Go on, take a look,' he said, holding up his lamp, gesturing to a high-sided wooden cart in the corner.

Chimes went first, followed by Hamish. Climbing up onto the driver's bench, they leaned into the back, rummaging about, inspecting the cargo.

'What is it?' asked Blakey, peering over the side, noting what appeared to be wooden barrels.

'Dear God!' exclaimed Chimes after a long moment. 'You wouldn't want to be sitting on this lot when it goes up. There's enough gunpowder here to sink the entire bloody Armada!'

Hamish frowned. There were several sacks wedged between the barrels and he quickly untied one, reached inside and pulled out what appeared to be a long metal tube.

'What in hell's fire is *that*?' asked Blakey.

'I don't know, but it's bloody heavy,' he replied, examining it. Both ends were sealed and a long string protruded from one end. 'I think it's made of lead,' he added thoughtfully.

'It's a pipe bomb,' announced Suzy matter-of-factly. 'And that's the fuse. It's a sealed lead tube packed with gunpowder and nails.'

Everyone gaped at her.

'And how do you know that?' growled Chimes suspiciously.

Suzy's reply was emphatic. 'Because that's what I instructed Robert Cecil to have made for us,' she said. 'And believe me, when those things go off, the Spanish will rue the day they ever set foot in England.'

*

'Do any of your men suspect anything?' asked Ramirez quietly.

Essex sipped from his glass, savouring the wine. 'No, I don't think so,' he said, surveying the panorama from the veranda of the governor's villa, high on the hill overlooking Ponta Delgada. 'My Commodore's perceptive but I've got the measure of him. I've ordered him to patrol these waters for the next three weeks hunting your treasure ships, so that'll keep him out of our way.' Below, bathed in silvery moonlight, he could see the harbour crowded with the masts of his ships and, offshore, the rest of his fleet lying anchored on the glassy ocean, silhouetted against the glittering night sky.

'Well, I hope he can handle disappointment,' Ramirez chortled. 'All traffic from our colonies has been suspended until the King's enterprise of England is successfully concluded.'

Behind them, a riotous chorus of singing erupted from the house, accompanied by accordions and loud cheers.

Essex smiled, thinking about the chests of treasure locked safely inside his cabin. 'And successfully concluded it will be,' he muttered to himself, taking another sip.

Ramirez chuckled caustically. 'So you still think the English will accept a Spanish Catholic as Queen?' he scoffed.

Essex glared at him. 'Don't ever doubt it, Ramirez,' he said warningly. 'As long as I'm their King, the people of England will take Princess Isabella to their hearts. They worship me, so when we're wed, England will rejoice. You mark my words, I'll bring them the glory they crave. My coronation will usher in a new beginning for our two nations. Just imagine it, England and Spain fighting together. By God, we'll build an empire of such unimaginable power and wealth that no nation on earth will be able to resist us. First we'll crush France, then we'll turn our guns on the rest of Europe.' He paused, laughing softly, and clapped the Spaniard on the back. 'Now come,' he said, 'enough of this. Let's rejoin the party and celebrate our good fortune.'

*

'What was that?' hissed Hamish, reaching for his sword, scanning the tall ferns at the side of the track. His heart was thumping and his mouth had gone dry.

'Probably a squirrel,' muttered Chimes, crouching beside him, gouging the damp earth with his knife. 'Here, pass me another pipe bomb.'

'It sounded too heavy to be a squirrel,' whispered Hamish, handing him one of the lead tubes, helping him to bury it in the shallow trench.

Just then another crack split the air and they both jumped, twisting around on the balls of their feet, scanning the undergrowth in the pale dawn light.

'Something's in there!' hissed Hamish, his senses on full alert. 'That was another twig snapping!'

Like statues, they crouched motionless in the middle of the track, holding their breath, listening for movement.

'It's all right,' whispered Chimes finally. 'It must have been an animal. It's gone now. Come on, let's bury this last one and get the hell out of here.'

Unconvinced, Hamish stood up warily, scanning the woodland beyond, but all he could see was fine white mist floating ethereally between the trees.

'Get down!' hissed Chimes, grabbing his sleeve, tugging at it furiously. 'Are you mad? We're behind enemy lines, for Christ's sake! Come on, give me a hand!'

Hurriedly, they buried the last pipe bomb and were camouflaging the ground with bracken when they heard a rustle in the ferns opposite and froze. Wordlessly, Chimes pressed a finger to his lips, motioning for Hamish to stay still. Then creeping forward, his knife gripped tightly in front of him, he took a deep breath and was about to lunge when out scuttled a hedgehog, which took one look at him and scurried straight back in.

Their relief was overwhelming.

'Come on,' sighed Chimes, shaking his head, 'let's get off this road and wait for the others. They'll be here soon and my nerves are shot!'

It was music to Hamish's ears. They'd been darting in and out of the woods laying booby traps for hours and he needed a rest before they embarked on the next stage of their mission south. But then he recalled what they'd be transporting and his stomach lurched.

How to disguise a consignment of gunpowder and smuggle it through enemy lines without detection: that had been the conundrum that had stumped them all. Their mission to destroy Penzance harbour depended on it, and Jeremiah had promised them a solution by the time they arrived at the inn. And boy, what a solution it had turned out to be, reflected Hamish. It was little wonder that the landlord feared the Reaper, because his methods were as repugnant as they were inspired. Hamish shivered involuntarily, recalling the events of last night and how the landlord had handed them each a linen scarf to cover their mouths and noses before ushering them into the stable block. It was the smell that had hit them first, the pungent stench of decomposing flesh coming from a second wooden cart. With gloved hands, the landlord had pulled back the tarpaulin and they'd all recoiled, first in horror and then in fear. For piled high were the filthy corpses of men, women and children, their waxen skin stained with black spots. Yet despite their revulsion nobody could dispute the ingenuity of the Reaper's plan. No Spanish soldier in his right mind would interfere with two carts laden with plague victims trundling through villages at first light amidst calls for people to bring out their dead, en route for a burial at sea.

Quickly, Hamish set off, heading with Chimes for the under-growth when they heard footsteps behind them and a voice yelled out, 'Alto, perros ingleses!'

Uncomprehendingly, they twisted around and stared in horror as two soldiers wearing the distinctive red of the Spanish army emerged from the woodland at the far side of the track. Their metal breastplates and curved helmets gleamed in the early morning sunlight and they stepped into the road scowling, clutching their pikes threateningly.

Hamish's bowels turned to water.

'I'm sorry, but my Spanish is a little rusty!' Chimes called out, stepping forward, drawing his sword and gesturing for Hamish to do the same. 'What did you say?'

'My friend here said stop, you English dogs!' translated the shorter of the two, leering at them malevolently. 'And drop your weapons,' he added gruffly.

'Now why in the world would we do that?' snarled Chimes sardonically, moving to the right with his sword extended, drawing the squat Spaniard away from his taller partner.

Gripping his sword with both hands, Hamish circled left, regarding his opponent warily. Conscious of the adrenaline surge running through his body, he knew that patience and timing would be just as crucial as speed if he was going to overcome the pike's superior reach. Behind him, a clang of steel on steel rang out as Chimes blocked his assailant's attack and Hamish stepped back, drawing his man away. The Spaniard lunged. Leaping aside, Hamish evaded the razor-sharp blade and brought his sword crashing down onto the pike's shaft, scoring it and almost knocking it from the Spaniard's grasp. Angered, the Spaniard thrust forward but Hamish moved back. Time and time again, the Spaniard advanced and Hamish retreated, biding his time, waiting for the all-important sign. Finally he saw it, a flash of impatience in his opponent's eyes, and like a bull the Spaniard charged. Patiently, Hamish waited, calculating and visualising his next move. *Trust your instincts*, he told himself, raising his sword high above his head, summoning up every ounce of strength in him – *not yet. Not yet. Now!* Pirouetting around, he slammed his blade down onto the pike's shaft and a loud crack split the air as the wood shattered and the weapon's blade fell to the ground harmlessly. Alarmed, the Spaniard back-pedalled frantically, discarding the splintered pole, fumbling for his sword. But Hamish was too quick. Dashing forward, he swung his sword in a wide arc and slashed the Spaniard's shoulder, tearing open his doublet and slicing through sinew. The Spaniard screamed out, staggering backwards, clutching his wound to staunch the flow of blood that was seeping between his fingers. There was fear in his eyes now and he dropped to his knees, pleading for mercy.

Hamish regarded him pitilessly, pressing his sword to the Spaniard's cheek, and then the outside world crept back into his consciousness and he heard Chimes calling his name.

'Hamilton!' he yelled. 'Hamilton, leave him! Don't kill him. We'll interrogate them!'

Hamish looked across at him blankly and saw that he was crouching over the other Spaniard, tying him up and gagging him, urging Hamish to do the same. Suddenly, a wave of exhaustion crashed over him and he stumbled backwards, feeling light-headed and faint. The 'fight or flight' adrenaline boost was wearing off and he started shivering, his arms feeling like lead weights. Blinking rapidly, he shook his head, trying to clear the fug from his mind when he noticed a look of alarm crossing Chimes's face. Time seemed to slow and as if having an out-of-body experience, he watched bemused as his friend's face twisted in fury and he bellowed something, springing to his feet and lunging towards him. But to Hamish his words sounded like a dull faraway drone and he looked around in confusion, noticing two carts approaching along the track. It was Suzy and the others, but for the life of him he couldn't work out what was so enraging Chimes. And then he felt it. Sharp and hot in his stomach. Bewildered, he looked down and thought his eyes were deceiving him. Something was protruding from the front of his doublet, and it took him a moment to realise it was a dagger handle. Then disbelief and alarm congealed into fear and he looked up, staring in dismay at the Spaniard, who was scrambling away smiling evilly.

The pain that erupted inside him was volcanic. Reflexively, he threw back his head and gasped as searing white-hot spasms tore through his abdomen, forcing him to double over and drop to his knees moaning in agony. Clutching his belly with both hands, his fingers closed around the wooden handle and he howled, wrenching the blade from himself and hurling it away. Momentarily, his pain eased but he could tell from the warmth on his hands that he was losing a lot of blood. His mind began to cloud and he closed his eyes, crouching forward, pressing his forehead against the damp earth when he became aware of Chimes helping him to lie down. Gratefully, he curled himself up into a ball, whimpering piteously, feeling his strength ebbing slowly away.

Disconsolately, Chimes sat in the road with him, murmuring the Lord's Prayer, watching Suzy throw herself from the cart and race panic-stricken towards them.

'Hamish, Hamish!' she screamed, flinging herself down beside him, patting his face, imploring him to speak. Tears rolled down her cheeks and she held him tight. 'Oh, Hamish, say something please!' she sobbed.

But Hamish didn't have the strength. Drifting in and out of consciousness, his breathing was becoming shallow and laboured.

'For God's sake, help him!' she wailed, shooting desperate glances at the others who were gathering around. 'Don't just stand there, do something! Call an ambulance!'

Frowning at her gibberish, Chimes placed a consoling hand on her shoulder. 'There's nothing we can do,' he said. 'He's mortally wounded. He's going to die.'

His words struck her like a knife to the heart and she cried out, burying her face in her brother's neck. 'Hamish ... Hamish, don't leave me!' she wailed. 'You promised ... you promised you'd never leave me.'

It was all too much for Chimes. Climbing to his feet, he drew his sword, glaring at Blakey. 'Look after her,' he muttered darkly. 'I'll be back shortly.'

Blakey shuddered, watching him go. He'd seen the rage in his eyes and knew that the Spaniard was about to pay horribly for his mistake.

Staggering away, stumbling from one side of the track to the other, the Spaniard was trying to escape but Chimes caught up with him quickly, dragging him off into the trees. Moments later, a shrill, blood-curdling scream pierced the air and when Chimes stepped back into the road Blakey could see clearly the grim satisfaction set into his face.

From somewhere far, far away, Suzy's anguished voice drifted into Hamish's consciousness. He couldn't decipher her words but he could tell from her tone that she was disconsolate. His own pain had subsided now and he felt strangely at peace. It was like he was floating and he wanted nothing more than to drift into blissful sleep. But Suzy's voice was troubling him, preventing him, and then he remembered. There was still one thing he must do.

'Hamish, say something, please!' she sobbed, cupping his face in her hands.

Fleetingly, his eyelids fluttered open and he smiled weakly, surprised and comforted to find her so close. 'I'm sorry, sis,' he whispered, his words as light as his fading breath. Then closing his eyes he surrendered himself to sleep; her panicked voice began drifting away, and fragments of memories flashed through his mind until finally there was only blackness.

'No!' she shrieked, shaking him. 'Hamish, don't leave me! Come back! Please! God damn you, Hamish, don't leave me!'

But it was no use. Her brother was dead and she fell over his lifeless body, weeping inconsolably.

Blakey's heart went out to her and he bent down, taking her gently by the shoulders, helping her to her feet. 'He's at peace now,' he murmured, holding her close. 'He's in a better place now. He's no longer in pain.' He paused, knowing that what he was going to say next would sound callous, but under the circumstances he hadn't a choice. Time was running out. 'We must continue to Penzance,' he said. 'England needs us. We'll hide Hamish's body here and collect it on the way back ...'

Instantly, Suzy stiffened and pushed him away, her eyes blazing with anger. 'No!' she screamed. 'This is where it ends! This is where our hideous journey comes to an end!'

Blakey frowned, taken aback. 'But we've got to complete the mission,' he protested. 'We can't stop now!'

Suzy glared at him. 'You're going to complete it without me. This is where we go our separate ways. You're going to continue on to Penzance, but Chimes is coming with me.'

Chimes stopped cleaning his sword. 'And where exactly are we going?' he asked guardedly.

'You're going to help me carry my brother's body back to Warfield,' she snapped, her tone leaving no room for discussion.

'You haven't answered my question,' he growled impatiently. 'I asked you where *exactly* are we going?'

Suzy was silent for a long moment, but her answer when it came unsettled him. 'To the place where our worlds collide,' she muttered bleakly. Then turning away, she began ushering everyone back to the wagons.

Watching them depart, Chimes waited until they'd disappeared from view before hoisting Hamish's body on to his shoulder and setting off after Suzy. Peering up at the darkening sky, he noticed slate-grey clouds rolling towards them and he groaned bitterly as the wind quickened, whipping at his hair and clothes. It began to rain and within minutes, the sky had turned oily black. Lightning flashes illuminated a cloud mass bubbling high into the heavens and cracks of thunder exploded with such force that the ground shook. The wind was howling now, driving horizontal rain into their faces, stinging their skin and forcing them to lean forward with their heads bowed. With the extra ballast slung over his shoulder, Chimes was struggling to make headway and the track underfoot was turning into a quagmire. Just then a lightning bolt struck a tree at the side of the track, shattering its trunk and engulfing it in flames. 'Sweet Jesus!' he exclaimed, ducking reflexively. He'd never known a storm like it, but what he found truly shocking was the speed with which it had descended. Like a divine act of brutality, it had come from nowhere, and for the first time in his life he felt genuinely afraid of the weather. *This is madness,* he thought. *We should be taking cover and waiting for it to pass.* But one look at Suzy's grim, determined face persuaded him otherwise. Even through the raging squall he could tell that she'd withdrawn into herself and was trudging doggedly on, oblivious to everything around her, everything but her own grief.

Once again, he played back her cryptic response: *To the place where our worlds collide,* and the more he thought about it, the more he sensed, inexplicably, that his life was about to change forever. And Warfield was the key, of that he was sure. Then a troubling thought occurred to him and he dismissed it as absurd. But the further they walked, the less certain he became because the storm's savagery seemed to be intensifying with every step they took. *Could it really be possible?* he wondered. *Could Warfield be at the eye of this storm?*

Suzy meanwhile was walking on automatic pilot. She'd retreated to a place of bleak and utter hopelessness, swinging from pathological despair one moment to barely-contained fury the next. Time and time again, she glanced across at Hamish's body slumped over Chimes's shoulder, hoping desperately that she would awaken to discover this had all been some hellish nightmare. But each time she saw his corpse a part of her died inside and by the time they reached the narrow farm track she no longer cared about anything or anyone, including herself. It was then she resolved never to return home. Not without Hamish. As far as she was concerned, her life back home was finished and explaining his death to their parents wasn't an option. It didn't even bear thinking about. *Mr McLeod can see to that,* she brooded, *and once I've returned Hamish's body to him, I'll lose myself forever here in the sixteenth century.*

'This storm's getting worse!' yelled Chimes, interrupting her thoughts. 'We should find cover. It's crazy carrying on like this.'

'We're almost there,' she mumbled flatly, staring ahead through blank, expressionless eyes.

Chimes saw her lips move but couldn't hear what she said. 'What did you say?' he bawled, stepping closer.

But Suzy didn't respond. As if in a trance, she turned off the road and began trudging down the waterlogged farm track.

Chimes grimaced, adjusting the dead weight on his shoulder, and hurried after her, slipping and sliding in the mud. 'Wait a minute!' he yelled. 'We need to talk! You need to tell me where we're going!' But his words were carried away on the wind and he staggered on, muttering to himself darkly.

The moment the farmhouse loomed into view Suzy's grief and despair exploded into rage and, half-running, she stumbled across the farmyard towards the front door. Suppressing an overwhelming urge to scream and pound it with her fists, she reached up to the metal lion's head and took hold of its hinged jaw, knocking three times as hard as she could. Instantly, the door swung open and standing there were two figures, concern etched deep into their gaunt features.

'Suzy, my dear, come in,' intoned Mr McLeod gravely, stepping forward, reaching out to her.

'Get away from me!' she screamed, leaping back. 'Get away from me!'

Her eyes were wild and Mr McLeod flinched as if he'd just been struck. 'Dear God,' he murmured, glancing at Genin. 'What have we done?'

Chimes couldn't hear them from across the farmyard but he could see the old men's faces lit up by the lightning and knew that something was wrong. Even through the squall, he recognised their torment and hurried over, heaving Hamish's corpse from his shoulder, laying it gently on the ground at the foot of the steps.

'He's dead and it's all your fault!' screamed Suzy, jabbing an accusing finger at Mr McLeod. 'You brought us here. If it wasn't for you, he'd still be alive. I hope you're satisfied. Now you can take his body back home and explain everything to Mum and Dad. But you're going to do it without me because I'm never going back, not now, not ever. I never want to see or hear of you again . . .'

Chimes saw the pain in the old man's eyes and wondered why she was blaming him. But intuitively he sensed there was more to her outrage than met the eye, so he kept quiet, listening and observing.

'Kindly take Hamish's body inside for us,' Mr McLeod instructed him, his eyes never leaving Suzy. 'Please, my dear,' he implored, 'come in out of this rain and let's talk.'

But Suzy stood her ground, refusing to move. 'Didn't you hear me?' she cried. 'I want nothing more to do with you! I've only come back to deliver my brother's body so you can see what you've done. I told you, I'm never going home. I'm staying here—'

'I'm afraid that's not possible,' interjected Genin, stepping forward. 'Your time here has come to an end. Your return to this site marks the completion of your journey's circle—'

'Oh, please!' she snorted derisively. 'You're just trying to trick me!'

Mr McLeod shook his head. 'It's true,' he said. 'Your time here is at an end. Your journey's circle has closed. If you set foot beyond the perimeter of this site, you will die for all eternity, lost between parallel dimensions in time and space. My dear, just as I am unable to leave this site, so too now are you.'

Bewildered, Chimes peered up at the solid but unprepossessing farmhouse, wondering what sort of magic lay within. But whatever it was, he felt strangely drawn to it and while he didn't understand what these two frail old men were talking about, inexplicably he trusted and believed them.

'I don't believe you!' snapped Suzy harshly. 'And even if I did, I'd rather die than go home without Hamish! At least then we'd be together in death . . .'

Chimes couldn't believe his ears. 'What are you saying?' he exclaimed. 'Have you lost your mind?'

Suzy shot him an irritated glance. 'Stay out of this, Chimes,' she muttered. 'It's got nothing to do with you.'

'Like hell it doesn't,' he growled menacingly. 'If you think I'm going to stand by and let you kill yourself then you're as deluded as you sound.'

Mr McLeod looked at him gravely, but inside he smiled. 'Please, Suzy,' he said. 'Let's all go inside for some—' but before he could finish what he was saying Suzy punched Chimes in the chest, knocking him out of the way, and bolted for the open gate.

Caught by surprise, Chimes sprawled backwards, stumbling but managing to retain his footing in the slick mud. Then with a howl of fury he launched himself after her, almost colliding with Mr McLeod, who'd hobbled down the steps and was looking on in horror.

Suzy ran as if her life depended on it, her long skirt clinging heavily to her legs, making it feel like she was wading through treacle. Behind her, she heard Chimes's splashing footsteps and could tell he was catching up. *Come on, come on,* she screamed inwardly, willing her legs to move faster. *Only six yards to go, then I'll be through and free.*

And Chimes *was* gaining on her, but he could also see that she was going to reach the gate first. Taking a deep breath, he gritted his teeth, knowing there was only one thing for it.

Suddenly his footsteps fell silent and Suzy glanced back, gasping in horror as he dived towards her, his outstretched hand homing in on her like a guided missile. And then she felt it – the tap on her ankle, slight but enough to destabilise her, and she sprawled forward, crying out as the ground rushed up to meet her.

*

Climbing back towards consciousness, Suzy heard distant voices growing steadily louder as a low hum of conversation swirled around her. Her head throbbed and she felt disorientated as she opened her eyes and flinched violently at the harsh sunlight flooding the room. Hurriedly, she pulled up her blanket, shielding her eyes.

'Welcome back,' said a woman's voice soothingly from somewhere above. 'That was some knock you took. I'd wager you've got a bit of a headache.'

Gradually, her eyes adjusted and she peered over the blanket, squinting at the ceiling. Mrs Potts's beaming face loomed into view.

'There, there,' she cooed, placing a cool damp cloth on Suzy's forehead. 'This poultice should ease the pain. Mind you, that sleep will have done you the world of good. My guess is you'll be up and about in no time. Now I'll leave you in the company of these good gentlemen while I go and fetch you some fortifying broth.'

Turning slowly, Suzy saw Mr McLeod and Genin standing beside the window, watching her anxiously.

'How long have I been here?' she asked weakly.

'My dear, you've been asleep for over two days,' replied Mr McLeod softly. 'You gave us quite a fright there.'

'Chimes sends you his best wishes and hopes to see you soon,' added Genin, smiling. 'He was distraught at having to hurt you like that, but he couldn't very well let you kill yourself, now could he?'

Suzy grimaced, feeling suddenly ashamed. 'I'm sorry, I don't know what came over me,' she whispered hoarsely.

Mr McLeod walked over and sat down on the edge of the bed, taking her hand in his. 'My dear, after everything you've been through, it's no wonder that all that stress finally took its toll. Chimes told us all about it. No words can begin to convey the depth of our sorrow for Hamish. His death is beyond comprehension but I swear to you, it wasn't in vain . . .'

197

The mention of his name struck Suzy like a slap in the face and she felt tears of pain sting her eyes. 'Hamish!' she gasped. 'Oh, my God, Hamish!'

'You must remain strong,' he said soothingly. 'Hamish might be gone, but always consider what he'd want you to do. Your parents are going to need you now, more than ever. To lose a child is the hardest thing in the world, but if there's one thing I do know, it's that they'll draw enormous comfort from having you home.'

Sniffing loudly, Suzy wiped her tears with her sleeve, noticing she was wearing a clean linen nightdress. 'Where's his body?' she asked. 'I'd like to see him before we take him home.'

'I'm afraid that's not going to be possible ...' sighed Genin sadly.

Suzy frowned.

'... His body's already been committed to Equilibrium.'

'Committed to Equilibrium?' she repeated, aghast. 'Are you telling me you disposed of his body before I could say goodbye to him?'

'I'm afraid we had no choice,' replied Mr McLeod quickly. 'The laws of harmony demand it. We had to commit his body to Equilibrium as soon as possible to ensure that his inner balance – his spirit – continues on its eternal journey. My dear, please draw comfort from the fact that Hamish is now on his way to another shallow pool where he'll continue defending harmony against the forces of chaos and order.'

Suzy stared at him wide-eyed, struggling to compute what she'd just heard. 'Are you trying to tell me that Hamish is still alive?' she ventured slowly.

Mr McLeod smiled at her. 'Yes,' he said. 'As well as living on in the hearts and memories of everyone who knew him, Hamish is now crossing over to another dimension in time and space.'

Immediately, he saw doubt and scepticism in her searching eyes.

But what Suzy saw startled and consoled her in equal measure. For gazing into his azure eyes, she was struck by their tender reassurance and in that moment she knew. It was true. Hamish *was* still alive, not here or at home but somewhere else in the universe, and although she still felt sick and hollow inside, that made her profoundly happy.

'Will I ever see him again?' she asked, sensing a huge weight rising from her.

'It's possible,' he conceded softly. 'But remember what I told you. The universe is far more complex than mankind currently understands. There are an infinite number of dimensions in time and space. And while chaos and order possess only enough energy to compete in six dimensions at any one time, they're shifting continually. So please don't raise your hopes too high because although it's possible, the laws of probability suggest that it's highly unlikely you'll ever find yourselves in the same dimension again.'

'But it *is* possible,' she repeated, more of a statement than a question.

Mr McLeod smiled at her. 'Yes, it's possible.'

'Then that's good enough for me,' she murmured, looking out of the window to the white clouds drifting serenely across the pale blue sky.

A tranquil calm had descended over her and Mr McLeod waited for a moment before continuing. 'Suzy, there's something else we must discuss,' he said, softly. 'It's quite possible that your parents will want to leave Warfield when they learn of Hamish.'

'They wouldn't do that,' she murmured, continuing to gaze out of the window. 'It's our home. It's our only connection to Hamish.'

'My dear, trust me. I know what I'm talking about. Often the only way parents can deal with the loss of a child is to move away.'

Startled by his certainty, Suzy looked up at him, remembering a story from long ago. 'You're the little boy, aren't you?' she said after a long moment.

Mr McLeod gaped at her. 'I *beg* your pardon?' he exclaimed, frowning.

'When you interviewed us for the house I remember you telling us that the last family to have it were happy there until they moved overseas but that the little boy still lived locally. And I just thought, well, after everything that's happened to me, you sound as though you might've experienced something similar. And I just thought maybe you're that little boy, that's all.'

Whether or not it was true, Mr McLeod was giving nothing away. 'Your recollection's impressive,' he said, 'but the point I was trying to make is that if your parents decide to move away then you have a decision to make. You can either go with them or you can stay. But either way, you should be aware that provisions can be made to facilitate both.'

It was Suzy's turn to frown now. 'So what you're saying is if Mum and Dad decide to leave Warfield, I can stay if I want to?'

'Yes, as a guardian of Equilibrium, your status here is assured for as long as you want it,' he explained. '12b Porchester Road will continue to be your home, with or without your parents.'

'But I'm not sure I'd like to live there by myself.'

'Then your decision's made,' he said. 'You must return home and convince your parents that their future remains here in Warfield.'

Just then Mrs Potts bustled back into the room, carrying a tray. 'Here we go,' she trilled happily. 'Pig's liver and trotter broth. Made it myself. Mark my words, this stuff'll have you back on your feet in no time.'

Suzy felt her stomach heave and she grimaced, looking at Mr McLeod, imploring him with her eyes to save her.

'Oh, don't be like that!' admonished the housekeeper, noting her revulsion. 'This stuff's lovely. It's a favourite among English soldiers. It puts fire in the belly and steel in their fight ...'

Suzy's blood ran cold and Mr McLeod saw the look of horror flash across her face. 'Don't worry,' he said quickly, waving the housekeeper away. 'Nobody's going to force you to eat it.'

But Suzy's mind was elsewhere. 'Two days!' she exclaimed, sitting up. 'I've been asleep for over two days! What about the Spanish invasion?'

Much to her surprise, Mr McLeod and Genin chuckled softly.

'The invasion failed,' Mr McLeod assured her. 'Don't worry. Harmony's restored.'

Her relief was overwhelming and she fell back on her pillow, closing her eyes and sighing heavily. Her mind was swirling with so many questions that she didn't know where to begin. 'Mr McLeod?' she asked finally.

'Yes, Suzy?'

'Can we go home now?'

*

Together, they stepped down into the silver pool and the warm liquid rose up, submerging their waists then their chests as they descended the terraced steps beneath the surface.

'Are you ready?' asked Mr McLeod, smiling at her. 'You know what to expect this time.'

Wordlessly, Suzy nodded and took a deep breath. Then, closing her eyes, she slipped under and was instantly enthralled by an irresistible white light drawing her effortlessly towards it. Its brilliance was mesmerising and she drifted weightlessly, basking in its warmth, until she began to hear a voice calling her name. Like an echo, it came to her in waves, faint one moment and clearer the next. Then slowly, ever so slowly, like swirling clouds, she noticed a face forming in the light and her heart soared. It was Hamish and he was calling to her. Grinning broadly, she willed herself towards him, floating on a tide of euphoria, sensing his aura embracing and enveloping her, making her feel whole again. And then she arrived. Smiling serenely, her head broke the surface and she opened her eyes, inhaling deeply.

Ascending the steps, she performed a full circle, surveying her surroundings, and her smile faded. The thought of climbing the spiral staircase at the far end of the cavern filled her with dread. How were they going to explain Hamish's death to Mum and Dad? And what about the school and police? Surely, they would need to be told too. And what about the body, or the lack of one? There was nothing to bury or cremate. There would be no final resting place or focal point for their parents' grief. Apprehensions and anxieties sluiced through her mind. *And what about the cause of death?* she brooded. *We can hardly say 'stabbed by a medieval Spanish soldier'.* Panic swelled inside her chest and suddenly the room started spinning.

Climbing the steps behind her, Mr McLeod saw her stumble and rushed over, catching her around the shoulders.

'I'm all right. I'm all right,' she panted breathlessly. 'But what are we going to tell Mum and Dad?'

'Don't worry,' he said. 'Calm down. I'll take care of everything. Trust me.'

Breathing deeply, Suzy felt her pulse begin to slow. 'But how?' she asked, anxiously.

Mr McLeod waited until some colour had returned to her cheeks before replying. 'Suzy, trust me. I'll take care of all the formalities. All I need you to focus on is your parents. When the police arrive later today to inform them about Hamish, you're going to have to be there to comfort them and persuade them not to leave Warfield. And, my dear, I can't stress this strongly enough, but you must never, ever tell them what really happened. The exact nature of Hamish's fate must always remain a secret. It's your duty as a guardian of Equilibrium never to reveal it. Do I make myself clear?'

Suzy nodded. Once again, she had the strangest feeling he'd been through this before.

'Good. Now, let's go and call the police,' he said, setting off towards the stairs.

Dispirited, Suzy followed, recalling the words of advice given by a removals man what seemed like an eternity ago. She felt relieved to be placing her trust in Mr McLeod. She couldn't imagine what he was going to tell the police but, whatever it was, she prayed that he'd be true to his word and that everything would work out fine. After all, she mused, recalling the fate of four council officials, if he could single-handedly save the house above from redevelopment then he could surely see to a missing person. And in that moment she knew precisely what he was going to tell the police and could almost have laughed had it not been so tragic.

Reaching the stairs first, Mr McLeod started up, but Suzy paused, taking one last look at the ancient stone circle, wondering where in the universe her brother was now. Marvelling again at the twelve titan blocks bathed in golden light, she resolved that if Equilibrium represented her only chance of ever seeing Hamish again, she would willingly and happily spend the rest of her life here.

It was Mr McLeod's insistent voice echoing down the stairwell, urging her to hurry, that broke her thoughts and she turned to go. Sighing heavily, she entered the stairwell and had started to climb when she heard a noise behind her and froze. Like a statue, she stood there motionless, holding her breath, beginning to wonder if she was imagining things when she heard it again. 'Mr McLeod,' she hissed, peering up into the darkness. 'Something's moving down here!' Her pulse quickened as she crept back down, stepping out into the open, scanning the cavernous void.

But apart from twelve immovable stones, nothing was there.

Mr McLeod reappeared, looking doubtful. 'What did it sound like?' he asked, surveying the hall.

'It sounded like something was shuffling or scrabbling about,' she hissed. 'Like rats!'

Mr McLeod shook his head. 'Trust me, there are no rats down here,' he said, 'or any other living organisms, for that matter. Equilibrium's peak surges see to that.'

'Well I definitely heard something . . .' she began to say but fell silent, staring in horror at Equilibrium. 'Look!' she gasped, pointing.

A hand had appeared over the ledge and was clawing the earth desperately.

'Dear God!' exclaimed Mr McLeod as a second hand appeared and they both rushed forward, their minds racing, struggling to comprehend what their disbelieving eyes were seeing.

Suddenly a shrill scream pierced the air and Suzy fell to her knees, clutching the hands, laughing and crying simultaneously, her frantic words ricocheting around them. 'Hamish! Hamish! Hamish!'

Mr McLeod was thunderstruck. 'It's not possible,' he breathed.

But however implausible, he couldn't deny reality. It *was* Hamish. The boy had returned and while he was very much alive, he looked exhausted to the point of breakdown, spread-eagled on the steps. Watching the ecstatic sibling reunion, Mr McLeod sighed wistfully, feeling a stab of jealousy, remembering

Rose, the sister he'd lost to Equilibrium over sixty years ago, and suddenly he felt tired. Hurriedly, he forced the memory from his mind, stooping down to help Hamish to his feet when he noticed Suzy examining the front of his doublet.

'It's fully healed,' Mr McLeod explained wearily. 'Just like your own cuts and bruises. Equilibrium's healed them.' He paused, looking at Hamish, and asked, 'How did you do it?'

Hamish frowned. 'Do what?' he asked weakly.

'How did you manage to return here, to this precise moment in time and space?' he demanded.

Suzy glared at him. 'For goodness' sake, he's exhausted!' she protested. 'Can't this wait until later?'

But Mr McLeod ignored her, his gaze fixed firmly on Hamish. 'Tell me, boy, it's important, I need to know,' he pressed. 'What did you experience in Equilibrium?'

Hamish hesitated.

'Tell me!' he snapped impatiently. 'I need to know! What happened in there?'

Taken aback, Hamish cleared his throat and began to speak quickly. 'Sir, I was floating. I was drifting towards an amazing white light at the end of a long tunnel. It seemed to go on forever but it was wonderful, really peaceful, and I was happy to be there. It was like I was in suspended animation. I could've stayed there forever just drifting along. But then something strange happened.' He looked at Suzy. 'Suddenly I sensed Suzy's presence and I called out to her, over and over again. It's hard to explain, but I felt her with me and for a split second we touched like we were holding hands. But then she let go and I continued drifting towards the light. I realised she was slipping further and further behind and I couldn't bear to be parted from her, so I resisted the light. I forced myself to turn away from it and went after her. It was really hard, like swimming against the tide, but as I continued on, I could feel her presence getting stronger and stronger. And then suddenly she disappeared and I thought I'd lost her. But as I continued on I sensed her shadow and followed it here.' His story over, he glanced at Mr McLeod anxiously, hoping it would pacify him, and noticed there were tears in his eyes.

Wordlessly, Mr McLeod pulled a handkerchief from his pocket and removed his spectacles. 'Extraordinary,' he muttered, wiping his eyes. 'Quite extraordinary.' Then, smiling sadly, he put his glasses back on and continued. 'I didn't think it was possible, but obviously I was wrong. You see, it's a fact of life that when someone dies, they can never again occupy the same dimension in time and space. Their spirit moves on. So, Hamish, because you died in 1597, that dimension is now closed to you forever. But when you consider that the universe consists of an infinite number of dimensions, the likelihood of you ever returning to this specific moment was virtually nonexistent. What's more, young man, you defied the will of Equilibrium and until now, I never thought that was possible. Which makes your return here all the more remarkable. Therefore the only conclusion I can draw is that . . .'

Hamish and Suzy were listening intently.

'. . . is that the strength of your relationship, your unique bond as brother and sister, is unparalleled. I always knew that you were two remarkable individuals with perfect inner balance – after all, that's why I brought you here in the first place. But until now, I must admit, I never truly understood the extent to which you complement each other. It's extraordinary. Not only have you saved the world we know from catastrophe but you've managed to return home safely, defying impossible odds. And for that I applaud you both.'

*

The first light of dawn was paling the sky when Mr McLeod came back into the sumptuous reception room carrying a neat pile of freshly laundered clothes. Hamish and Suzy recognised them immediately.

'You'll need to put these on,' he said, laying their pyjamas and dressing gowns on the elegant writing desk set between the two sash windows. 'You can change behind that screen over there and leave your clothes. We don't want your parents finding them, now do we?'

'Mr McLeod, how did the Spanish invasion fail?' asked Suzy, studying the giant globe in the corner of the sumptuous room. Set in its heavy oak cradle, the ancient leather sphere's gold markings glinted in the room's radiant light, clearly outlining the earth's borders and boundaries. Pushing the sphere gently, she noticed that the red blush on its worn surface had grown, spreading across the Middle East into North Africa.

'My dear, the answer to that question can be found in any decent history book,' he replied, crossing over to one of the tall bookcases and withdrawing an innocuous-looking tome from the shelf. 'Now let's see,' he murmured, leafing through the pages, retracing his steps to stand with his back to the fire. 'Ah yes, here we are. *On learning that Lord Essex had taken the English fleet to the Azores, King Philip II of Spain ordered his Armada to set sail from Ferrol on 18th October 1597. England was defenceless and four days later on 22nd October, a hundred and forty galleons appeared off the coast of Cornwall. But that night, fierce storms shattered the Armada ...'*

Suzy gasped as he continued reading. '*... This disaster left King Philip prostrate with disappointment. He was bankrupt, his people were weary of this fruitless war, and now he was forced to face the fact that his great enterprise of England would have to be abandoned forever.'* He stopped reading and looked up them, smiling. 'So you see, were it not for Hamish's death, the resulting tempest would never have thwarted the Armada.'

Hamish got up from the burgundy sofa and crossed to collect his clothes from the desk, deep in thought. With his pyjamas and dressing gown in hand, he wandered over to the elaborately painted screen in the corner. 'What about Cuffe?' he asked, unbuttoning his doublet. 'What happened to *him*?'

Mr McLeod shook his head. 'There's very little mention of him,' he replied. 'He's an irrelevant footnote in history. He was jailed as a common criminal and executed for treason.'

'And what about Lord Essex?' asked Suzy, crossing the room to collect her garments and slippers. 'Whatever happened to him?'

'Ah, now, there's a story,' said Mr McLeod, with a knowing smile. 'Believe it or not, Lord Essex returned from the Azores as England's hero, much to the Queen's displeasure. The people refused to blame him for their failure to sink the Spanish fleet at Ferrol, blaming instead his officers. And eventually, even the

Queen herself forgave him. She missed his presence at court, so it wasn't long before he was back to his old tricks, getting away with things that other people would have been thrown into the Tower for. And, of course, he still harboured military ambitions. He even managed to persuade the Queen to raise the biggest army of her reign and put him in charge of quashing a rebellion in Ireland. But after six long months of appalling losses and failure, he deserted his command and returned to England, whereupon he burst into the Queen's bedchamber unannounced, begging for forgiveness. It was the final straw. The Queen had had enough and he was found guilty of disobeying her orders and sentenced to indefinite house arrest. But it didn't stop there. Lord Essex became so embittered that on the 8th February 1601 he tried staging a coup, leading his friends and supporters through London, expecting to trigger a popular uprising. But he'd overestimated his popularity and the people stayed indoors, leaving him to flee home in panic. And this time the Queen showed him no mercy. He was arrested, thrown into the Tower, and on the 25th February 1601, he was beheaded for high treason.'

Suzy whistled softly but Hamish frowned, stepping out from behind the frieze wearing his black and white striped dressing gown. 'If Cuffe was only a civil servant, where did he get the money to fund his Great Salvation?' he asked.

Mr McLeod laughed softly. 'Well, that's one question you won't find the answer to in any history book,' he said, watching Suzy disappear behind the screen. 'But what would you say if I told you it was the Queen?'

'The Queen!' they chorused in dismay.

Mr McLeod nodded. 'Indirectly, yes,' he said. 'The Queen was a generous benefactor to many people, but there was one person in particular to whom she was especially generous . . .'

'Oh, don't tell us,' groaned Hamish, rolling his eyes. 'Lord Essex!'

Mr McLeod smiled at him. 'Correct!' he said. 'Despite his great wealth, Essex lived way beyond his means and exploited his place in the Queen's affections by asking for loans. Of course, she had no way of monitoring how exactly the money was spent, but most of it went to fund Cuffe's Great Salvation. In funding Cuffe, Essex was effectively hedging his bets. All he cared about was removing Elizabeth from the throne and becoming King himself. So he devised two plans to guarantee success, one with the King of Spain and the other with Cuffe. It was very clever really because if one plan failed, the other was bound to succeed. Either way, he would become King and his debts to the Queen would be written off with her death. So it didn't matter to him how much he borrowed, he was never going to pay her back. Or so he thought. But when he was sentenced to house arrest, the Queen called in all her loans. She wanted her money back. Financially, he was ruined. He'd had to return the Spanish treasure to King Philip for fear of being exposed as a traitor on his return from the Azores. And he had no other means of paying her back. So in desperation, he tried staging a coup.'

Hamish and Suzy were lost for words.

'Now, my dear people, it's time you were heading home,' he added as Suzy emerged from behind the screen, wearing her blue dressing gown. 'But in order to complete your journey's circle, you must return home via the same stairs that led you to Equilibrium.'

Their heads spinning, they accompanied him to the door in silence. He opened it and they gazed into the hallway, smiling. Once more, it gleamed brilliant white.

CHAPTER TWELVE

'Ugh, this milk's off!' complained Mr Hamilton, grimacing at the curdled globules floating in his coffee.

'It can't be. I only bought it yesterday,' insisted Mrs Hamilton, placing the replenished toast rack on the breakfast table. 'Having said that, the bread's quite stale too,' she added, sniffing the milk carton and pulling a face. 'I'll have to have words with the shop manager next time I'm in. It's disgraceful!'

Glancing at each other across the table, Hamish and Suzy continued eating, pretending not to hear.

'Mind you,' said Mr Hamilton, pouring himself another coffee, 'I feel great this morning. It just goes to show what a good night's sleep can do.'

'Me too,' agreed his wife. 'I was worried we were all coming down with something last night. I can't remember the last time I slept so well. Suzy, would you mind passing me the butter, please, and, Hamish, the marmalade. Thank you.' She buttered her toast and took a bite, looking at each of them in turn. 'What time did you two get up this morning?' she asked. 'Your beds were empty when I woke up.'

Hamish stopped chewing.

'Oh, it was about six o'clock,' replied Suzy quickly.

'And what have you been up to?' she asked, taking another bite.

Suzy hesitated, glancing at Hamish anxiously.

'Exploring,' he said casually.

'Yes, that's right,' sighed Suzy. 'We didn't want to disturb you, so we went exploring the house.'

'Did you find anything of interest?' asked Mr Hamilton, reaching for the butter.

Determined not to look at each other for fear of giggling, they shook their heads, concentrating on their toast.

'Hamish, if you've finished, would you mind popping upstairs and fetching the post, please?' asked Mr Hamilton, buttering his toast. 'I think I heard it being delivered when I came down for breakfast.'

Relieved to escape, Hamish got up and Suzy watched him hurry out. Sighing contentedly, she sat back in her chair, smiling fondly at her parents. 'Do you know something?' she said. 'It's great to be home.'

Mr and Mrs Hamilton smiled at her.

'My darling, you're right, it's absolutely wonderful being home,' agreed Mrs Hamilton, reaching over and stroking her arm. 'It's been a difficult time leaving Northumberland and moving here. But here we are, in our new house, and I think we're all going to be very happy here, very happy indeed.'

Upstairs, Hamish was crouching over the front doormat, rifling through a pile of newspapers, thunderstruck. There were twelve in all – twelve editions of the *Warfield Daily Chronicle*, and their headlines were astounding. '*Snow in Summer!*' '*Blizzard Chaos Blights Cornwall!*' '*Prepare For Worse!*' '*Warfield Paralysed!*' '*Emergency Services Overwhelmed!*' '*State of Emergency in Warfield!*' '*Army Rescues Tourists!*' And so they went on until the eleventh day when the newspaper declared, '*Here Comes The Sun!*'

'Dear God,' he breathed, picking up the twelfth paper, the most recent. The front page was dominated by a picture of delighted holidaymakers playing on a beach under the headline '*Harmony Restored!*' No wonder the milk was off, he thought, shaking his head in wonder. Mum and Dad had been asleep for twelve days. Then he remembered something that a silver-haired removals man had once said and he chuckled to himself, knowing that the weathermen would be scratching their heads for years trying to figure out what caused it.

'Hamish, what's taking you so long?' came his father's voice, calling up the stairs.

Quickly, he gathered up the newspapers, stashing them in the cupboard under the stairs, and hurried back down.

'That's a lot of post,' observed his father as Hamish dumped the letters on the table, motioning for Suzy to come quickly.

Excitement gleamed in his eyes and Suzy pushed back her chair, about to get up when Mr Hamilton handed her a golden envelope. 'Here, this is for you,' he said.

Suzy frowned, noting the flamboyant handwriting and postmarks. 'It's from London,' she murmured, nonplussed.

'And this one's for you,' announced Mr Hamilton, handing an identical letter to Hamish.

Intrigued, they tore them open and each withdrew what appeared to be a single white card fringed with gold borders.

'What are they?' asked Mrs Hamilton, noting their surprise.

But neither replied. They were lost in thought, reading and re-reading the cards over and over again.

'Well, what have you got there?' asked Mr Hamilton after a long moment.

It was Hamish who found his voice first. 'It's an invitation,' he mumbled distractedly.

More silence.

'An invitation to what?' pressed Mrs Hamilton, a hint of impatience entering her voice.

This time Suzy replied by reading the inscription. '*Peacock & Mayther are proud to sponsor an exhibition of the Private Collection of Queen Elizabeth I and cordially invite Suzanne Michelle Hamilton to attend an exclusive preview at Warfield museum ...*'

'My, but how lovely!' exclaimed Mrs Hamilton, interrupting. 'That's very kind of them. You remember, Peacock & Mayther are the legal firm who represented the seller when we bought this house, so they're obviously keen to help us settle into the local community.' She looked across at her husband. 'Darling, are there some for us?'

Mr Hamilton shook his head.

'Oh, that's odd,' she murmured. Then, brightening, she said, 'Never mind, I'm sure ours are still in the post. Anyway, when is it?'

Hamish hesitated and looked at Suzy. 'Today,' he announced pointedly, observing her surprise.

*

Hamish spotted the distinctive blue and white lorry first. Parked in a narrow street running down the side of Warfield museum, its rear doors were open and several figures were milling about, ferrying boxes from the vehicle into the ornate building through a side entrance.

'I wonder what Chimes & Sons are doing here?' he pondered, as they crossed the cobbled marketplace.

'I've no idea,' replied Suzy, admiring the stately building. 'But I can't help feeling it's more than just a coincidence.'

An architectural gem, Warfield museum had been bequeathed to the town as a parting gift by Queen Elizabeth I on her deathbed in 1603 and it dominated the town's main square. Resembling a classical Roman villa, its white stone portico was supported by four giant Doric columns. Built entirely from Portland stone, its white walls reflected the warm afternoon sunshine, causing Hamish and Suzy to squint as they climbed the sweeping steps to the building's main entrance. Intrigued, they joined a short queue of smartly dressed people and filed into the refreshingly cool marble hall, handing their invitations to a suited lady at reception.

'Ah, Hamish and Suzy Hamilton,' she said with a smile, ticking their names off a list. 'We're delighted you could come. Someone will be across to join you shortly but in the meantime, please proceed into the main hall and enjoy the exhibition.'

'I wonder who's joining us?' whispered Hamish as soon as they were out of earshot.

'It's all very strange,' muttered Suzy, glancing back and noticing that the woman was talking animatedly into a telephone.

Crossing the polished marble floor, they reached the entrance to the main hall and stopped dead in their tracks.

'I don't believe it!' gasped Suzy, staring at a tall glass exhibition cabinet.

Hamish whistled softly. The gold and silver coronation gown glittered spectacularly under the halogen spotlights.

'Over four hundred years old and impossible to wash, yet it looks as amazing today as it did the last time we saw it,' whispered Suzy, circling it, admiring the intricate needlework and recalling the indomitable woman who'd last worn it.

'It's quite beautiful, isn't it?' came a cultured voice from behind, causing them to spin round. Startled, they looked down at an elderly gentleman in a wheelchair. 'Please allow me to introduce myself,' he said, smiling up at them. 'My name is

Mayther, Sterling Mayther, and I'm the senior partner at Peacock & Mayther, the proud sponsor of this fascinating exhibition. I'm delighted to meet you finally. I've heard so much about you.'

As befitting his profession, he was wearing a pinstriped suit and was immaculately groomed. His black shoes gleamed. Hamish noted his slicked-back white hair, sunken cheeks and the liver spots on his taut, parchment-like skin and estimated him to be in his nineties, if not older, but his resonant voice and piercing black eyes could have belonged to a man half his age. They shook his hand, sensing they'd met him before. But try as they might, they couldn't remember where.

'We have some important business to attend to today,' he announced affably. 'But first, please enjoy this wonderful exhibition. It's quite remarkable what the Queen collected privately.' He paused, pointing to the far side of the hall. 'I suggest you begin over there.' And without further ado, he turned away, propelling himself across the polished floor and calling out to a group of visitors entering the museum.

Hamish and Suzy watched him go.

'What do you make of that?' asked Hamish.

'I don't know,' she replied, shaking her head. 'But today is getting stranger by the minute.'

Anxiety and intrigue stirred in the pits of their stomachs as they set off across the hall. They were following the walkways intersecting the glass exhibition cabinets when something caught Suzy out of the corner of her eye and she whipped round, grabbing Hamish's sleeve. 'Look!' she hissed, barely able to believe her eyes.

It took Hamish a moment to work out what she was looking at, and then he saw it. 'Sweet mother of God!' he whispered, approaching the glass box.

It was a rough charcoal sketch.

'It's Chimes!' whispered Hamish incredulously. 'Sis, it's from your sketchbook!'

Suzy felt her pulse roaring in her ears. Although the paper had yellowed over the centuries, the portrait itself remained as clear today as the day she'd drawn it and she stared at it, recalling

Chimes's awkward self-consciousness posing for her beside the cart and his subsequent indignation at the words she'd inscribed on its side. And there they still were, over four hundred years later.

'Hello, you two!' boomed a familiar voice from behind. 'I thought I might see you here.'

'I don't believe it!' exclaimed Hamish as the silver-haired removals man clapped him on the shoulder.

Bob Chimes stood resplendent in his blue and white overalls, his smile fading as he noticed their astonishment. 'What?' he asked innocently. 'Have I said something wrong?'

Suzy shook her head. 'No, Mr Chimes, you haven't said anything wrong,' she said. 'It's your timing, that's all.'

'My timing?' he repeated, puzzled. 'What's wrong with my timing?'

'Nothing's wrong with your timing,' said Hamish, smiling. 'It's just, well, it couldn't be better, that's all.'

'Now you've lost me!' he muttered.

Hamish and Suzy stepped aside, pointing to the exhibition cabinet.

The senior removals man frowned, stooping forward, and read the caption aloud. 'Local Boy by Unnamed Artist, 1597,' he muttered, then all of a sudden his face paled and he exhaled noisily. 'I don't believe it!' he cried, reading the words on the side of the cart. 'Chimes & Sons, Discreet Removals, Established 1597!'

Hamish and Suzy laughed. If they hadn't known better, they could have sworn he'd seen a ghost. His eyes were like saucers.

'I . . . I can't believe it!' he stammered. 'Just look at the resemblance! He's the spitting image of my Amos!'

Just then the woman from reception came hurrying across. Unsmiling and serious, she looked flustered, and for a moment Hamish and Suzy worried that their laughter might have offended her. 'Please, come with me,' she said. 'We must hurry. Mr Mayther has to return to London and needs to see you.'

Disquieted, Hamish and Suzy glanced at each other and followed her out.

Chimes was so preoccupied by his discovery that he didn't notice their departure. Fumbling in his pocket, he pulled out a mobile phone and punched in a number. 'Hey, Bert, it's me,' he said excitedly the moment it was answered. 'Yeah, that's right . . . You know that family debate of ours . . . yep . . . yep, that's right . . . well, wait till you get a load of this . . .'

Their minds boggling, Hamish and Suzy were ushered into a large conference room and asked to wait.

'This place looks like it belongs in the headquarters of a large corporation, not in a provincial museum,' observed Suzy, surveying the light, modernist room with stark white walls, green-tinted windows and a huge chrome glass-topped table running down its centre, surrounded by twelve black leather chairs.

Moments later, the door opened and in glided Sterling Mayther, a slight frown creasing his brow. 'Sorry to keep you waiting,' he said, positioning himself at the head of the table. There was a briefcase on his lap and he placed it on the table in front of him. 'Please sit here,' he said, gesturing to the two chairs nearest to him.

Compliantly, they sat down and watched him open the briefcase, unsettled by his grave, business-like demeanour.

'Before I execute the final wishes of Peacock & Mayther's founding partner, I need you to sign these documents,' he said, sliding a single page of densely typed words to each of them. 'It's a mere formality,' he added, handing a fountain pen to Suzy. 'By signing them, you acknowledge safe receipt of what I'm about to give you and agree to the strictest confidentiality.'

Suzy's hand was shaking as she signed her name and handed the pen to Hamish.

When Sterling Mayther was satisfied that everything was in order, he returned the contracts to his briefcase and withdrew two items, both of which he placed on the table in front of Suzy. One appeared to be an ancient-looking scroll, and the other a modern brown manila envelope.

'These items have graced our vaults for over three hundred and fifty years,' he explained, closing the briefcase and placing it on his lap. 'They were put there by our founding partner addressed to you, Miss Hamilton. And now that I've executed his final wish, I'm afraid I must return to London post-haste.'

Hamish and Suzy were so transfixed by the objects on the table that they didn't notice him manoeuvring away and it was only when he'd reached the door that they finally looked up.

'Hang on a minute,' called Hamish, his mind swirling with questions. 'Can't you stay until we've opened them?'

Sterling Mayther hesitated. 'I'm sorry, but I really have to go immediately,' he insisted. 'Something's arisen that requires my urgent attention.'

Hamish frowned, feeling the frustration rising up inside him. 'All right, but please, just answer one question . . .'

The senior lawyer raised an eyebrow.

'When we bought our house, you represented the seller,' Hamish said. 'Please, I'd like to know who that was.'

Sterling Mayther smiled to himself, regarding him thoughtfully. 'There's no point,' he replied.

'No point?' repeated Hamish in surprise.

'That's right, there's no point,' he reiterated, a hint of a smile playing on his lips. 'Because even if I told you, neither of you would believe me.' And before either of them could protest, the door opened and he glided out.

As they glanced at each other in dismay, their gaze fell upon the objects in front of them.

Suzy picked up the scroll, examining the seal. Pressed into the red wax was a coat of arms she'd never seen before and carefully, very carefully, she prised it open. Her pulse quickened as she unfurled the yellowed parchment, scanning the black spidery handwriting. Then, after taking a deep breath to steady her nerves, she began to read aloud.

'*For the attention of Miss Suzy Hamilton on this day August 12th 1654. My dear friend, now that I am in the twilight of my years I feel compelled to span the centuries and bid you proper farewell. When I reflect on all that we are forbidden to reveal – about those dark and dangerous times – it warms me to know how privileged I am. While history will never recall our exploits, though grave and historic they surely were, nothing can ever take away from us what we achieved and who we were. And I for one would change nothing were I to have my time again. For I have benefited greatly by our association. Under the stewardship of Robert Cecil,*

Jeremiah Graves and Her Majesty the Queen, I trained as a lawyer and have dedicated my life to the defence of harmony and fair justice for all. But alas, I am the only one left. All the others are gone and now I too must prepare to follow, which brings me to the main purpose for writing. There is an item in my possession that was bequeathed to me by Robert Cecil on his deathbed, a unique treasure that I have nobody to leave to. Before he died earlier this year, Chimes recommended, somewhat curiously, that I should entrust it to history addressed to you. My dear friend, I know not what came of you following that most grievous day but I pray you found peace. As for me, I will rest easier when this treasure is delivered into the safety of your hands. Sincerest farewell, Blakey (Robert Blake).'

Mystified, Suzy laid down the scroll and reached for the manila envelope. Her mouth was dry and her pulse raced as she opened it, peering inside to discover what appeared to be a small, dark cube.

The suspense was almost too much for Hamish to bear. 'What is it?' he asked impatiently.

But Suzy didn't reply. Wordlessly, she tipped up the envelope and frowned as a crimson leather box fell into her hand, scuffed and worn from centuries of use. She lifted the lid and gasped. Inside was a ring, a gold signet ring, and etched into its shiny flat surface was the Sign of Equilibrium.